IN JOAN'S DEFENSE

RON CARTER

Palmyra Press

Printed and bound in the United States of America:

ISBN 0-9755080-4-0

Library of Congress Control Number: 2005906046

This is the story of a trial. Or rather, it's the story of a woman on trial. You may find yourself reading along and thinking that this story seems pretty close to what a courtroom must be like (at least from what you've seen of *Law & Order*), and if you think that, you're thinking right. Because, though it's been fictionalized somewhat, this is basically how an actual murder trial went down. And if a certain attorney in this book starts to sound an awful lot like an author you've read, you have a pretty good idea why.

Trials are perhaps our greatest unscripted dramas, full of theater, acting, posturing, sleights of hand. The drama is heightened by the fact that somebody's money, property, or life is on the line inside the courtroom, and that somebody's peers determine what happens to those items.

Even with the theatrical accounted for, it's ironic that witnesses are sworn to "tell the truth, the whole truth, and nothing but the truth." No trial has ever revealed "the whole truth and nothing but the truth." Every trial has evidence—actual facts—that are not admitted in court. Further, the feelings, the motivations, the raw human emotions that drive our actions can only be hinted at in a courtroom, and the ways in which they can be described are carefully limited. This is all for the best, I suppose. After all, we want juries to rule on facts, we want to protect people from unlawful searches and seizures, and we want defendants to be judged according to the evidence, not bias-inducing emotions and opinions. Even so, at the end of a trial, I can't help but feel that there was more lurking just below the surface, things obscured by the roar of the combatants, things that were hinted at, but could never be fully explored. That's just how it is, though—there's a natural limit to what a trial can reveal.

Ultimately, this story is much more than the account of a trial—it's a tragedy. It's the story of a marriage gone suddenly and inexplicably bad, a marriage that appears to end with the firing of two bullets from a hunting rifle. Like the trial, which can only hint at the full truth, the printed word can only suggest the full depth of emotion that flows from a tragedy like this.

But you'll notice that I said that the marriage only *appears to end.* The whole truth of this marriage, the reality of what Les Carson was, only partially made it to the courtroom. To me, that reality is the real story, and the implications that flow from it may very well stretch beyond the grave. The printed word can't fully capture the depth of the tragedy, nor can it adequately explain the hope, tinged by sadness, that ultimately surfaces in this story.

So you'll have to forgive me. I've had to rely on the trial to paint you the picture. Hard questions lurk beneath the surface—Was it really murder? How do we define murder in our society? Did the marriage of Les and Joan Carson end? What will Joan's life be like hereafter? What will the afterlife be like for Joan and Les? Those questions . . . well, you'll have to be the jury and answer them for yourself.

··

THE SHOOTING
September 18th

CHAPTER ONE

. . . .

IT WAS EARLY DAWN. SHE COULD see the dark outline of the door to the construction office to her left, and the door to the apartment directly in front of her.

She tried to control her trembling fingers as they identified the apartment key and slid the blade into the lock. The door opened and she stood in the doorway with white knuckles and a pounding heart. Her eyes adjusted to the gray interior of the room and she suddenly understood that there were boxes stacked near the archway to the kitchenette—boxes with her things packed inside, piled in rows and ready to be moved.

To the left of the doorway were shadowy shapes she could not identify. She stopped all motion, and for ten seconds did not breathe. Again she searched for sound or movement before she turned the light on. There were none. She stepped into the familiar room and reached for the light switch. Her hand stopped as she sensed, more than heard, the footfall behind her.

She turned as he took the last step between them. Even in the dark with his face away from the gray-black of the doorway, she could see his eyes, wide and insane.

Silence still hung in the air as he raised his right hand and as she lifted both her arms to shield her face. He swung his open hand and struck her left cheek. The force of the blow jerked her head to the side and threw her off balance. His left hand caught her right arm as she started down. He held her erect and her arm grew numb in the vice grip, as warm blood oozed from her nose and trickled onto her lips. He struck her again and again, closing his hand, clubbing her with his fist. The blows landed on both sides of her face and neck as he struck first forehand, then backhand. The pain dulled and her mind began to drift. Her knees buckled and her weight sagged forward. He grabbed her left arm and momentarily held her erect by her arms, then violently threw her back away from him. Her back slammed into the edge of the archway to the kitchenette, and the force of the blow knocked the first grunting sound from her as she slid down the doorframe to a sitting position. Her left knee bent high in front of her and her right leg slammed against the floor.

The impact of her body hitting the archway shook the wall and the object leaning against it began to tip, then quickly slide toward her, coming to rest against her leg. As she tried to push it away, she realized that her hand was touching the stock of her rifle.

He was standing in front of her, perhaps ten feet away, making a faint silhouette in the doorway. He made a strange sound and moved toward her.

She could no longer focus her thoughts. The terrifying fear that gripped her as she had unlocked the door and entered the room, followed by the savage, mindless beating, had drained any capacity for conscious, rational action.

Instinct asserted itself. With her hand on the fore grip of the rifle, her right hand worked the action, levering a live cartridge into the firing chamber. She could not see the gun sights. She could hardly see the barrel. He approached her, twisting slightly to the right. She raised the rifle. With her left hand helping to aim by feel alone, she triggered the first thundering blast. The bullet struck his lower left rib cage, traveling upward through the upper right side of his back and through the open door.

The flame from the muzzle flash showed his face to be filled with an expression of wonder and a hint of surprise. She worked the lever, ejecting the spent cartridge, chambering a new one. She waited for her eyes to adjust to the darkness again. He took a half step backward and sat down heavily on the floor. His arms were moving slightly, his head twitching. As her ears stopped ringing, she could hear his struggled breathing and see the slight movements of his body.

Again she raised the rifle, brought it to bear on his head, and squeezed off the second deafening blast. The bullet struck him in the left temple and snapped his head to the right, as it passed through his brain and buried itself in the wall beyond. His body toppled onto its right side, quieted and became still.

She waited, working the rifle action from habit, chambering a new cartridge, watching, waiting, rifle still half-raised. He did not move or make another sound.

The instinct that had risen from within her began to subside and surrendered control back to her own thoughts and reason. As it faded, she felt the beginnings of disbelief for what she had done during the horror of the past few seconds.

....

Chapter Two

"DAD, THERE'S A CALL FOR YOU. I think it's David at the office." It was Laura, her voice sleep-fogged, standing on the front porch in her bathrobe and slippers, looking to be certain he had heard above the rushing sound of the garden hose.

At dawn, Ben Cooper had begun work in the shrubs and flowerbeds in the front yard, preparing them for the approaching winter. He was crouched down, whistling softly to himself, feeling the warmth of the rising sun as he worked the hose nozzle back and forth to wash down the driveway.

The flowerbeds were raked clean; the leaves and rose bush and mum trimmings lay in piles on the grass, waiting to be picked up.

As Ben was momentarily caught up in the gentle rose and yellow colors of the sunrise, his thoughts again drifted back more than eight years to when Elizabeth had worked in these flower beds at his side. A sense of peace always surrounded her like an aura as she handled the flowers with a feeling akin to reverence.

Almost seven years ago, Ben had first noticed the fatigue, soon followed by the weakness and the discomfort in her: the forced smiles, excuses, and finally the slight hollowness in her cheeks and the sallow, waxen look of her skin. Two days of tests by the experts at Johns Hopkins University Hospital confirmed the cancer. The day they learned of it, Ben withdrew from every other activity in his life except his work at the office, so he could be home with her.

They had faced her dying squarely, with no pretenses between them. As she became unable to leave the house, Ben would work at the office only until noon each day, coming home to prepare any food she wanted, and finally, any food she could eat and hold. He read to her, played recordings of her beloved music, sitting beside her bed until she would close her eyes and drift into a quiet sleep. When she could no longer move about the house, his partners in the law firm called an early morning meeting; they told him to take a leave of absence from the office until his home circumstances had been resolved. His share of the partnership profits would be paid regularly in the meantime, no questions asked. From that day on, he remained at home and tended her every need, feeding and bathing her, and changing her clothing and bedding. At night he would gently gather her close and hold her to him, listening to her shallow breathing until she relaxed and slept, finding her only peace in the familiar security of his arms.

He never remembered her as the eighty-six-pound, wasted being who died in the spring nearly a year later; he only saw the vibrant, beautiful, full woman whom he had loved and married, and with whom he had shared twenty-eight years of his life. She had blessed him with three children—two sons, married and away from home, and then the last child, Laura.

Ben accepted Liz's passing with the stolid resolve typical of his upbringing. The unbearable pain in his soul was seen by few. He spoke of it only twice, with Laura. Ben and Liz had not withheld the truth from Laura; after the first four months, there was no point. But knowing of her mother's impending death did not spare her the near total disorientation she suffered when she saw her mother's coffin lowered into the ground and then returned home to the silent emptiness in a house that had been filled with family sounds since the day of her birth. For months Laura withdrew inside herself. Her performance in school dropped dramatically; she became morose, silent. Her usual carefree, easygoing attitude became depressed, sullen.

Then one day, as though she suddenly realized what she was becoming, she seemed to cast about for something to fill the void that was within her. Her appearance slowly began to improve, and she guardedly began to talk with others about her feelings, probing for a way to cope. Just after her fifteenth birthday, she suddenly discovered the cathartic, miraculous healing power that comes to a woman when she gives herself to the needs of others; and she found her father. She lavished on him her deep need to give. She became an efficient, dedicated housekeeper; she studied his wants and needs for meals, and had them waiting when he needed them or wanted them. She constantly checked to be sure the closets and drawers in his dresser were full of clean, mended clothes. She talked to him, haltingly at first, then voraciously, about anything—his business, his hurt, his pain; her school, her dreams, her desires. Inevitably they drew closer than any of the other family members.

At twenty, Laura was tall and well formed. She had her mother's classic looks. The price she'd paid for the loss of her mother had been compensated in part by an unusually deep insight into the people and affairs around her. Ben had come to trust her intuition and instincts; they became confidants.

In the six years that had passed since the funeral, Ben had learned to live with the feeling that he was an incomplete human being. He had come to realize he could never entirely let go of Liz. Working in the earth and the flower beds she had loved somehow eased the ache that still lingered.

● ● ●

Ben glanced at Laura, seeing Liz's eyes and smile as he always did, and nodded acknowledgment. "I'll be right there."

He twisted the nozzle shut and dropped the garden hose into the shrubbery lining the driveway. He paused to watch Laura turn and disappear back through the entryway, and then he straightened from the crouch to his full six feet. Walking across the driveway toward the side door, he slapped at the front of his ancient Levi's and old, battered sweatshirt, brushing fragments of leaves and shrub clippings loose. He glanced at the large wall clock as he walked into the kitchen, and his pace slowed momentarily as his forehead wrinkled and he ran his hand over his graying brown hair.

If it was David calling, what was he doing at the office at 6:15 on a Saturday morning, and why was he calling here? Ben was looking down, picking at the tiny flakes of crushed leaves still clinging to his sweatshirt, as he raised the phone.

"Ben Cooper speaking."

"Ben. David." Ben detected strain in the young voice, and his movement stopped, his eyes still cast downward.

"David, what's wrong?"

"I'm at the office. Joan Carson just walked in. She says she's shot Mr. Carson. She's killed him."

Ben's head jerked up violently.

"She's WHAT?" Ben was nearly shouting.

"Joan says she just shot Mr. Carson and killed him. She's here with me now, listening to this. She's all right. Maybe a little too calm. Get down here, Ben. She's been beaten pretty badly. She's bloody. I don't think we should be handling this over the phone."

"Keep her there, David. Don't take any calls and don't make any. Lock the office doors and let no one in. Don't let her clean up. I'll be there in about ten minutes."

As Ben turned, Laura burst into the room, her eyes inquiring at the outburst that had startled her. She sucked in her breath and her

hand involuntarily covered her mouth as she saw the wild look on
Ben's face. In her twenty years of life with her father, only once had
she seen him this shaken, and that was when her mother died. Now
she was seeing it again. Ben barely glanced at her as he jammed the
receiver back on the hook.

"If anyone calls here, I can't be reached." His face was white.
Laura could only stare as Ben covered the few feet to the side door
and barged outside.

As Ben slid behind the wheel of his Oldsmobile, his mind rejected
the thoughts of the killing. He hit the ignition, jerked the car into
reverse gear, and the screeching tires left black on the cement as he
backed out of the driveway. All four wheels squealed as he made the
left turn at the stop sign at Chambers Road, then sped on toward his
office. The car leaned violently as it turned into the parking lot and
skidded to a stop across two parking spaces.

David swung the big door open as Ben approached, and Ben did-
n't stop moving. Both men silently trotted to Ben's office. Joan was
seated in the chair facing Ben's large desk. She didn't rise. She turned
her head slightly to acknowledge she knew the men were there, but
did not look up. Ben stopped at her side, drew up a chair and sat
down, wiping sweat from his face with his sleeve.

"Joan, are you all right? Are you coherent?"

"Yes, I'm all right, Ben." She turned her head and faced him.

Ben clamped his mouth shut on a groan as he looked at her. Her
left eye was swelling shut. Blood had dried in both corners of her
mouth and there were spots of dried blood on her chin. Blood had
trickled from both swollen nostrils and dried. Her right cheek was
badly swollen and her face and neck were beginning to show bruises.
Her shoulder-length brunette hair had been tied in a loose ponytail,
but was now all askew. There were spots of dried blood on the rose-
colored sweater she was wearing and a few on the front of the legs of
her jeans.

Ben blinked his eyes in disbelief, his mind momentarily going
blank. "Joan! Joan-in God's name, who . . . who did this to you? What
happened? What did David mean about Les?"

As she spoke, he caught the sick fear in her voice. She began
speaking as though she were reciting from a book or a script. Ben
went cold inside, watching.

"Well, Ben, you know that in the last little while, trouble has been
developing, and—"

Ben interrupted. "No, no, Joan. Who did this to you? Where's Les?"

"I shot him."

"No, Joan. You couldn't do . . . Where? Where were you when you shot him?"

"In our apartment at the construction office building."

"When?"

"About forty-five minutes ago."

"What gun . . . what gun shot him?"

"My .300 Savage."

"How could that happen? How could you have shot him with your old rifle from the ranch? Don't you mean there was an accident with a pistol? A handgun?"

"No, my rifle." Ben fought to maintain his composure.

"Where did the bullet hit him?"

"The first shot went through his chest at kind of an angle. The second shot went through his head."

Ben's mind froze and he felt his thoughts begin to disintegrate. TWO shots? Joan shot Les with two shots? Her old lever-action rifle? This is a farce! You can't have a two-shot accident with a lever-action rifle!

"Joan, you've had an accident—something's happened—is Les dead? Do you know he's dead? Who beat you?"

"Yes, I'm sure he's dead."

Ben broke off the conversation, looking at Joan as though he was looking at a total stranger. Something desperate, something unbelievable has happened. She's not remembering it right. She's confused.

His eyes never left her face as he spoke to David.

"I don't know what's happened, but it must have been bad to put her in this condition. I've got to know, right now. I'm going out to that apartment. It's just not possible she shot him, but something might have happened with a gun."

David was standing to his right, immobilized by what he was watching, trying to understand what the conversation between Ben and Joan meant.

Ben let his gaze fall briefly to the floor. His mind was nearly numb, his reasoning capability reeling. It just wasn't possible Les was dead at the hands of Joan, the woman he loved more than life itself. Something horrible has happened, and Joan's blaming herself. But who was it that beat her half to death? Fighting to stabilize his thoughts, Ben suddenly stood and spoke to David.

"Call city-county law enforcement's emergency number and ask for Charlie's office. Tell whoever answers that it's possible we've got a dead man at the construction company apartment at the east end of the building. Get the address from Joan. Have them get someone out there as quickly as they can, and bring an ambulance. Tell them I'm on my way there and might get there before they do. If they want more details, they'll have to talk with me. You stay here with Joan until you hear from me. Track down Wylie Benoit by phone and ask him to go to his office and wait for me there, and say that it is critical."

Ben paused, then looked directly at David.

"Any better ideas?"

David's thoughts were beginning to become more coherent.

"Ben, if there really was a shooting and Les is dead and you get there first, you're going to run the risk of becoming a material witness. Maybe they'll even charge you with something if they don't buy your story."

Ben dropped his eyes for a second, weighing the risk against his overpowering need to know.

"I'll risk it. I've got to know."

"Don't do it, Ben. Don't go out there. At least wait until they get there, so you've got protection. If she told us the truth and you have to defend her, you'll be disqualified if you become a material witness."

Ben looked at David, seeing the near panic showing in his serious young eyes. Then he shook his head and turned to leave.

"I'll be in touch as soon as I can." He turned his eyes to Joan, his teeth gritted at her appearance, shaking his head slightly.

"Joan, can you hold on for twenty minutes? Can you just hold on until I get back?"

Her expression was still too calm, too detached. She could only nod. Ben muttered, "Hang on, Joan. Hang on," as he ran back to his car.

As he hit the ignition, he was mentally laying out the fastest route to the apartment. Back on East Colfax, headed west, he jammed the gas pedal to the floor and pushed the horn. He paid no heed to traffic lights or stop signs as he drove wildly, changing traffic lanes with sudden, twisting turns. He was scarcely aware of the shambles the big white Olds was leaving behind it in the early morning traffic. The car fishtailed as Ben turned off State Highway 6 into the company parking lot and raced the last 100 yards, stones flying. The tires dug trenches in the gravel as the car slid to a stop, and Ben was out and running before the car quit rocking.

Grabbing the doorknob to the apartment, he found it locked. Hardly pausing, he decisively took one step back, raised his foot, and kicked with all his weight. The doorjamb splintered around the lock, and the door swung open.

Despite what he had been told, Ben wasn't prepared. The drapes were all closed, and the room was totally dark, save for the light from behind him, framing the doorway. About eight feet inside the door, lying on the floor, was the body of Leslie Carson. Ben felt the odd, creeping, prickly sensation of being in the presence of a killing. A large circle of blood stained the carpet around the chest, and a second stain surrounded the head. The front of the pants was darkened by the wet of urine. Ben involuntarily sucked in his breath as his eyes adjusted to the dimness of the room and the full impact of the horror smashed into him.

The body was on its side, facing toward the door. The head, caught in half-light, half-shadow, was grotesque; the face looked nearly inhuman. It appeared as though some sudden, terrible force had exploded inside the skull, pushing everything outward. The cheekbones were broken and out of alignment. The jaw appeared to be unhinged on the right side and the mouth sagged open. The tongue was partly visible on one side. The right side of the head was a gaping hole, turned toward the floor and only partly visible. The eyes were open and protruding, as though transfixed in some great, horrible surprise, with the flat, lifeless stare of the dead. Had Ben not been told who it was, he would never have recognized Leslie Carson, whom he had known from birth and loved from his earliest memory.

Ben sagged against the doorframe, his head down, his eyes closed, for just a moment. That's not Les—can't be Les—no accident—he was killed—someone killed him—Joan killed him. As the certainty settled into his heart, he felt pain he had endured only once before: when Liz had wasted and died.

He straightened and opened his eyes against the dim light. By force of will, he again looked at Les and then glanced around the room without entering. To the right of the door, close to the floor-length drapes, leaning against the wall, was the rifle. Ben stepped backward, closed the door as much as possible against the splintered jamb, and stood there for several seconds to let his mind accept the shock.

He slowly walked back to his car. As he opened the door, an unmarked county car came screaming through the parking lot, ground to a stop in the gravel, and the plainclothes officer came running. Behind him came an ambulance, siren howling. As the assistant investigator approached, Ben nodded to acknowledge him and spoke.

"It was my office that called you, Reed. You'll find the body just inside the room. I had to know if he was dead. I forced the door and broke the jamb, but I didn't enter the room. Everything is just as I found it. I will be in touch with your office sometime later this afternoon."

Detective Reed Jenkins paused, puzzled and alarmed at the lack of color in Ben's face and the shallow expression in his eyes.

He started to say something, then reconsidered, and hurried on into the apartment.

Ben got back into his car. He slowly interlaced his fingers at the top of the steering wheel, leaned his head forward against his hands, and closed his eyes. He sat for several minutes while he let his mind grapple with the unbelievable, impossible events of the last half-hour.

Joan, beaten and bloody; Les dead, his body almost unrecognizable. Where could there be an answer? For just a moment, it was simply a mistake—a gigantic, sadistic mistake. Les and Joan. Part of the foundations of his life; he had known them and loved them both. How could this possibly have happened? How?

Finally Ben raised his head and opened his eyes, and by force of will pushed the shock and his feeling of anger behind him. He turned the key in the ignition and slowly started back to his office. Mechanically he moved through the traffic, working in his mind to somehow sort out the best way to proceed with the soul-wrenching ordeal he must now face with Joan.

He parked in front of the two-story brick office building he and his partners had built in suburban Aurora, and entered through the heavy door, his mind just beginning to stabilize.

CHAPTER THREE

BEN PUSHED HIS OFFICE DOOR OPEN and entered. Joan was still sitting in the same chair. She turned her face to him. David stood, waiting. Ben walked to the chair beside Joan and sat down.

He began quietly, staring at the carpet. "Les is gone. A detective, Reed Jenkins, is at the apartment now, beginning a full-blown investigation."

Ben looked at Joan and cleared his throat. As gently as he could, he led Joan into the questions he knew had to be answered. "Joan, seeing you in this condition, and Les—what I saw back at the apartment, is hard for me to accept. You have to tell me everything you can, and let me sort it out. What happened? What happened this morning?"

Joan began slowly and deliberately, speaking with unnerving control.

"After I woke up in the rocking chair, it seemed to me best if I could get out to the apartment and get my things before Les got there. I didn't want to meet him there because I didn't know what he would do—whether he would beat me again. I thought if I got there early enough, I would be loaded and gone before he arrived. I didn't . . ."

Ben was preparing to reach for the phone to call Wylie. It was clear that Joan was beyond shock, in a strange, tortured new world. She's repeating herself, Ben thought. She's not making sense, and she doesn't know it. She's in trouble. "Joan, what rocking chair? Load what things? Why?

Joan suddenly set her jaw closed and abruptly stood. "I'm not making sense. Let me get—give me a minute to get hold of myself. Have you got some water or something?"

Ben nodded to David. He then looked back at Joan, realizing she was gamely refusing to buckle, and was determined to hold herself together. Ben felt a surge of hope as he saw her visibly take charge of herself. Maybe, he thought, maybe she's got the strength. She might make it.

In seconds, David returned with a pitcher of ice and water and glasses on a tray. Slowly Joan poured a glass half full of water and took a sip, paused, and then drained it. She took a deep breath and started to work her hair with her hands, brushing at her sweater, straightening her clothing. She glanced up and spoke.

"Is there a rest room somewhere I can wash up and clean myself?"

"Joan, don't fix your hair. Don't worry about it. Leave yourself just the way you are. Just tell me what happened. And why."

She didn't sit down, but began talking while she stood, gesturing with her hands, moving a step or two from time to time. He watched her eyes and knew she was regaining some sense of perspective, beginning to find her way back to the realities of the world.

"Last night, Les came home after being gone for two days and told me he wanted to live alone at the apartment. Without me. He told me he would be out on a project overnight and would be back at the construction office apartment about noon today to load my things and be rid of me. I was scared to be alone with him, so I got out as quickly as I could, and when I got home at 10, he was gone. I sat up all night, afraid he would come back, but he didn't. So I thought if I got to the apartment before he returned from the project I could load my things myself and avoid him. So I drove out to the apartment and got there about 5:20 or 5:30. It was still dark. "

Ben stared at Joan. "What do you mean, you were afraid to be with him at your home? And you wanted to avoid him at the apartment? What's going on here, Joan? What are you telling me?"

Joan put her hand over her eyes and began to rub them, then winced slightly in pain. She drew a deep breath and let it out. "I have to remember you don't—Ben, I think I've made a mistake coming here. I can't do this to you. I'll have to tell you things about Les that you won't believe. You'll think I'm lying. I can't mix—you don't want to get mixed up in this. Help me find . . ."

Ben cut her off. "I'm already mixed up in this, Joan. Clear up to my chin. Heavens, woman, don't talk to me about staying out. Now, what in the world are you trying to tell me?"

She stopped a moment, sobered slightly by Ben's explosive words, dreading the responsibility of destroying the image Ben still carried of Les. She continued.

"Last week—probably ten or twelve days ago now, I called Les from the front room to come to supper and suddenly, for no reason I know of, he got so violent, he knocked me down. I couldn't believe it. When I tried to get up, he knocked me down again. Never, not ever, had he even raised his hand to me in anger before that day. Then he walked out and was gone for a couple of days, and I didn't know where he was. When he came back he seemed like Les again, so I asked him what had happened. He got furious again. He knocked me down and kicked me in the head. Then he stormed out of the house swearing and saying crazy things. He left me on my hands and knees in the kitchen, bleeding." Joan paused and searched Ben's eyes, desperately needing to know if he believed her.

Ben let his eyes drop, then met her gaze.

Satisfied that he knew it was true, Joan continued. "That was just the last part of it. For weeks before that, Les had been doing things and saying things that were just unbelievable. He couldn't remember things. He started drinking. He would be gone for two or three days and never let me know what he was doing or where he had been."

Ben couldn't control his expression. He didn't try to mask his shock. He could only look at her, waiting for the story to unfold, having to repeat to himself that it was true.

"I swear to you, Ben, there was some kind of demon in Les. It took control of him a little at a time, until these past three or four weeks it possessed him. I can't find—there aren't words to tell you the look that came across his face when he lost control of himself and started doing, started being brutal. Ben—his eyes—the look in his eyes—Ben . . ."

Her mouth trembled and the thought flashed in Ben's mind: "She's going. She's going to lose it." He started to rise.

She set her jaw and shook herself and somehow asserted control again and continued.

"I've never known terror until I had to look at Les these past ten or twelve days. I don't think I'm a coward, but as God as my witness, I couldn't control the terror in me when I had to face him."

What is she telling me? Ben asked himself. She was terrified of Les? He loved her—nearly worshipped her. Beat her? Never! He'd kill anyone who even *tried* it.

"Joan, tell me about this morning. What happened this morning?"

"I couldn't face him this morning. If I didn't get my things out of the apartment, and he got mad and lost control again—God only knows what would have happened." But something had happened. Something inconceivable had happened. Joan shook herself as if trying to wake up from a nightmare.

"So you went out to the apartment this morning to get your personal things?"

"Yes."

· · · · · · · · ·

"What happened? What led to the shooting?"

"It was still dark when I got there. I didn't see him, and I didn't see his pickup. I thought it was all right. I opened the door to the apartment and stood there still, so I could hear anything that moved. I was afraid to turn on the lights, for fear he was there. But I didn't hear anything. I could just barely see the packing boxes stacked around one side of the archway to the kitchenette. I started into the room and reached for the light switch, when I heard just a whisper of sound behind me. I turned and he was in the doorway."

Her eyes widened as she remembered the horror of the moment. She groped for the words that would make Ben understand.

"He was only a silhouette, but even in the dark I could see his eyes." Her breath caught in her throat. "I could smell the liquor on him. He had about a two-day growth of beard and his hair was messed. But his eyes. They were wide, like a maniac. He raised his arm and I put my hands up to protect my face. He hit me and then grabbed my right arm and held me up, and he just kept hitting me with his right hand. The fourth or fifth time, the pain stopped, and I can't remember much of what happened next. I tasted blood from my nose and mouth. I thought he put my eye out. I couldn't keep my legs under me any-more. He grabbed me and threw me backwards, real hard, and I went down. I hit the archway to the kitchenette backwards, and I remember sliding down the doorframe until I was sitting."

She stopped talking. She was breathing hard, and swallowing, try-ing to keep from tears.

"Something bumped my right shoulder and slid down my arm, and ended in my lap. It was my rifle. Les had leaned it against the wall with my other things.

"He started toward me and I chambered the first bullet. I guess he heard it and he turned right. I fired the first shot and it hit him on his left side, and he went down backwards, sitting." Her mouth trembled and her hands started to shake. "When my ears quit ringing and I could see again, I heard him still trying to breathe and I could see his head moving. I chambered the second bullet and I shot him through the head."

She stopped. Her hands steadied and she closed her mouth, star-ing at Ben.

"How much time between the shots?"

Almost as if in a trance, she replied. "I don't know. I thought about six or seven seconds, but I don't know. It must have been longer. Maybe longer."

"Did you see his face on either shot, in the muzzle flash?"

"Yes. Both times."

"On the second shot, what did his face—was he still alive?"

"Yes. His head was moving. All I saw was a profile. When he went down, he sort of turned and was nearly facing the door."

"Why did you fire the second shot?"

She looked startled, as though she somehow thought the answer to the question was obvious.

"Ben, I would have emptied the gun if he had kept moving." She shook her head violently, as though she couldn't believe what she had just said. "My goodness. I can't—it doesn't sound right when I say it here to you—but I know that there, in the dark, it was right. There was no question. I knew I had to put him down to stay. It was right." Her voice was rising, defiant.

Her eyes broke from Ben's, and she sat down. Ben could see her own words had terrified her. She started rocking back and forth, and suddenly clasped her hands together, interlacing her fingers, jamming her hands to her lap. Her shoulders shook as she battled to hold the tears, and she couldn't. She started to sob. "I killed him, Ben. My God, I murdered him. I murdered him. I murdered him." She was repeating it, like a chant, as she rocked. Her eyes were wide, staring straight ahead.

"The kids, Ben. The kids. What will they do to me? What will the law do to me? How could I do it? How? How?"

Ben smothered the lump that rose in his own throat as he saw her making her first feeble, heart-wrenching attempt to admit to herself what she had done. He controlled the panic he felt at the thought it might snap her mind. Ben groped for something to do, something to say, but could think of nothing. Haltingly, he spoke, hoping he could help her rise above it if he could keep her talking, keep her mind working.

"After the second shot, what did you do?"

She paused and swallowed hard, raising both hands to wipe away the tears. Ben could see her pull herself into control.

"I sat there. My legs were so weak I couldn't get up and my ears were ringing so bad I couldn't hear anything. I remember the smell of the burnt gunpowder. Finally I got onto my feet, stepped over Les'ss legs, leaned the rifle against the wall, and walked out the door. I think I set the lock behind me. I got into the car and drove here."

"Joan, did you think I'd be at work at 6 o'clock on a Saturday morning?"

She looked at him, and he watched as her eyes slowly showed understanding that her thought processes had been borderline irrational. She didn't answer. Ben continued.

"Did you touch anything in the room but the rifle?"

"No. I don't think—no."

"Did you intend to murder him?"

"I shot him twice, and I knew where both shots were going. I knew they would kill him."

"Joan, try hard to understand my words. Did you intend to murder him?"

She opened her mouth to answer, then realized what he was asking. "I don't know what the law considers murder."

"I know you don't. Just answer the best you can."

"No. I did not intend to murder him. I don't remember having intent to do anything. I just knew I had to stop him and the rifle was the only way I could do it. I didn't stand a chance against him without the rifle."

"Was he armed with anything? A club or a bottle?"

"No. Nothing." She bowed her head and covered her face. "Just his hands." Suddenly she broke into unrestrained sobbing that filled the room.

Ben moved quickly from his chair, knelt in front of her, and put his arm around her. She rested her forehead against the front of his shoulder as she wept uncontrollably. Ben moved his arm and put his hand gently on the back of her head. He didn't move until her sobs diminished and finally stopped.

Ben looked at David and signaled for the box of Kleenex with his eyes. David brought it and stood waiting until Joan raised her head from Ben's chest. She took a tissue and gingerly dabbed at her left eye, which was now nearly closed and turning black. She started to wipe at the blood on her face, but Ben tenderly stopped her hand. He spoke quietly, almost as if he were pleading, a look of deep sadness in his eyes. "You can't clean your face until you have been seen by a doctor." She nodded her head.

"I'm all right now. Ben, I didn't mean to put this off on you. How can I—what's going to happen to me, Ben?" The calm expression in her eyes begged him for help.

He slowly drew his chair to a position nearly facing her, and slowly sat down.

"We're going to take care of you, Joan. You're going to be all right."

She let out her breath, almost as though his saying it had made it so. Ben could see she wasn't yet the Joan he had known all his life, but she was able to talk coherently, to answer questions.

Ben waited a moment, then gently continued. "When did this all start, Joan? And how?"

"I think it started last May, when Glenn Tolboy, Les's partner, had his heart attack and had to quit work. From then on, it's just a mess, Ben. It gets all confused with the business going downhill, and the state department of transportation, and the newspapers pressuring Les to run for governor. What part of it do you want me to talk about?" She was working the tissues in her hands, gently folding them and refolding them.

"We'll take time for all of it, Joan, but up front, I need to know if all these business reverses and the other pressures can explain this whole thing."

"No. It doesn't explain it to me."

"Nor to me. Now let's start at the beginning."

CHAPTER FOUR

BEN SAT QUIETLY FOR A MOMENT after Joan finished, then stood and walked toward the office door a couple of paces. His mind was swamped, utterly numbed by her story. He began pushing the entire scenario a little way out, trying to get enough distance to see it as a whole. Regaining perspective, he turned as he spoke to both David and Joan.

"Joan, there are some things we must do now. David, take her to Denver General and check her into the emergency room. Get a seasoned doctor to give her a thorough physical examination. Let him know she has been the victim of an assault and you need medical proof. Don't let Joan clean up until the exam is over, and don't say a word about the shooting. Understood? I'm going back to the apartment to see if I can work out something with Charlie Fawcett. Then I'll come to the hospital and expect you to be in the emergency room. Any questions? Okay. Joan, David and I will be gone for just a minute to get a camera so he can take pictures of your injuries. Please wait here."

As they passed into the adjoining library and opened the cabinet for the camera, Ben spoke quickly and quietly to David.

"Watch and listen. If she starts to break down, get to a phone and call me."

David nodded. They walked back into the outer office and Joan rose, ready to go, as Ben spoke once more.

"Take David's car. And be careful."

As they started to the door, Ben impulsively caught Joan's arm and turned her to face him. "Will you be all right?"

She looked him in the eyes and realized his need to know. "I'll be okay, Ben. I know where I was thirty minutes ago, but I'm past it. I'll be all right." She held his eyes until she knew he believed it, and then she and David were gone.

Ben touched the number for the hospital emergency room as he watched the door close behind David and Joan. Emergency came on the line, and Ben told them what was coming. Then he went to his car.

Seated behind the steering wheel, Ben suddenly took his fingers off the ignition key and leaned back. He closed his eyes and took a deep breath and let it out slowly, taking stock of himself. He slowed the headlong, racing pace of his thoughts and forced himself to probe for the starting place, to put the case in focus.

He turned the car key and entered the traffic on East Colfax. Driving slowly, he let his thoughts run. The starting place? It had to be the irreconcilable gap—more like an abyss—between Joan's verbal portrait of the man she'd killed and the man Ben had known all his life. That was the juncture where the two Les Carsons met, creating a mind-breaking Jekyll and Hyde dichotomy for which Ben could see no resolution. Ben carefully began sifting through his memory, trying to put together anything, any combination of things that might help him understand what had happened.

The marbles. That was the earliest clear recollection of Les that Ben could pull from his memory. In the tiny town of Caldwell, in Jackson County, Colorado, there was precious little that could be called commercial entertainment for the adults, and nothing for the children. So the boys played marbles, carrying their winnings around in homemade blue denim marble bags with drawstrings to keep them closed. The girls played jacks with any ball they could find that would bounce, using rocks for jacks if they didn't have the real thing. Les was usually with the other boys, his marble bag, dangling from the brass button that closed his bib overalls at the side, banging off his leg. He was just another tow-headed kid in a homemade shirt, with a homemade bowl-over-the-head haircut and high-topped, lace-up shoes. But when he grinned and spoke, he was irresistible.

There was a second boy, Joshua Albertson, who felt a close kinship to both Ben and Les. Josh was clearly a gifted scholar, tending to be slow and quiet and thoughtful, adding a dimension to both Les's bright, easygoing personality and Ben's sober, serious side. Les was two months older than Ben, Josh the youngest by five months. At their entry into the first grade in the small frame schoolhouse, they had already innocently formed the bonds that would, in time, strengthen and join them together for the rest of their lives.

A faint smile tugged at the corners of Ben's mouth as he thought about the social structure in Caldwell, remembering there wasn't one. It wasn't a town—at least no one thought of it that way. People didn't think of Caldwell; they thought of "the Carson place," or "the Albertson place," or "the Cooper place."

The character of each of the people and the families, and consequently Caldwell, was directly related to the harsh, brutal climate in
which the families lived. The winters at the 6,700-foot level on the
east slope of the Continental Divide in the Rocky Mountains were
unforgiving; the summers short and hot and dusty. No one living
there expected life to be other than a never-ending contest with
nature for survival. Inevitably, it hammered and tempered people
into a tough-minded, tight-lipped independence that reached into
and colored their every attitude and thought.

Ben shook his head slightly as he remembered the accepted and
unchallenged inner structure of the families. Father stood at the head,
the source of the law and the enforcer, assuming the responsibility of
facing a raw world, carving out a living for his own. Mother was the
heart. Hers was the love-work of bearing children, cooking, mending,
washing, arbitrating, nursing, wiping noses, bandaging, setting bones
occasionally, transporting, sewing, canning, counting the pennies,
and always, always quietly standing beside her husband—watching,
reading him, becoming the mortar that held the bricks of their life
and the family together.

The kids were growing reflections of the parents, from birth to
adulthood. As soon as they could walk, they began assuming their
share of the load, each according to his size and capability. And once
begun, the process never stopped. It had never occurred to them that
life should be otherwise.

Serious trouble for one neighbor was considered serious trouble
for all the neighbors. No one asked for help; it just arrived in time of
need—no questions asked, no thanks expected.

Ben called up his memories of Les as a teenager. Big frame, strong,
quick-witted, and rapidly developing the habit of ignoring those tasks
he couldn't do quickly, that required him to grind out effort a day at
a time. School studies, football practice, working in the summer hay,
or rounding up the cattle for the winter feeding—if he couldn't do it
quickly, he tended to lose interest. When teachers or coaches or his
parents cracked down on him for his lackadaisical irresponsibility, he
manipulatively used his charm and wit. One could get angry at Les,
but not stay angry. He was increasingly beginning to show the insta-
bility and unsteadiness that were to become his cross to bear. Yet,
when something meant enough to him, he would do anything to
reach his goal.

Ben knew that despite Les's tendency to drift with whatever
winds were blowing, if Les could find something good in life that cap-

tured him deeply enough, it would be the making of him. If he could stabilize and commit, his other qualities would make him a natural, gifted leader who could write his own limits.

Ben remembered the rise of hope he felt for Les when he learned Les was becoming serious about Joan Albertson, Josh's sister. Three years younger than the boys, Joan had always just been there in the background, hardly noticed, sharing the harsh life of their community along with the boys and their neighbors. She had learned from life that its joys and sorrows came mixed, on their own schedule, and each was to be accepted. She always seemed to know what her direction should be, and knowing, she never considered another course. She had never consciously decided to "be a good girl"; being such came naturally. She had learned all the attitudes and skills to create a solid home. And when it was needed, she could saddle a horse and work the cattle right along with the men. Carrying the old Savage .300 rifle, she was accepted by them as an equal on their fall hunts for venison.

As a young man coming home from his first year of college, Les had shown the good sense of seeing Joan for what she was: a beautiful, strong young woman who saw the best in people and drew it out of them. That summer, by the luck of the draw, Josh was drafted into the army to help serve in Vietnam. Eight months later the Albertsons received a telegram: "Greetings from the United States Army. We regret to inform you . . ." Ben and Les both came home from college for the funeral, and during their two days at home, Les realized how he felt about Joan. He waited. After his second year of college, when she had graduated from high school, he told her he loved her; she told him she had loved him since the eleventh grade. Her world was complete. They told her father and Les asked permission to marry her. Jesse told him to wait one more year, to stabilize and overcome his tendency to drift. Les stood and looked at Jesse and shook his hand. "I promise you and Joan this day I'll do it." He kept his promise. His grades improved dramatically and he became more responsible.

The next year they were married. Ben stood as best man and he couldn't have been happier for both of them. From the day of their marriage, Les took hold, as Ben knew he would. Les loved Joan more than he could say and she was becoming the center of his life.

Ben shifted his frame of reference to the crucial years after college, after their marriages. At the university, Ben had won regional second place in the National Collegiate Rodeo Association competition and became president of the university rodeo club during his junior year;

he also was a member of the student Intercollegiate Organizational Council, the student group that ran campus affairs. There, he had met Elizabeth Bowden, from a wealthy family in Oak Park, Illinois. She found Ben's common sense and intense independence to be something she admired and needed in her own life. During their senior year, they married, and Les had stood as Ben's best man. Until she died, Liz had remained totally fascinated by Ben's hands-on practicality, while Ben had never lost his reverence for her sense of culture and refinement, and her classic beauty.

After their marriages, the two couples had gone where their dreams and plans took them, but they stayed in touch. When children were born, telephone calls were made, and there were occasional visits through the years. When Les and Joan moved to Denver to go into the construction business with Glenn Tolboy, they visited Ben regularly for the first several months; then the visits dwindled as they settled into their routines. Ben could see that Les had matured; Joan had drawn out the best in him. He was becoming an outstanding, natural leader—steady and firm. She had become a beautiful, serene, fulfilled woman.

When Liz sickened with the cancer, Les and Joan respected her need for privacy, but they watched and waited. When she died, they attended the funeral. Les came to Ben after the service and impulsively put both arms around him. Ben held onto him for several moments. With tears in her eyes, Joan also held Ben close, and though she said nothing, Ben could see the shared pain in her eyes.

In their lives, the three of them—Les, Ben, and Joan—had never talked of their feeling for each other. Expressing emotions through words just didn't come naturally. Instead, their fondness for one another was displayed with a deep loyalty. Each one did for the other. The roots of their beginnings were intertwined by the joys and sorrows they had shared in the harsh outdoors. There would always be a common bond between them.

Months after Liz's funeral, just before Thanksgiving, Les called Ben.

"What are you doing Thanksgiving, and the two or three days following?"

"Nothing special. Why?"

"Pack your gear and your kids. We're going home. Joan wants to see Jesse and your kids need to visit your folks. You and I are going after elk and deer."

For three days, the two of them lived in an old line shack in the mountains, working the frigid, snow-covered peaks and valleys during the day for deer and elk, returning exhausted in the late afternoon, warming themselves with firewood they had to cut, and eating what they fixed with their own hands. They talked into the night, in the light of a flickering fireplace, before pulling their blankets up to their eyes and dropping into a deep, dreamless sleep. The evening of the third day they returned home with two deer and two elk, and Ben felt better able to deal with the pain and bitterness of losing his wife. Though neither of them ever put it into words, two men were never closer.

● ● ●

Ben shook his head, pulling his mind back to the reality of Les being dead.

It wasn't there. No memory, nor any combination of them, even remotely suggested an answer to the question "Why?" Rather, his memories confirmed Ben's conviction that somehow a great, horrible piece of the puzzle was missing. It didn't occur to Ben to do other than try to find it; he knew he could not rest until he had the answer.

He slowed the car to make the turn into the large parking lot of the construction company, and he neared the cluster of police cars and people gathered around the plastic orange posts with the yellow ribbon protecting the apartment.

As he parked the car and got out, Ben centered his thoughts on what he was facing with Charlie Fawcett, the chief of criminal investigation of the city-county law enforcement department. The splintered doorjamb, Reed arriving while Ben was leaving—how was Charlie going to take it?

He quickly walked through the few silent onlookers to the yellow tape. Inside he could see Charlie's figure, towering above all the others as they silently worked, each pursuing his specialty in homicide investigations. Ben spoke to the nearest uniformed officer.

"I'm Ben Cooper. I called in the report on this homicide. Would you let Chief Fawcett know I'm here?"

The officer turned and walked into the room. Ben watched as he spoke briefly to Charlie, and Charlie nodded. The officer returned to Ben.

"He'll be out in just a moment." Charlie glanced at his notepad, closed the cover, and dropped it into the inside breast pocket of his jacket as he emerged from the dark room into full sunlight. He squinted for a moment, picking out Ben, then walked directly to him. His expression was tentative, testy.

"Hi, Ben. I've been waiting to talk with you. Reed said you were here earlier. You know some things I need. Got a minute?"

"Yes. You've got some things I need too, Charlie. What can I help you with?"

"How did you know Carson was inside, shot to death?"

"I had an unexpected visitor this morning, about 6 o'clock. I was told about the shooting." Ben stopped, waiting.

Charlie paused, his eyes narrowing as he mentally arranged a question that would not step over the ethical lines of inquiring about confidences Ben could not reveal.

"I don't suppose you'd be able to talk about who it was or what was pushing you so hard?"

"You know I can't do that."

Charlie broke off, studying Ben, impatient at his refusal to show any sign of cooperation. As he turned, he spoke mechanically, as though to quit wasting further time on a hopeless effort.

"Thanks, Cooper. That's all. See you around."

Ben reached out and gently caught his arm.

"If I was told the truth, Charlie, there are some things you will have trouble putting together. I can help you with this. All I need is to confirm that my informant was telling me the truth, and that the person's psychiatrically sound. I've already arranged for Wylie Benoit to examine the person this afternoon. If you will let me ask your people a couple of questions, I'll know if I got it straight. If I did, and Wylie gives my informant a clean bill of health, I will be in your office tonight, and either let you know what went on and who did it, or let you know I can't be involved. How about it?"

Charlie reacted quickly, coolly, his words firm.

"No, I don't think so. We'll have it worked out in the next thirty-six hours, or at least enough to go for a warrant."

"I think I can save you some time, and some guesswork. Your decision isn't whether or not to share your facts with me, Charlie. Your decision is *when* to share. I'll get it all now, or I'll get it later under my Rule Sixteen rights. I'll save you some time and cut your margin of error if you'll save me some time. Think about it."

Charlie looked harried, anxious to be finished. All that was holding him from walking back inside was the fact Ben could tell him in ten seconds the things his department would spend a day and a half to develop, and then not be absolutely certain. He had long since learned that professional considerations had to override his own feelings. Looking sour, he turned to the uniformed officer and spoke.

"Let him inside the barrier. Cooper, follow me."

CHAPTER FIVE

"MR. DUPREE, THIS IS SHARON AT the switchboard. You had a call from law enforcement. Urgent. Do you have the number?"

"Yes, I have it. What's it about?"

"There's been a homicide. They're investigating it now."

Dupree glanced at his watch, puzzled at getting a homicide call at the odd hour of 8:25 on a Saturday morning. "Did they mention who had been killed? Who was involved?"

"No. Want me to get more information?"

"No, that's fine, Sharon. I'll call them right now. Thanks."

Alonzo J. Dupree, chief of criminal prosecution, felony division, Denver city-county prosecutor's office, pushed down the disconnect button on the phone cradle and ran his free hand through his thick, black, curly hair, annoyed at having his only free Saturday in four weeks interrupted. Impatiently he released the button and dialed the numbers for the city-county law enforcement office, anxious to be finished with the interference. He paced while the circuits clicked, wiping perspiration from his face onto the sleeve of his sweatshirt. His breathing was still a little labored from his daily four-mile run. The phone was answered on the fourth ring.

"Al Dupree. I'm returning a call concerning a homicide."

"Hi, Mr. Dupree. I have the following message for you. Let's see— 'Homicide in the early hours of this morning at the offices of Tolboy Construction Company on State 6, west, near Sheridan. County coroner's office is notified. Detectives and Chief Fawcett are at the scene.' That's the message. Charlie's waiting for an answer. What shall I tell him?"

"Wait for a second, Betty." Dupree's brow knitted as he searched his memory. "Isn't that the company Glenn Tolboy owned, west of town? Didn't he recently die?"

Quickly she scanned the note and responded. "Yes, well, it's named Tolboy—I presume owned by someone named Tolboy. The deceased isn't that name . . . he's a male named Leslie Carson." She waited, tapping her pencil, her short blonde hair moving slightly with the rhythm of her hand movement.

"Did the report state cause of death?"

"Let me see what else . . . It says he was shot twice at close range with a heavy caliber rifle."

"A rifle? Shot twice with a rifle?" Dupree was staring, his brow wrinkled, as he waited for the answer.

"That's what Reed Jenkins said when he called in his first report. That's when Charlie decided he better go out there himself. What shall I tell Charlie?"

Betty paused, knowing that Dupree was going out there if Charlie Fawcett, chief criminal investigator, was there. Dupree sighed.

"Tell Charlie I'm on my way in ten minutes. Thanks, Betty. You do good work."

Dupree dropped the receiver into the cradle and wrote a brief message to his wife on the small blackboard on the kitchen wall. Then he walked quickly to the bathroom and turned the shower on. He pulled the sweatshirt over his head, dropped it into the hamper, then started working on the knot in the drawstring of his damp sweatpants while the water warmed. As he stepped into the steaming shower, he quietly repeated to himself, "A rifle?" His forehead was still furrowed. He had that familiar, uncomfortable feeling that something wasn't right.

After finishing his shower, he leaned over the washbasin to shave. As he stood in front of the mirror, he idly wondered if he would be back before his wife, Joyce, returned from Boulder. She'd made the drive yesterday morning, to visit their daughter, Angela, attending college at the university. The Associated Women's Unit on campus was sponsoring a mother-daughter weekend affair.

A twenty-year-old junior, Angela was the vice-president of her sorority, and in charge of getting moms to attend. Joyce and Angela had planned the visit for weeks, both excited and eagerly waiting for their two days together. Mike, their eighteen-year-old son, had gone along to drive the car for Joyce. Mike couldn't wait to use the Friday night ticket his dad had reserved to watch the Colorado football team play the University of Wyoming. For Mike, an athlete himself, there were only two things worthy of time and thought: cars and athletics. His only regret was that his dad couldn't go and "bum around with him," as he put it. Dupree wanted to go, but his office responsibilities came first.

Dupree let his mind drift to Angela, wondering how she was. He wished he could be there, just to see the two women together. He knew how they treasured their relationship; when they got together, they talked about everything known to the world of females, and you couldn't tell which was the mother and which the daughter. He smiled at the thought.

Suddenly he stopped the razor and sucked in his breath as the horror of the unwanted memories of twelve years ago involuntarily flooded into his mind. After years of concerted effort, he could hold the memories out of his consciousness most of the time. Only in unguarded moments did they ambush him.

Once the terror and rage revisited him, he couldn't block his mind. He felt the sweat start on his face as the image again burned across his brain from that grotesque, unbelievable day in Los Angeles twelve years ago.

Born and raised in south-central Los Angeles, he had watched portions of his city and neighborhood degenerate to a war zone after he became a deputy district attorney, assigned to handle minor criminal matters in what was called Compton. He left work twenty minutes early that awful afternoon, telling himself he just needed to get a jump on the traffic, unwilling to admit he had a premonition something was wrong at home. A block from home, he involuntarily touched the brakes when he saw the black-and-white in his driveway, lights flashing. He parked in front of the house and ran up the driveway, alarmed at seeing the black youth in the back seat of the police car, handcuffed to a uniformed officer.

With a sense of panic, he charged into the house, banging into two uniformed officers just inside the door. In the front room, Joyce turned to look at him, his face white, eyes wide with questions. The doctor, standing next to Joyce, turned to talk to Dupree.

Screaming "Where is she?" Dupree ran into his bedroom, finding Angela in their bed, asleep under heavy sedation. Barging out of the bedroom, past the doctor and Joyce, Dupree dropped his briefcase on the dining room table, fumbled with the locks, grabbed the pistol and started for the door. The two uniformed officers caught his arm, wrestled him to the floor, and pried the pistol from his clenched fist. Dupree was held screaming, blind with rage, wanting only to kill the black youth in the car. The officers helped him back onto his feet, one on each side holding him firmly, trying to calm him, waiting several minutes until his tears and rage began to subside.

When Dupree regained control, the officers told him as gently as they could how the fifteen-year-old boy had assaulted Angela on the way home from school. He had jerked her into an alley and vented all his hate on her eight-year-old body. They caught him just as he finished; they brought Angela home as soon as she could tell them where she lived.

For the next ten months, Joyce cowered behind the locked doors of their home, wide-eyed, silent, feeling no emotion other than fear. She left the house only to deliver the children to school, and she waited in the car, its engine running, at the front of the school when the children came out. The children were never out of the house alone. And without good reason, they never left the house at all.

Dupree knew they couldn't stay. He put out feelers for a position with a prosecutor's office in several surrounding states. The office in Denver responded.

Their eleven years in Denver had brought them to a near-normal life. The two years of therapy had helped. They never spoke of the rape anymore. From all appearances, Angela was a happy, normal, well-adjusted young woman. Only Dupree and Joyce were aware of the small, occasional things she said and did that made them remember.

Through it all, Dupree had been there for both Joyce and Angela. For the first two or three years, he was the first in Angela's room when she awoke in the night screaming. Holding her, he would talk quietly to her, telling her he was there and everything was all right. He would lie beside Joyce in the dark, listening to her breathe. He learned to tell when she had been awakened by a dream. He would quietly, gently reach for her and hold her, making no demands other than to let her know he was there. During the second year in Denver, she gave up using sedatives.

The bitterness and outrage were more than Dupree could handle for a time. For three years, he refused to prosecute a rape case, knowing that the violence inside him could erupt at any time. For five more years, his intense hatred for crimes of violence was controlled, but his detached, methodical, exhaustive preparation and presentation of the criminal cases he tried made him feared in the courtroom. The last four years he had begun to mellow, as time and experience worked their cathartic healing. But in the courtroom, he remained an impassioned, impersonal prosecutor—sometimes guardedly referred to by those who had faced him as "a machine" in his systematic, devastating presentation of a case. Dupree closed his eyes, took a deep breath, and turned the razor on again. He brought his thoughts back under control and finished shaving, pushing the nightmare back into its place. He quickly dressed and walked out to the car, ducking his head to get his stocky, five-foot-ten-inch frame into the Chevy.

● ● ●

"Hello, Charlie. Looks like we have a little bit of a different one here." Dupree was watching his feet while he entered the dark room, carefully avoiding the masking tape and overlapping electrical cords on the floor. He nodded to the detectives silently finishing their work of taking fingerprints, photographs, and videotapes.

"Hi, Al. Yeah, this one is different." Charlie paused and waited. He spoke slowly, deliberately, pulling his mind back from the intense concentration demanded in conducting a primary homicide investigation. He turned his large, round face to Dupree, waiting. Dupree picked up the conversation.

"This looks like an apartment. Carson lived here?"

"Yes, him or his partner Glenn Tolboy. They used it for convenience, when the work load prevented them from going home."

Their conversation was quickly becoming typical of people who lived by the one simple rule of primary homicide investigation: Get the facts. Their sentences were terse.

"Mind if I look around for a minute, Charlie?"

"Go right ahead. Be my guest." Charlie turned back to his work. Dupree drew a breath, feeling his mind settle for the task ahead. Not wanting to disturb the investigating team by unnecessary movement, he remained silent as he walked among the rooms, examining everything before him.

The masking tape outline on the gray carpet showed where the body had been. Dupree eyed the two massive, round bloodstains. He flared his nostrils slightly and caught the faint, acrid smell of burned gunpowder still hanging in the air. Dropping to one knee, he studied the outline briefly. Then he looked toward the door to the apartment and back to his left, toward the kitchenette. He walked over to a small table against the front wall, and leaned over, carefully examining the old Savage .300 rifle, two spent casings, and one badly misshapen bullet. He continued slowly through the living room, studying the ragged edges of the crater in the wallboard and the badly splintered pine two-by-four stud beneath it, where the detectives had dug out the spent bullet. Around the hole, in a fairly uniform circle about six feet in diameter, Dupree noted the concentration of blood flecks and tiny shards of tissue, now dried and clinging to the wall.

He moved quickly to the several cardboard boxes labeled "Hubbard's Orchards" stacked around the archway, opening a few of them to examine their contents; then through the kitchen, and into the bathroom, noting the absence of women's toiletries. In the bedroom, he glanced at the rumpled bed, the closet with men's clothing, and the dresser, with four drawers empty, two others with men's clothing.

Finished, he slowed his thoughts and began the mind-draining work of sifting through and weighing all that was there.

"Charlie, when you've got a minute . . ." Dupree moved to a corner in the living room that was away from the equipment and the detectives.

Charlie nodded, and set a drinking glass down on the table, careful not to disturb the black fingerprinting dust showing in splotches. He turned his full attention to Dupree as he stepped toward him.

"What can I help with, Al?" Dupree held his voice low.

"I think I have most of it figured, but there are two or three things that won't come together. Where's the second bullet, or bullet hole?"

"We think it went out the door. We think the entry door was open, and the first one went through Carson, and right on out."

Dupree glanced out onto the gravel, thick enough to support heavy construction equipment and provide water drainage during the spring snowmelt. It would be nearly impossible to find the bullet if it was out there.

"Where did the bullets hit Carson?"

"The first one went through the torso, the second one through his head."

Dupree's forehead wrinkled as he struggled to fit it together.

"Then that hole in the wall was made by the second bullet. At what angle was it traveling when it hit the wall and the stud?"

"Nearly level."

"What angle for the first shot?"

"Upward. It caught him just under his ribs on the left side, and exited just at the lower edge of his right shoulder blade."

"What time of day?"

"The coroner says about 5:30 this morning."

"Were the lights on or off? Any way to establish that?"

"We think off. The drapes were drawn."

Dupree paused, looked toward the kitchenette, and then to the open entry door, and finally at the bullet hole in the wall.

"That translates into someone firing from a low position right there"—he pointed at the kitchenette archway—"at Carson while he was standing about right there." He pointed just ahead of the blood-stains.

"In the dark. An ambush?"

"Possibly. We don't know."

"Any signs of a struggle? A fight?"

"None."

"What condition was the body in?"

Charlie's face showed revulsion. "Unrecognizable. We found a photograph in the bedroom that must be him with his wife and family, but you wouldn't know it was him by looking at the body. The head and its contents were about half gone. The slug we dug out of the wall was about a 150-grain soft-nosed hunting bullet. At that range—you'll have to see the photographs when they're developed."

"Did the coroner's people get the tissue picked up? The pieces the bullets took with them?"

"Yeah, as best they could. With tweezers."

After a pause, Dupree continued. "Two shots in the dark. How accurate?"

"Both smack on the button. The first one was good, the second one expert. The gunman knows how to handle a rifle."

Dupree's thoughts continued to race. "Which one killed him?"

"Either one was fatal, but we think the second one killed him. We don't know yet, because the coroner hasn't come up with an opinion."

Dupree nodded his head, tracking Charlie's words.

"Fingerprints?"

"Mostly his, except on the rifle. We found a second, smaller set around the trigger area. We think they belong to his wife; they match those on that drinking glass over there and a few other places in the apartment."

"His wife? A woman could shoot that accurately?"

"Surprised us too. But we don't argue with fingerprints."

A few seconds passed as Dupree digested the conclusions they had reached, and then he continued with another thought.

"Any witnesses to any of this?"

Charlie paused, knowing the impact the answer was going to have.

"Yeah—well, we don't know. When Reed got here, Ben Cooper was just leaving."

Dupree's head jerked around, his eyes instantly alive with shock and disbelief.

"Ben Cooper was here? Before Reed got here?"

"Yes. Ben told him he had kicked the door open, to be sure Carson couldn't be helped, but he didn't enter the room or disturb anything."

Dupree's head swiveled around and for the first time he noticed the splintered doorjamb. He quickly turned back to Charlie, a look of amazement on his face.

Over the years, the natural course of their professional work had brought Ben and Dupree into opposing positions in a number of heavy criminal trials, some of them first-degree murder. Inevitably, under the terrific stress and strain of the intense, emotionally charged combat of a courtroom, they had collided violently from time to time. But there had been no personal offense taken by either—no vendettas. In the process, each had developed a healthy respect for the other. The fact that Ben arrived before the police and kicked the door open was unbelievable.

Before Dupree could respond, Charlie continued.

"Ben came back later, just a little while ago, actually. He's had an interview with someone this morning, and whoever it was knows what happened here. He wanted to be certain he had been told the truth. He asked about some of what we had developed."

Recovering his composure, Dupree continued,

"If he knows who did it, what did he think was important?"

"Just the basic stuff. He wanted to know where the empty casings were, and the origin and the ending place of each shot. He wanted to know which shot came first and which of the two killed Carson, and the time interval between the shots. And he asked for a photograph of a mark on the wallpaper over by the kitchenette."

"Show me." Dupree started toward the doorway.

Charlie stooped over and identified and traced a faint, almost unnoticeable, arcing mark beginning at about the forty-two-inch level and rounding downward toward the archway, ending at a point on the doorframe that showed a slight bruise on the paint.

"Is that what I think it is, Charlie?"

"I imagine it is. We think it is a mark made by the blade on the front sight of the rifle as it slid toward the doorframe. The lab will tell us later today."

"Did you ask Cooper just what was driving him to kick the door open before you guys got here?"

"I did, and all he said was 'personal'."

"Personal! Personally involved?"

Charlie's eyes temporarily showed his surprise. "No, nothing we've found would support that."

Dupree moved his feet, interrupting his thoughts, then continued.

"Think you'll see Cooper again tonight?"

"Yeah, if what I gave him checks out with what his client gave him, and if Wylie Benoit declares the client competent."

Dupree nodded. "Thanks, Charlie. Cooper's name goes to the head of the witness list. If I have to call him as a prosecution witness, I will. I'm heading to the coroner's office."

"You call if the coroner gives you anything, okay?"

Dupree nodded and started toward his car. Squinting against the bright sunlight, he waved to Charlie.

"And you let me know if Cooper gives us anything."

Chapter Six

DUPREE WALKED THROUGH the nearly deserted emergency room of Denver General Hospital and took the stairs to the basement. Opening the sliding door, he stepped into the small foyer of the coroner's office.

"Something I can do for you?" The hesitant, tentative, small, gray-haired woman behind the counter, employed only for Saturday mornings, hoped the man was here on a routine matter she could cope with.

Dupree smiled and said calmly, "I am Mr. Dupree, chief of criminal investigations from the district attorney's office. I understand a Mr. Leslie Carson was brought here earlier this morning, dead from gunshot wounds. I would appreciate seeing the body."

"Do you have some identification?" Dupree produced his card.

"You can go on down to the autopsy room—-you know where it is?"

"Yes, I know. Thank you." He turned through the big double doors marked AUTHORIZED PERSONNEL ONLY, wrinkling his nose against the sterile smell of formaldehyde.

Two white-gowned men were bent over the big stainless steel table, V-shaped to allow drainage to the center. One was dictating medical jargon into a hand-held recorder, his tie loosened, sleeves pulled back. The other man, tie immaculately knotted, gown fully buttoned and sleeves extended, was hunched over a nude male body covered with a surgical drape from the waist down. The body was propped on its left side, exposing a gaping wound on the right shoulder blade and a sickening crater in the right side of the head. The man was taking careful measurements of the wounds and writing them on a meticulously hand-drawn sketch of the body.

Dupree glanced at the trays of bottles and surgical steel equipment, and the pile of swabs and blood-soaked gauze pads as he walked toward the two men. He was mildly surprised he recognized neither one.

He showed them his identification, then spoke.

"Hi. I'm Al Dupree from the district attorney's office." He extended his arm, and they shook hands. As they did, the man with the neat tie spoke.

"I'm Alfred Pinnock, deputy forensic pathologist. This is Dr. Robert Lowe." Pinnock was smiling expectantly. "I presume you came to examine the corpse of Leslie Carson." Dupree glanced at the body. "Yes, I did. Mind if I take a look?"

"Not at all." Pinnock stepped back to allow Dupree room, bumping one of the wheeled tray stands in his eagerness to accommodate.

Dupree leaned over silently looking closely at the gaping cone-shaped hole in the head. Then he looked briefly at the wound in the back.

"Were both of these wounds fatal?"

"Either one would have killed him. The one through his torso would have killed him in seconds. The one through the head was instant."

Dupree's eyes momentarily scanned the clipboard. The sketch was exact, the notes in precise handwriting.

"Any way to determine which came first?"

"It was the torso shot."

Without an indication to either man, Dupree was noticing everything about Pinnock, silently evaluating him as they moved through the interview, formulating some idea of what kind of a witness he would make and how to handle him. Dupree knew all too well the consequences of presenting a case through sloppy, ineffective witnesses.

"What is the official cause of death?" Dupree turned his gaze directly into Pinnock's face.

Pinnock caught the sudden seriousness and glanced at his notes, sensing a slight tension in the bottom-line question.

"Death resulted from a gunshot wound to the cranium."

Dupree paused to allow the information to settle in. The killing shot was the fulcrum on which the case would finally be balanced; on which conviction or acquittal would be decided.

"Is there anything else remarkable? Any indication of alcohol or drugs or anything?"

"His blood shows about a .04 alcohol content. He'd had a little to drink but was not legally intoxicated. We found no evidence of drugs or any other substance that would affect his senses—nothing remarkable other than the wounds. It's been difficult making a written report of the head wound. As badly as the cranium and the brain were damaged, we had trouble identifying some of the fragments of material in the opening. There was tissue that went with both bullets out into the room. We had to gather that up and we have it in a container." Pinnock gestured to one side of the table.

Dupree walked to the workbench where the tools and bottles were clustered and Pinnock showed him the shreds of tissues on a metal tray. Dupree looked carefully and then glanced at Pinnock.

"I presume you intend to save it?"

"If you want it, yes. We'll bag it and freeze it."

Dupree walked toward the foot of the table and turned. "Could you have your people take good eight-and-a-half-by-eleven color images, high-resolution, and make enlargements about three to one to be used in court? Both wounds, entry and exit? It looks like you'll need good light to show the depth of the cavity in the head."

"We'll have it done in a little while. If you'll have your office contact us next week, they can pick up the report and the photographs."

"Mr. Pinnock, were there any marks on the body, perhaps the hands, that suggested a fight?"

Pinnock tipped his head forward as he carefully searched through his notes. Then he glanced at the body.

"No. Nothing I discovered. He was a good physical specimen, in sound condition, other than the bullet wounds. There were no marks on his body or his hands."

Speaking slowly for emphasis, Dupree asked, "Do you have an estimate of the time lapse between the first and second shot?"

Pinnock again referred to his notes, beginning to realize Dupree was not going to waste time with unnecessary formalities or trivia. "Our estimate is that it would have been about eight or ten seconds."

"Based on what factual evidence?" Pinnock was impressed with the direct, nearly impertinent manner. He continued his mode of precise, accurate statements.

"Partly on the size of the bloodstains on the carpet. The heart had been shocked but not entirely stopped when the first bullet went through, close to but not touching the heart. It pumped some blood out and was still pumping when the second bullet went through the head and stopped everything. Also, the amount of blood the heart pumped into the cavity will give us a pretty good idea how long it continued to beat after the torso shot. We'll know more when we open the chest for the autopsy."

Dupree shifted his foot so he was squarely facing Pinnock. "After the first shot went through his body, could Carson have presented a threat to anyone? Could he have delivered any physical harm to anyone?"

Pinnock slowed his speech, giving thought to the weight of the question.

"No, no. Absolutely not. For all practical purposes, he was totally and permanently disabled when the first shot left his body."

Dupree's eyes dropped, and he slowly nodded, a hint of smile showing.

"Thanks for your help. Would you let my office know if anything unexpected shows up?"

As the heavy stainless steel doors swung closed behind Dupree, Pinnock heaved a sigh and glanced at his notes, unconsciously beginning a mental review of them in response to his dominating inner compulsion for meticulous accuracy and orderliness.

Dupree felt his spirits lift a little as he left the autopsy room. Pinnock would be a good witness. It never crossed Dupree's mind that he might also make a strong witness for the defense. He entered the elevator and pushed the button for the ground floor, his head tipped slightly forward as he slowly, carefully integrated the facts he had just learned with the legal framework in which they would be tested. When the elevator doors opened, his brow was knitted, his mind preoccupied. He stepped out and walked through the emergency room toward the exit doors. With his head still tipped slightly forward, brow furrowed in thought, he only peripherally noticed the four people standing near the exit door, nearly in his path. He made a slight adjustment to walk around them when a faint sense of warning told him something was familiar about one of the men standing with the group of people, three men and a woman. The man had his back to Dupree and was talking to a doctor, examining a medical report. The size and build of the man and the sound of his voice were familiar.

At the moment Dupree passed them, the man suddenly shook the doctor's hand, thanked him, and made a slight turn to his right, his shoulder brushing against Dupree's. In that instant, Dupree realized it was Ben Cooper.

His head jerked left as Ben's jerked right, and the men stood there stunned, staring at each other for what seemed minutes, unable to rally their thoughts or presence of mind to say anything. Dupree had the advantage; he knew Ben was involved, but at that point, Ben didn't know Dupree had entered the case.

Instantly the realization came to Dupree: He's here because of the killing, but why?

It took slightly longer for Ben's mind to connect Dupree with the killing. He visibly recoiled as it registered to him that Dupree was investigating the killing and had been down to examine Les. Dupree's eyes instantly swept the other three faces, and despite his deeply ingrained habit of showing no emotion, his mouth opened for a second, then closed, as he saw Joan. He paused, taking in the total impression of her battered, bruised face in less than a second. He knew instantly who she was and why Ben was here with her. Most of the questions he had raised back in the apartment were being answered.

His eyes came back to Ben's, and Dupree spoke first.

"Hello, Ben."

Ben nodded. "Hi, Al."

Neither man knew what should be said next; professional ethics prevented either from inquiring of the other about his presence in the hospital. Dupree couldn't ask for introductions, nor could Ben volunteer them without risking a breach of confidence. Each instantly realized he had simply blundered into one of those bizarre, explosive, chance events that can abruptly change the course of lives.

Dupree recovered first, and said the only thing he could think of that would be ethically acceptable.

"Nice seeing you, Ben."

Ben nodded, holding his expression blank while his mind raced. Dupree continued out the emergency doors, his pace and manner deliberate, not looking back. Ben's eyes trailed him until he turned and was out of sight.

Quickly Ben looked back at the doctor, thanked him for the report, and assured him he would be in contact regarding the nature of the case and his possible appearance as a witness in a trial. Then Ben caught Joan gently by the arm and signaled David with his head to step back to the phone bank opposite the reception desk.

He fumbled for a number in the directory, inserted a coin into the phone, and dialed.

"This is Ben Cooper speaking. May I speak with the coroner on duty, please?" He pursed his mouth and waited a moment, eyes locked with David's for a second.

"Hello. This is Ben Cooper speaking. May I speak to Mr. Dupree, from the prosecutor's office? I believe he was coming over to examine the body of Leslie Carson."

He paused. "No, I'll talk with him later. Thanks."

He turned, making an instant assumption as he faced Joan and David. Joan spoke first.

"Ben, what's wrong? Who was that man and why such an odd thing between you two?" Her face showed her fear.

Ben nodded his head, seeing her concern.

"That man is Alonzo J. Dupree. He's the chief prosecutor in charge of felony cases and he is one tough gentleman in a courtroom. He knows about Les and I'm sure he knows I was involved. I'll bet he's been at the apartment and talked with Charlie or Reed. Or both."

His face nearly blanched as he continued letting his thoughts run.

"Oh my, I think we just unwittingly gave every missing piece in the puzzle to them."

Joan drew a sharp breath, not knowing the legal consequences of what had happened, but aware that it sounded ominous. Ben read her gasp and the startled, probing look in her eyes.

"No, Joan. Don't get alarmed. It's certain he recognized you from the photographs they must have found there, and if he did, he knows who you are. And he certainly knows you took a bad beating this morning. If he knows that, he knows you shot Les, and he thinks it was because he was beating you. He has probably figured out why the shots were fired from a sitting position and the sequence of the shots."

Joan steadied her gaze and with a forced composure in her voice she asked, "Ben, is it all over for me? What do I . . . is it all over?" She didn't show outright panic, but a controlled fear.

"No, Joan. Get a hold of yourself and settle down. He won't move on this until he has it all in hard facts in a written document from Charlie Fawcett's office, called an 'Information.' What he saw here won't be in that document; it will just considerably speed up the process of getting a warrant."

Ben paused and reflected, his mind sorting out the consequences of the startling development.

"I don't think it hurt us, at least not in the long run. I think it put us on a pretty fast timetable, but that's about all. Come on. We've got to get to Wylie Benoit's office for the psychological evaluation as soon as we can."

● ● ●

Dupree drove straight to his office, his mind going over the implications of the chance meeting. Once seated behind his desk, he picked up the phone and in seconds had Charlie Fawcett on the line. He came straight to the point.

"I know who shot Carson and I know the immediate reason he was shot. Cooper will be defending her and I know what the defense is going to be. I even have a pretty good idea what the jury will do with this."

There was a pause as Charlie swallowed, his eyes widening as he realized what he was hearing.

"A confession? Cooper came in?"

"No. Maybe better. By sheer accident, I walked right into them in the hospital emergency foyer. Mrs. Carson—is her name Joan?—was there, and Cooper and his associate were just finishing a conversation with a doctor. Cooper was holding a medical report."

Dupree paused to give emphasis.

"She was badly beaten this morning. Her left eye was almost closed, her nose was swollen, her cheek and mouth swollen, and she was black and blue from the shoulders up. She must have gotten into a donnybrook with her husband this morning at the apartment, and he must have really worked her over. I think he knocked her against the wall, the rifle slid over against her, and she just used the opportunity to stop the fight. Okay so far?"

Charlie was tracking, step by step. "Yeah. I can guess the rest of it. But go on."

"She knocked him off his feet with number one, waited until he was down and quit moving, then blew half his head away with number two."

Dupree was reciting like a machine now, reverting to his style of presenting facts with a cold, relentless accuracy that was overpowering.

"Cooper is going to defend her on the claim of self-defense. The problem is, self-defense might explain the first shot, but not the second one. She might get away with one, but not two. She had too much time to think, and she did too good a job on accuracy. She's looking at a minimum conviction of Manslaughter One, maximum of Murder Two."

In Dupree's mind, the facts were being set in concrete and doors were closing. In his certainty, he was forming opinions that he would not again open for discussion.

There was a long pause while he gave Charlie time to think. Finally he got a response.

"It all fits. What a crazy development. You got the missing piece and the puzzle came together. I can't mention this in the Information, which means I'll have to finish it the usual way, on the hard facts we have. But it will sure speed it up. I'll let you know when it's finished. It will probably be sometime early in the morning. I have to wait for the usual lab reports to go with it to support a Murder One charge. Are we going Murder One?"

"Yeah. With Cooper representing her, we'll have to. I'll need all the elbowroom I can get to bargain down to a lesser charge. I'll let the on-duty judge know we'll be in to see him sometime tomorrow to get the warrant signed. Oh, and one more thing. If Cooper does come in tonight to make any deals, be sure you protect your rear end and mine. If the media gets into this thing, I don't want any questions about sweetheart deals. I really wouldn't like being on *Sixty Minutes*. Okay?"

"I hear you. I'll be in touch if lightning strikes."

● ● ●

"I need to have you examined for certification that you are mentally and emotionally sound," Ben explained to Joan as he drove toward the tall buildings of downtown Denver. "I'm sure you are, but it is something that has to be done. The man I want you to see is Wylie Benoit. He's a psychiatrist—one of the best."

As they entered the modern building and took the elevator to the sixth floor, Ben continued conversing with Joan.

"Don't be fooled by your first impressions of Dr. Benoit. He's quite small and you'll notice his ears stand out too far from his head." Ben was nearly smiling as he considered the contradictions that were wrapped into Wylie. "He dresses in the latest fashion—a real Dapper Dan. He is a textbook gentleman—will nearly overpower you with his ingratiating manners—and at times you can't find his off button. He might talk your leg off. But don't let that lead you away from what's inside. He's probably the keenest psychiatric mind in the western part of this country. He's a guest lecturer at the annual International Psychiatric Convention, where the best talent in the world comes to listen and learn. Tell him everything he asks for. Okay?"

Joan nodded, intrigued and now impatient to meet him. Leaving the elevator, Ben directed Joan and David a few steps down the hall and opened the large door to Wylie's office, stepping aside to allow them to enter ahead of him. Wylie was walking to meet them when Ben closed the door and turned. Startled at Joan's appearance, Wylie stopped, his eyes growing wide, waiting for an explanation from Ben.

"Wylie, this is Joan Carson. Joan, this is Dr. Wylie Benoit."

Joan put out her hand and nodded as she spoke, immediately aware why Ben had taken the time to describe Wylie and prepare her for this meeting. Even attending this unexpected emergency appointment on a Saturday, he was wearing a full three-piece suit with French cuffs and cuff links showing in just the right proportions at his wrists. She had to look down two inches into his eyes.

"Hello, Dr. Benoit."

Wylie paused, quickly sensing that a direct approach would probably help disarm a rather tense, embarrassing situation.

"I am not yet aware of the entire problem, Mrs. Carson, but I can obviously see part of it. It's what I can't see that perhaps I can help with." Wylie smiled and waited, his sense of confidence and ease serving to calm the others.

Ben gently spoke. "Joan, my—our chief concern is you. Considering what you've been through, we will both understand if you are reluctant to go through an examination by Dr. Benoit right now, but if it is possible, it is essential. How do you feel? Can you make it?"

Joan looked indecisive. "I don't know what the examination entails, but if it's necessary, I'll handle it."

"Wylie, where can we all sit down?"

Wylie turned immediately, and with a flourish to his hand gesture, invited Joan to enter his inner office first, then Ben and David. Wylie followed, closing the door as they all sat down around his large desk.

Ben leaned slightly forward, while Wylie waited expectantly and Joan wondered. David was still, watching.

"Wylie, the past few weeks Joan's husband Les began a change in his conduct that got bizarre, crazy. It came to a head this morning, about 5:30. Joan went to an apartment at the construction building where her husband is a partner, to get some of her personal things. Her husband surprised her, and for reasons which she still doesn't understand, he gave her a beating."

Wylie glanced at Joan for a moment; she lowered her eyes, embarrassed at her appearance.

Ben continued. "By pure accident, an old rifle fell across her lap after he knocked her down, and without thought, she used it to stop him. She fired two shots, about six or eight seconds apart. The first through his torso, the second through his head."

Ben paused, knowing he had to give Wylie time to absorb the details. Wylie sat motionless and looked inquiringly at Ben.

Ben continued. "There's a second part of this that we must consider. By sheer coincidence we bumped into Al Dupree—the prosecutor on this case—at the hospital after I got Joan checked out for injuries. He saw Joan and her condition." Ben paused to look at her for emphasis. "Dupree's pretty sharp. There isn't a question he put it all together two minutes after he saw her.

"That incident reduces the time for obtaining a warrant, and puts me on a pretty tight timetable. I don't want them to arrest Joan right now because I don't want her in jail—for a lot of reasons, but the important one is the loss of time right up front, while this thing is fresh and developing.

"So, I need your help on two things. Is she competent and can she help make some heavy decisions this afternoon?"

Ben paused, and Wylie caught his earnestness and intensity.

"I want to make an offer to the sheriff's office this evening to bring her in voluntarily on Monday, if that's what we decide to do. Can we get that far yet today?"

Wylie stood and paced toward the ceiling-to-floor sheers that partly obscured the window-wall of his office. He pursed his lips, considering.

"Yes, we can. Anything else?"

"No, not for now." Ben turned his eyes to Joan, continuing in his paced, controlled tone.

"Joan, this will not be difficult—in fact, probably easier than what I've put you through already. I'll be back as soon as Wylie finishes."

Joan nodded, her developing understanding and trust beginning to emerge in her expression.

Wylie spoke his reassurances to Joan. "All I need is a little time to carry on a conversation with you. I think you will be surprised at how easy this will be. I think I can be finished in an hour, hour and a half. My biggest concern is that you'll be concerned. Please don't be, Mrs. Carson." He turned to Ben. "I'll call you, Ben. Okay? Your office?"

Ben nodded. "Wylie, here's the medical report from Dr. Winters at the hospital for whatever use you might want to make of it. I'll get it later." He looked at Joan and reached for her arm, taking hold for a moment, then patting it reassuringly. Joan set her jaw, then smiled to give Ben a little comfort. "I'll be okay."

Joan was puzzled that Ben had failed to mention their lifelong friendship, but her trust that Ben knew what he was doing kept her

from asking. She watched as Ben and David left, then turned and
took the seat indicated by Wylie.

● ● ●

"Ben, what's a Savage .300 rifle and when did Joan have time to
load it before she shot Les?"

David was quietly pacing the floor in Ben's office, where both
were waiting for Wylie's call.

"Savage Firearms makes the .300. It shoots a .30-caliber bullet
about 2200 feet per second. Makes a horrible wound. As for when she
had time to load it, she didn't need to. It was already loaded. I bet
that old rifle hasn't been unloaded in eighty years. It stood behind
the Albertsons' kitchen door up at their ranch ever since I can remember. I've seen it there five hundred times, with cartridges in the magazine, ready to go. When Joan moved to Denver it naturally came with
her; so far as she's concerned, it's just a standard piece of equipment
or furniture."

David paused, filing the information in his mind, then continued
his slow pacing. Ben was seated at his desk, eyes blankly staring at the
glass-covered desktop, one finger idly tapping as he reflected on the
wild events of the day. He glanced at David, briefly wondering what
his thoughts were at this moment.

Ben contemplated David. He tended to be quiet—perhaps a sign
of lingering sadness. He had been orphaned when he was fourteen
but he still was persistent and steady and rose to challenges with a
passion. He had maturity beyond his years. An aged uncle and aunt
took him in while he worked his way through high school, then he
was on his own. He got through college and law school by earning
athletic scholarships and taking after-hours work during the school
year wherever he could find it. During the summers, he took the
highest-paying job he could find, no matter how tough or dirty the
work was. Ben knew that David's maturity and gritty determination
would be needed to handle what was rapidly becoming a difficult,
maybe impossible case.

In the silence of their thoughts, the ring of the phone sounded
too loud, jolting them back to the present. After receiving the brief
message, they headed for the door.

CHAPTER SEVEN

"MR. COOPER." WYLIE HAD JUST opened the door to his office and motioned toward his foyer, inviting Ben and David to enter.

Ben entered, nodding to Wylie, and his eyes appraising Joan.

"Joan, you all right?" She pursed her mouth and nodded.

"I'm fine." It was more a declaration of determination than a statement of condition. Wylie closed the door and began talking as he walked a pace or two forward to address them all.

"I believe Mrs. Carson has survived the last hour." He smiled at Joan, his eyes inviting a response.

"I'm surprised at how easy it turned out to be," Joan admitted.

Ben looked at Wylie, eyes narrowed, his smile fading, impatient to get to the bottom line now that he knew things had gone well. Wylie took his cue.

"For the benefit of all of us, I want you to know Joan is fine. She experienced a dramatic trauma this morning, but she is handling it very well. At this moment, she is absolutely within normal limits and I am certain she will continue to be so. I might say, she has a strong—in fact, very strong—constitution. It goes without saying she knows right from wrong, and did throughout the early hours of the morning. I am certain her judgment is competent and sound at this time, and that she can assist in making any decisions necessary to prepare her defense."

He paused and looked at Ben waiting for a signal he had covered all the bases.

Ben considered and nodded. "Good. Very good." He waited for Wylie to continue.

Wylie directed himself to Joan.

"Joan, as I mentioned to you, there are a few things I need to discuss with Ben and it is probably better if he and I do it privately. Would you excuse us for just a few minutes? Be assured these matters are not secret, nor negative—just things we must discuss professionally, which require some discretion and confidentiality. I'm sure you understand. Please be seated and help yourself to some of the magazines." He gestured to the large, glass-topped, ornately designed table.

Joan nodded, offered her thanks, and she and David sat down as Wylie escorted Ben into his inner office. Ben spoke first as he sat down.

"Is she all right? Are there any cracks in her personality, down deep?"

Wylie's smile faded, and his face took on an inquisitive look, almost stern. "No. She's sound. You didn't tell me she and her husband have been your lifelong friends. Was there a reason?"

"I just wanted you to analyze this case as objectively as possible. I thought that might start you out a little slanted."

The smile returned to Wylie's face as he nodded his understanding. He raised his eyebrows and looked directly at Ben, still smiling.

"Not bad." His expression settled down to business as he continued. "I need some things from you, Ben, to give me a stronger sense of confidence in just a few areas. Will that be all right?"

Ben nodded. "What's up?"

"First, I'm not too comfortable with the shooting sequence she described. I mean, this woman is a real classy lady, not by acquired graces, but by her very nature. Is she really able to shoot a rifle with sufficient skill to place two shots with accuracy, in the dark, after having been beaten?"

Ben's answer came instantly.

"Absolutely. Understand, Wylie, she comes from the high mountain ranch country. She's been shooting guns since she was about ten or twelve, and the one she used this morning was the one she's used for big game since she was about thirteen. I won't multiply words unnecessarily. The answer is yes. Don't doubt it for a second."

Wylie bobbed his head up and down, his smile widening as something he felt to be humorous crossed his mind. "The next thing you will be giving me is your standard 'tougher than saddle leather' statement in describing this woman, right?"

Ben ducked his head for just a moment, grinning, knowing how Wylie thrived on the stories Ben was continually telling him from his childhood and youth, seldom missing an opportunity to needle him about them.

"Nope, I won't have to. You did it just fine."

"I gather you and Les were inseparable friends until you left for college, and you've stayed in touch since. From what I learned from

Joan in this short time, I understand he began a radical change of conduct months ago that culminated in this morning's shooting. Without going into detail, would you have suspected him capable of beating Joan?"

Ben shook his head, then spoke. "Not under any circumstance."

Wylie paused to give emphasis.

"Would you have suspected Joan capable of shooting him?"

"Not in my worst nightmares. Never."

Wylie dropped his eyes and his brow wrinkled in thought, then he continued.

"Ben, I also need to know—"

Ben cut him off. "Wylie, don't leave that subject yet. Did Joan tell you about the business reversals? The problems they brought down on Les?"

"She did. A business grossing one hundred million dollars per year could do horrible things to a man if it suddenly came apart at the seams. That's understandable."

Ben's eyes narrowed with intensity. "Do you think it can explain what went wrong with Les?"

Wylie looked thoughtful. "I doubt it. If he is of the same cut as yourself and Joan—I mean, with a constitution that has much in common with a blacksmith's anvil—it might have made him a little nervous. But I don't believe it's the answer. That has yet to be explored. My basic mission here today is Joan, not Les. Let's put that on hold for a few days, okay?"

Ben nodded. "Right. What else was it you needed from me?"

"Ben, I need to know your stake in this thing. I knew when you walked in something was different. I know now it is what these people mean to you. Specifically, have you ever had any romantic interest in Joan? Any intimate, sexual relationship?"

Again Ben's answer came immediately.

"None. Ever." Ben stopped, waiting.

"Ever been in love with her?"

"No, Wylie, not romantically in love with her. Not the way you mean it. My feelings for both Joan and Les run pretty deep. I've never been asked to put them into words. In the classic sense, I suppose I love them. Both of them."

Wylie looked at Ben, and for several seconds a silence hung between them as he probed Ben's eyes and let the words sink in. He paused, sure he had the answer he needed, but asked one more question to be certain. The smile was gone, his expression earnest.

"Is that why you're taking this thing on?"

Ben paused, dropped his eyes and nodded, knowing what the next question was going to be.

"Can you handle it, Ben? Right at the top of her list of heroes, Joan Carson has included the names of Joshua Albertson, Leslie Carson, and Joseph Benjamin Cooper. You're the only one she has left. That's just a little frightening, isn't it?"

Ben didn't respond for several seconds, as he reached deep inside himself for the answer.

"It's heavy, Wylie. I can tell you right now this case is probably going to go against her, one way or another. I mean, a conviction for some degree of murder or manslaughter. It's that damned second shot. I know the risks—the legal axioms against representing someone close to you under these circumstances." Ben paused, covered his eyes with his hand and began rubbing them, feeling a weariness settling over him. He continued softly. "What about it, Wylie? What should I do?"

Wylie looked at him intently for several moments, then rose and walked toward the window. He clasped his hands behind his back, still looking out over the street below, lost in deep concentration for several seconds.

"I can't tell you that, Ben, but let me give you what I can. I analyzed the shooting sequence just the way you did. The prosecutor will hang his case on the second shot and that's going to be hard to beat in a courtroom. If another attorney defends Joan, who doesn't have the reasons you do to help her, he's going to do his professional duty in the standard, objective way. That means he'll get her into a plea bargain that will conclude by her having a felony record and probably some prison time."

Wylie turned and walked back toward Ben, sitting down as he finished.

"The problem I have is, I don't think this woman is guilty of the intent necessary to commit a homicide."

Ben's eyes narrowed, incredulous. In one stroke, Wylie had laid the case wide open, revealing the question on which it would ultimately come to rest. Wylie's expression didn't change. He continued.

"I don't know if we stand a snowball's chance in hell, Ben, but the bottom line is, I think she reacted on instinct peculiar to the female of our species and in my professional opinion, she *couldn't* form the necessary intent. After eighteen years of forensic psychiatry, I respectfully submit I am qualified to make that call and I'm making it now, foolish as it may be with just an hour's interview."

He changed his expression to one of finality and made his conclusion. "Anyway, if I were Joan, considering your motivations in this case, not to mention your scholarly and gentlemanly courtroom demeanor, I would give anything I had to get you into this case. It might be the only thing standing between her and some other safe, objective defense counsel selling her up the river." He rose, offering as an afterthought, "Your legal axioms to the contrary notwithstanding."

At the mention of his "scholarly and gentlemanly courtroom demeanor," a wry smile flickered across Ben's face. In the past sixteen years, Ben had used Wylie professionally more than a dozen times, six times in first-degree murder cases. Wylie had vivid memories of the many times Ben had gone head to head with opposing counsel in open court, tenacious, occasionally loud, giving no thought to being gentlemanly or scholarly.

Ben slowly leaned back, realizing they were now making the first major decision of the case. As his conclusion began to form, his head began to nod slightly.

"For now, I think I better hang with it. Let's see what develops."

Wylie nodded, satisfied. Ben continued.

"To keep her from an immediate arrest that would put her in jail until she could be arraigned, I want to get to Charlie's office as soon as I can. The plan is to tell them she was involved in the shooting and in exchange for their not arresting her now, I'll bring her in Monday morning for booking and arraignment. What I need to know from you is whether or not she can competently help me make that decision and whether you approve of it."

Wylie considered. "Yes, she can competently help you. Shall we go on out and take care of it now?"

Ben rose, pausing only to ask, "Anything else we need to handle here?"

Wylie shook his head no as he opened the door, standing back in his most gentlemanly manner, as he allowed Ben through the door first.

Wylie took charge. "Joan, Ben and I agree that you should consider a proposal he has to make. Ben?" He turned, smiling, having focused their attention.

Ben sat down on the overstuffed sofa near Joan and turned to her. "Joan, I think you understand the sheriff's office will be obtaining a warrant for your arrest in the next several hours."

Joan was silent, listening to every word. "If they do arrest you, the procedure is to take you to the city-county jail, kitty-corner from the courthouse, and hold you there until they can find a judge to arraign you and set your bail. Once bail is set, you'll have to remain there until it can be arranged. All that might take a day or two. I don't want that to happen to you."

Joan nodded, waiting now for the alternative.

"I propose that I go down to the sheriff's office soon and make an offer to Charlie Fawcett, their chief investigator. You remember?" She nodded and he continued. "The deal would be to have them hold off on serving the warrant, on my promise that I would bring you in Monday for booking and arraignment and posting bail in one transaction, so to speak, which would last about two hours and result in no time in jail."

He paused, trying to get a reading on Joan's reactions. She closed her eyes for a second, then opened them.

"Does this mean I would plead guilty?" She was calm, focused.

"No. It means I would tell Charlie you were involved in the shooting, in fact, that you did shoot Les. However, when you do enter your plea, it will be not guilty. There will be no confession of guilt."

"Do I have to go through a booking and an arraignment, as you call it?"

"Yes. Either way, the process requires it. The difference is that I think I can arrange it to suit my schedule, not theirs, and I think I can keep you from spending any time in jail."

She suddenly leaned forward, bowing her head slightly, speaking almost as though to herself. "This is just unreal. I can hardly keep up with the events since early this morning. The apartment, the hospital, a psychiatrist, a lawyer . . ." Then she raised her head and spoke with resolution.

"I agree with you, Ben. Do what you think is best. Do I go with you?"

"No. I go alone. I will call you as soon as I know whether Charlie will accept the offer or not. I can't force it if he won't."

"Okay, I understand. Dr. Benoit, is it all right?"

"It certainly is. I agree with Ben."

Ben looked at Wylie, waiting for any final advice. Wylie stood and started for the door.

"Ben, please call me at my home number—I presume you still have it—when this thing is finally resolved tonight, will you? Joan, my secretary Maggie will be in touch Monday to set up a schedule of visits and tests that I will need if I am to help you in a trial. Will that be all right?"

Joan nodded and paused, thrusting out her hand. "Dr. Benoit, thank you very much. I wish our meeting could have been under other circumstances, but we have to take it as it comes." As Wylie shook her hand, he responded.

"Making your acquaintance is welcome under any circumstances, Joan. Call me at either of these numbers if you need me." He handed her his business card.

Wylie opened the door to the hallway and the three of them left. Outside, the afternoon light was beginning to fade. As they entered the car, Ben turned to Joan.

"Where would you like to go while I visit with Charlie Fawcett?"

She shook her head. "I hadn't thought that far. I guess home."

Ben thought for a minute.

"Do the twins know about this yet?"

She closed her eyes and laid her head back against the headrest. "Oh Lord, no. I hadn't even thought of them. They're up at Boulder in school. I probably won't be able to call them until tonight—it's Saturday."

"Come on to my house. Laura's there by now. She can handle this thing. Call the twins from there and tell them to come directly to my home, no matter what time it is. You'll stay there in the guest bedroom tonight. I don't want you in that big house of yours alone and I want to be there when we have to tell the twins. Okay?"

Joan shook her head, a slow smile coming. "The Carsons are in trouble, so here come the Coopers to help. Ben, do you think we'll ever get out of Caldwell?"

He chuckled at the thought. "You mean, get Caldwell out of us." He waited a moment. "Settled? You'll come and stay with Laura while I'm gone?"

She nodded assent.

● ● ●

"What can I do for you, Cooper?" Charlie looked rumpled and sounded distant. Ben took a second before speaking, concluding he'd better come straight to the point.

"Let's get right to it, Charlie. I'm authorized to tell you Joan Carson is responsible for the death of her husband Leslie Carson. There isn't much point in discussing the details because after my chance meeting with Dupree this morning, you've got them all put together. I just want to make an offer that will save you some trouble and spare me a scramble over the weekend."

Charlie nodded. "We've got enough for the warrant. There are still a few things we don't know, but that's okay. We'll get them." He stopped, making it clear he was willing to take it further, or drop it right there, depending on Ben.

"What is it you lack?" Ben kept it going.

There was a cutting edge in Charlie's answer. "What demons were driving you this morning, Cooper? I mean, kicking that door down was a little extreme, wouldn't you say?" Ben felt his defenses rising, sensing what was coming.

"No. Under the circumstances I don't think so." His words were clipped, dispassionate.

"What circumstances, Cooper? What was Les Carson to you?"

Ben's eyes narrowed. "A friend."

"What is Joan Carson to you?"

"A friend."

"What is your justification for knowingly interfering with standard police procedures? Wake up and smell the coffee, Cooper. What is Joan Carson to you?"

Charlie suddenly stood, his chin thrust out, his great frame leaning forward, knuckles on the desk and his massive, stiff arms supporting his upper body.

Ben walked directly to the front of the desk until the front of his legs were touching it. He leaned slightly forward, purposely bringing himself face to face with Charlie. His words were soft, but terse and forceful.

"A friend. A lifelong friend. Les was my buddy from as far back as I can remember. Les and Joan have been in love since high school and I couldn't have felt happier when they got married. And that's all."

Ben stopped and his eyes locked with Charlie's. Neither man moved.

Three seconds of stillness passed before Charlie cut loose.

"Come on, Ben, don't you realize where you've put us?" he roared. "A high-profile citizen was shot to death today in one of the most bizarre murders in recent history around here. Our people get a call, go directly to the scene, and what do we find? A 'friend' of the wife leaving the scene, the front doorjamb splintered where he forced entry, the murder weapon carefully leaned against a wall, and a shooting job that *had* to be done by an expert, which you are. And all we are getting from you is that you romped out there at 120 miles an hour to have a look, just because she happened to be a 'friend' of yours. Now you're here and have neatly boxed us in.

You're her defense counsel, so we can't examine you like a regular witness, and your little escapade of getting there first and kicking the door open gives you the best of both worlds. You got the facts and you don't have to tell us. Right this minute, I can make a pretty convincing case of her getting a beating, you finding out about it and going out there in a rage and killing Carson yourself because you're having an affair with his wife. That didn't happen, but I hope you're starting to understand why we're just a little irritated with this cowboy routine of yours. What do you think the news media would do with this if we pass it off just because you're one of the good ole boys?"

Ben didn't move, nor answer, waiting to let Charlie get it all out. Charlie grappled for a moment, then his face sobered as he brought his frustrations under control.

"So now we've come full circle. What was Joan Carson to you?"

"I've answered that. Anything else?"

"A friend? That's it? You want me to believe that?"

"I answered you. Believe what you want." Ben's face was set, impassive, still showing no emotion other than a total unwillingness to be intimidated.

He waited, but Charlie didn't speak. Ben continued.

"Let's get back to my offer."

"Make it."

Charlie's snapped response nearly clipped Ben's words. His face was without emotion.

"I doubt you'll have your warrant ready before tomorrow, probably noon or after. If you'll hold back serving it until Monday morning, I'll have Joan Carson here, 8 o'clock sharp, for arrest and booking and the arraignment. In return, I'll waive the preliminary hearing and save Dupree the trouble of showing probable cause for holding Joan to stand trial."

"And we get butchered when the media finds out."

Now Ben showed temper. He leaned forward, his voice rising.

"Charlie, for once, just tell the media to go shove it up their damn noses if they don't like it. For goodness sake, we're dealing with a dead man that was as close a friend as I ever had, and his widow whom I've known since the day she was born. If the media makes any mistakes in reporting that, I'll sue the living hell out of them. Count on it. Now can you and I get that out of our craw and try to make sense of this? Come on Charlie, *be the chief investigator!*" Ben's eyes were flashing, his head thrust forward, the last words exploding.

Charlie held his stance for a moment, then slowly relaxed and eased back, straightening and dropping his hands. The fire slowly subsided from his eyes. He dropped his head forward and pursed his lips for a second.

"For the record, no deal. I'll make just one concession. We'll go through the normal process of getting the warrant issued, and then I'll take it for service myself and call you when I'm ready. If it gets too late in the day tomorrow, I'll hold it for service Monday, which is normal under these circumstances. Our records will show a perfectly normal process. If you haven't heard from me by about 8 o'clock tomorrow night, have her here at 8 o'clock sharp Monday morning. At 8:05 I come looking. Understood?"

Ben's stance eased.

"Understood. Charlie, can you give me a little benefit of the doubt until you get into this case? I know the risk I took this morning, and I know where it put you. I think you'll understand it better a little later on."

Charlie didn't respond. Ben turned to go.

"Thanks, Charlie."

"O eight hundred, Ben. Not one minute later."

As they approached the car, David walked to the driver's door.

"You ride passenger. You look beat and you still have a long night ahead of you at home. I'll drive."

Ben gratefully sat down in the passenger seat and leaned his head back against the headrest, closing his eyes, beginning to think through how he would handle the arrival of Joan's twins at his home sometime in the middle of the night. As the car started, he shivered slightly, feeling the chill of the evening air.

CHAPTER EIGHT

"SIT DOWN FOR A MINUTE BEFORE you go, Joan. I need to talk with you about a couple of things." Ben dropped his overcoat on the side of his desk, helped Joan remove hers and seated her, and motioned to David to take the chair next to her. He backed up to the front edge of his desk and rested against it, facing them. "Joan, did you understand most of what went on at the courthouse this afternoon? You understood the trial will begin November 29th, a Monday?"

"Yes, I got that." Joan was attentive, waiting.

"Was there anything about the proceedings today you didn't understand?"

"No. Setting the trial date was a lot easier than the booking and arraignment we had last week. That was just a nightmare of moving from one room to another, people giving orders, and being handed papers I still don't understand."

Ben dropped his chin, a slight smile of sympathy passing momentarily. "Was I able to explain most of it, or is there something about the arraignment that still concerns you?"

"No, I survived it. Can I ask more?" They both smiled.

"All right." Ben eased forward and walked around his desk, sitting down in his large office chair. "The judge for your case is Randolph Boyd. He's pretty much his own man. Gritty, but a people judge—by that I mean he sees the law as being the servant of the people, not vice versa. I feel okay about him. I hope you do."

He waited. Joan nodded. "I don't know enough about him yet, but he seemed to know how to move things along."

"He will in the trial, too. Joan, I need to know how you are getting along with Wylie. How do you feel about him?"

She looked up, eyes widening slightly. "Fine. Why? Has he said something?"

"No. Not at all. I have a phone message to visit him this afternoon and I wanted to have a feel for how you see your relationship

63

before I do. No problem. Has he covered most of the facts? Has he gotten most of the story?"

"Yes, he's thorough. And I think very intelligent."

Ben nodded agreement. "How are Chad and Sharlene handling this by now?"

"They're getting their feet back under them. Heavens, Ben, I don't know what I'd have done if you and Laura hadn't been there when they drove in that Sunday morning. Sharlene walked around for a day or two with that dead, blank stare in her eyes. Chad got back to the real world a little faster, but both of them have pretty well got it under control now."

"Any sign they're harboring hard feelings against you?"

"No, not that so much as being torn between a feeling of loyalty for Les and for me. They believe there has to be some reason behind the drastic change in their father. They're being pretty fair about it, and they're walking in on me all the time asking if they can help with supper or make beds or anything, just to let me know they're in support. They're okay."

"Are they going to return to school?"

"No, they're staying home this semester. We talked it over—I think it's best. Is that all right?"

"I think it's right. They should be here for the trial. How about yourself, Joan? Are you back to the real world?"

"I'll never be back to the real world that used to be. I'm in a new 'real world,' and I'm learning to live with it. I'll be okay. I just hope some day I'll understand what went wrong."

Ben paused and nodded in agreement. "Joan, I think I'll have to talk with some of the people out at the construction company as I investigate this case. Who are the main players out there?"

"Ann Fenton is the office manager. She's been there since before Les's time. Glenn Tolboy is gone, as you know. The number two man out there under Les—the number one man now—is Tom Price. He's a prize. You'll find those two can help you with most of what I imagine you'll need. If they can't, they'll help you find who can."

"Can you call and tell them they may be hearing from me?"

"I can. I don't know what kind of a reception I'll get. They might feel pretty . . . awful about me." She lowered her face for a moment as she worked to hold her composure.

Too late Ben realized he had embarrassed her. "I'm sorry—you're right. Never mind. I'll make the call." He paused. "Well, I think that covers it." He stood up and walked around the desk, helping Joan with her coat. "Call me if you need to and I'll do the same. Be careful driving home."

"Thanks, you two." She smiled as she turned and walked out the office door.

Ben turned back into the room and spoke to David as he walked to his desk chair. "I'm going to need some pretty heavy research, David. You got the time?"

David nodded, both men smiling, knowing David would take whatever time was necessary.

"Start with the annotations in the revised statutes. I think section 18.3.101 is the definitions section. Get into the current case law on intent. Scrutinize everything you come across, clear through the advance sheets. And I think it would be smart to get hold of the criminal law professor at Boulder and the student editor of the law review to see if they have anything new. Okay?"

"Got it. No problem."

"Oh, and would you get a porcelain board from the supply room and a tripod and a few dry pens? Set it up over there, out of the way, by the windows. I'm going to be making some diagrams before this is over, sure as the sun rises."

"Anything else?"

"No, not for now."

"I'm on my way."

As David left the room, Ben reached for the phone message slip, picked up the phone, and touched Wylie's number. On Wylie's invitation, Ben drove to his office immediately.

Wylie was waiting for Ben when he arrived. When both were seated in his office, Wylie leaned forward, his fingers interlaced, forearms on his desk, eyes alive and serious. "Ben, would it be admissible evidence if it could be proved that something was drastically wrong with Les?"

Knowing Wylie seldom scheduled sudden appointments and never spoke lightly on those occasions when he did, Ben was listening intently. Suspecting Wylie might know something that would explain Les's conduct, and consequently Joan's, Ben narrowed his eyes and locked them with Wylie's. "Under the present state of the law, probably not, no. But regardless of that, I want it. I want it all."

Wylie nodded his understanding, let a second go by, and continued. "It took me a while to realize it because I wasn't expecting it, but the answers I am getting from Joan's examination keep leading back to Les, and if one pauses to put it all together and look at it, his conduct becomes a sequence of confusing contradictions to say the least." He paused a moment to let Ben's thoughts focus.

Ben quietly asked, "Specifically?"

"It lacks consistency. By that I mean the change in him was limited, selective. If it had to do with the sudden pressures of having the entire construction business come down on him when his partner collapsed, you would expect the change to appear with some consistency in *all* his dealings with *all* people. It doesn't. I checked with the office manager, a Mrs."—he quickly opened his file and located the name—"Ann Fenton, and she confirmed that she knows of no brutal or violent acts, or outbursts of sudden, nonsense sentences. Except one. Apparently Les came to the office late one afternoon, went into Glenn Tolboy's office, and provoked a pretty loud argument about money. Mrs. Fenton heard it through the door. Les accused Glenn of mishandling—nearly stealing—company money. Mind you, this was between two men who had reportedly *never* passed a harsh word in thirteen years."

Wylie paused and Ben sat motionless, deep in concentration. Wylie continued.

"Tom Price, Ben's right-hand man for nine years, confirmed Mrs. Fenton's observations. The conclusion is that his physical violence seemed limited to the one person he loved above all, and that was Joan. The circle of verbal violence spread slightly to include his partner, Glenn, whom he regarded almost like a father, and loved, if that is the proper term. It does not include anyone else so far as I know. And even with Glenn and Joan it was irregular, coming and going in a pattern that defies predicting. The result is an inconsistency that I suddenly realized is staring at us, trying to tell us something about Leslie Carson."

Now Wylie slowly unlocked his hands and stood, walking to the window and looking down at the street. "My guts tell me we're into something strange with Les. Understanding him is the key to understanding Joan. This woman's instincts are so pure, so predictably female, that when she uses words like 'total stranger' and 'possessed' in describing him, I listen. And when she describes her reactions to him with words like 'terror' and 'fear,' I start looking for something in Les that was so violently maladjusted that it reached into her subconscious with such power that it put her beyond her coping ability."

Ben was nearly holding his breath, staring as he listened intently. Wylie glanced at him and continued. "The possible explanations are divided into two categories at the first level of analysis: physical and psychotic." Wylie's eyes narrowed with intensity, and his head thrust slightly forward. "This leads to you, Ben. Your investigation."

As though not to break the intensity or the flow of thought, Ben nodded, his eyes telling Wylie to proceed.

"Go to the coroner's office and get a copy of everything they have on Leslie Carson. Take it to Bill Heyrend for an opinion regarding whether the documents show *anything* that will support the possibility of a stroke, a brain tumor, or perhaps an accident involving the head—anything that might suggest brain damage. Remind him to look for a high protein content in the fluid in the dura or an irregular reading in the sodium content. Have him go over the blood analysis to the last dot and period. You do remember Bill Heyrend, the brain specialist?"

Ben nodded, and Wylie continued. "When you interview other persons, listen for the mention of an accident or blow to his head that occurred about the time his partner collapsed. Be sensitive to any hints of alcoholism or drug abuse—just anything that might tell us what happened to him physically. If I had any closer definition or notions, I'd give them to you, Ben, but I don't. We just have to spread the net as wide as we can and hope it catches something that will tell us what it was. Okay so far?"

"Okay. What about the second possibility?"

"The second possibility is that he had a psychotic episode, which I doubt. I just don't think he was that type. But we can't rule it out. Look for anything that might have given him a guilt complex he couldn't live with. Embezzlement, commission of a murder or some other horrible violence, Mafia involvement, racketeering with government contracts, payoffs to high government officials for road construction contracts—just anything."

Wylie paused, and Ben realized he had finished. Ben's eyes dropped and for a few seconds he let Wylie's words sink in. Then he rose. Wylie spoke one more time. "Ben, you've got to remember I'm leaving for Geneva in mid-November to speak at the international convention. I won't be back until"—he glanced at his daily appointment register—"December 12th, a couple of days before I'm to testify. If anything breaks before that time, get to me with it. If it comes after I'm gone, and it's an emergency, Maggie can reach me over there. If not, I'll see you the day I get back, which I think is a Sunday. Okay?"

Ben nodded. "Thanks. Wylie. I'll get David onto the coroner's files today and I'll start with the personnel out at the construction office as soon as I can myself." He paused, then added, "I just hope we'll recognize what we're looking for when we see it."

CHAPTER NINE

DUPREE PRESSED DOWN THE BUTTON on the intercom and leaned over. "Sharon, could you get Charlie Fawcett for me? And have Bruce Dayley come in at first opportunity, would you?"

"You bet, Mr. Dupree. Anything else?" she said cheerfully, waiting.

"Nope. Thanks."

Minutes later, Dupree raised his head at the rap on his door.

"Come on in."

He watched Bruce walk in and take a seat, clipboard and pencil in hand, wordlessly waiting for Dupree's instructions. At twenty-eight, Bruce had a quiet nature which seemed to accent his aura of competence. He was well placed as a researcher who could also draft the legal documents needed by Dupree. Six years of experience made him a valuable man to Dupree, and their nearly opposite natures made each a natural complement to the other.

"Bruce, how's your time? We've got a live one going—the Carson homicide case. Heard about it?"

"Yes, generally." He smiled slightly, speaking with a habitually slow drawl.

"I'm going to need a state-of-the-art brief on intent. We've got a woman who was beaten pretty badly by her husband and then shot him twice with a deer rifle. The second shot was about eight or ten seconds after the first, and it went through his head. I need to know if there's enough intent implied by the time gap to make the second shot a homicide. The facts are in this file," he dropped a file on the front edge of his desk, "and I'll need the memo reasonably soon. Okay? Can you run with it?"

Bruce picked up the file. "Sure. No problem. Anything else?"

"No. Get back to me if you have any trouble with the facts. Okay?"

Bruce rose to leave just as the desk phone rang. Dupree waved a good-bye to Bruce as he picked it up and pushed down the red intercom button.

"Yeah, Sharon, what's up?"

"Oh, pardon me, Mr. Dupree, I forgot Bruce is here. I'll have Charlie call back."

"No, no. Bruce is just walking out. If that's Charlie, I'll take it. Thanks."

He pushed down the flashing incoming line button.

"Charlie, I need your help. One of the heaviest issues in the Carson case has to do with the time lapse between those two shots. I need two real sharp guys to set up some kind of a test that will give us that time frame as accurately as possible. Got two men who can figure how to do it and run the test?"

"Yes, we do. When?"

"ASAP."

"Day after tomorrow?"

"Fine. I also need to know how well Joan Carson could handle a rifle. Do you suppose someone up in her hometown—Jackson County somewhere—would remember well enough to tell us?"

"Yeah, I think Don Qualls will remember. He's been in the sheriff's office up there for thirty-five years. I'll give him a call."

"Let me know when you've got the arrangements for the test set up."

● ● ●

Two days later Dupree and Charlie arrived at the apartment a little early, and were admitted by Tom Price.

"When are Adamson and Two Boys expected to be here?" Dupree asked.

"Five-thirty," Charlie answered. He picked up the old rifle and pulled the lever down, checking to be sure the magazine was empty. The front door of the apartment was standing partly open, and both men paused and looked out into the predawn blackness as they heard the faint sounds of a car engine and tires hitting gravel.

"I think they're here." Dupree walked to the doorway and looked. He waited the few seconds it took for the black-and-white to cover the distance to the apartment and then spoke into the darkness. "Hi. This is the right place. Glad to see you. Come on in." Both men called their greeting and Adamson opened the back door of the vehicle and removed a large, dark gray, nylon zip-shut bag. They both entered the apartment, squinting their eyes against the light as they came in from the darkness.

Charlie put the rifle on the table and walked toward the men. "Hi, guys. Thanks for coming. Your gear?" Charlie nodded toward the large bag.

"Yeah. What's the setup?" Adamson was looking down at the large bloodstains, studying his youthful face and blue eyes, concentrating as he continued. "This is where the shooting took place? And the light conditions right now are about the same?"

"Yes. The rifle was fired from about here by Joan Carson, the wife of the victim." Charlie walked over and stood by the archway. "We think she fired it from a sitting position." Adamson nodded, silent.

Carefully pointing to each place as he proceeded, and positioning himself to demonstrate, Charlie explained to the men the parts they would play to reenact the shooting sequence as closely as possible. When he finished, he looked at them to see if they understood. "Anything you need to clarify?"

Two Boys had watched and listened intently. He walked over and took his position where Les had been standing when the first shot was fired, then took a pace backward and bent his knees, imagining himself falling backward into a sitting position, then tipping onto his right side with his head falling onto the designated spot. He looked at Charlie.

"When do you want to run the first test?"

"As soon as you two are ready. We have to be finished before first light. Got your flak jacket and helmet?"

Two Boys walked over and unzipped the bag. Adamson drew out a small plastic bag with sixteen rounds of wax plugs in the shape of Savage .300 ammunition, and looked at Two Boys.

"Two Boys, want to check the ammo?"

"I already did. Just be careful."

Two Boys took off his coat and quickly slipped the large, three-quarter-length flak jacket into place. Adamson worked with the straps and buckles until Two Boys' vital organs were all protected, and then he took a step back to check his work. Satisfied, Adamson took off his own bulky, red jacket and worked with the sleeves and buttons of the sweater he had been instructed to wear until he had it on and it felt comfortable. He picked up the rifle. In seconds he had two rounds of ammunition in the magazine, the lever closed, the rifle pointed to the ceiling, his trigger finger laid across, but outside of the trigger guard. He looked at Two Boys and nodded his readiness.

Dupree stepped forward and raised a hand to stop the proceedings. "I need to take a minute before we start and let you know the
weight this test is going to carry in how we decide to handle the first-
degree murder trial of Joan Carson. To do that, you will need to
know some of the laws of self-defense. In this case, the law will allow
Mrs. Carson to use deadly force to stop her husband only if she is
convinced he is about to inflict mortal or near-mortal injury on her,
and she has good cause to see it that way. Okay so far?" He paused
while the two men nodded. "In this case, he was apparently giving
her a real beating when this old rifle somehow got mixed up in the
action and she got possession of it. She shot him with it, the first
shot traveling from his lower left side through his chest and out the
upper right part of his back. He went down backward to a sitting
position, mortally wounded. The shot totally and permanently disabled him; I mean, after that hunting bullet went through him, it
was all over for him."

Dupree's voice dropped a little as he approached the crucial element. "Then she chambered a fresh cartridge, and some time after he
hit the floor, she shot him a second time through the head. He was
still alive, and that one killed him instantly. We're giving her the benefit of every doubt on the first shot and calling it pure, legal self-
defense. But the second shot? We don't know what to call that one.
Do you see our problem?" He looked at each of them inquiringly.

Adamson answered. "Your problem is you don't know how much
time between the shots?"

"Exactly. If the time lapse was two seconds, the second shot
would probably fall within the self-defense rules; if it was fifteen seconds, it was murder. We've got to establish some realistic time frame
before we can make that call. That's where you enter the picture and
why what you establish here is critical. Got it?"

The two men exchanged glances and their expressions clearly
showed they understood. They didn't hesitate.

Adamson stepped toward the kitchenette archway. "What ya say
we give it a walk-through?"

"Fine," said Two Boys.

Adamson sat down, his back against the doorjamb. Two Boys
walked to the entrance door and turned, waiting for Adamson's nod.
Then he took the three steps necessary to put him in the position
Charlie had first indicated. Adamson did not operate the lever on the
rifle, but did run his hand through the motions. At the proper
moment, he said "bang." Two Boys took a step backward, his knees

buckled, and he sat down heavily, turning as he went, ending in a sitting position facing the door. Adamson again went through the motions of working the lever and again said "bang." Two Boys snapped his head to the right and tipped over, his head coming to rest almost in the center of the large bloodstain.

Adamson looked at Charlie. "That comes close to what you want?"

"Good. Ready for the first timed test?"

Adamson looked at Two Boys and they both nodded. Charlie placed his hand on the light switch. Dupree held the stopwatch ready.

"Okay, this is a live run. Two Boys, don't start until all our eyes have adjusted. Let's give it a try."

Two Boys walked out, turned, and stood in the doorframe. Seconds after Charlie switched out the lights, he said, "I'm coming."

He took the three steps into the room and paused.

From the archway came the metallic sliding sound of the lever working. Adamson brought the gun muzzle to bear on the silhouette and triggered the first popping shot. The wax plug from the cartridge thumped onto the flak jacket. Two Boys took a step backward, his legs buckled, and he sat down heavily. Adamson again ran the rifle action. When he could define the head well enough to place his shot by feel, he triggered the second shot. The wax plug smacked onto the helmet, and Two Boys tipped over. Charlie flipped the light switch. Two Boys' head was a few inches from the designated spot. Two Boys sat up, unharmed, and removed his helmet. The wax plug showed red on the shiny black surface, but the spot was well behind where his temple would have been.

Adamson quickly stood, walked over and examined the flak jacket. The first shot had been a little high.

He looked at Dupree.

"You're telling me a woman did the shooting, in conditions near identical to these?"

"As identical as we can make them."

"What time did the watch show?"

"Eight point eight seconds. Did you fire the second shot as quickly as you could define his head for a target?"

"Yes."

"Ready for the second test?"

Four more times, the men performed their functions. Then they gathered around Dupree as he totaled the times and averaged them.

"An average time of eight point four seconds." He looked up from his notepad and slowed his thoughts, pausing before continuing.

"Now I want to ask you a couple of questions and the answers will be critical." He looked intently at them for emphasis.

"Adamson, if you intended *only* to defend yourself against an attack from Two Boys, would you have fired the second shot?"

Adamson didn't answer, but instead asked, his voice level and eyes steady, "I think you mean if I just meant to defend myself, *not* murder him?"

"Yes. Exactly."

"No, I wouldn't have fired the second shot, but I've got to say that if Mrs. Carson didn't know what the first shot did, she might have thought he could get up."

"She knew what the first one did. Now what's your answer?"

"No. The second shot wasn't necessary for self-defense."

Dupree continued without hesitating.

"Could she have fired the shots in a shorter time interval?"

Adamson glanced at Two Boys, and a silent message passed between them. Adamson answered.

"No. She couldn't have."

"All right, next question. After a time lapse of eight point four seconds, should she have known the second shot wasn't necessary?"

Adamson answered without waiting.

"Yes, she should have known."

"All right, last question. Was the second shot a lucky one?"

Adamson's answer came instantly.

"No, it wasn't. No way. For whatever it means, that lady can *shoot.*"

Dupree looked at both men for a second, letting the answers sink in. Then he closed his notepad and broke the hush of their deep concentration.

"Thanks, men."

He turned to Charlie.

"Any leaks? Any holes? Anything I missed?"

"Nothing I can see. Solid all the way."

Dupree considered further, then spoke.

"Do we still go for Murder One?"

"Yes, I think we have to give the jury the option."

Dupree nodded his agreement and looked at Adamson and Two Boys.

"That was good work. Can we help you pack your gear? One of us better go up to the construction company office to tell Tom Price we're through and thank him for coming early to let us in."

CHAPTER TEN

"BEN, I GOT SOMETHING." BEN WAS holding down the button on his desk intercom, waiting for David to continue, but the silence held. Ben suddenly realized it was serious.

"Get on in here, David."

With controlled intensity, David walked in and sat down opposite Ben, forgetting protocol. He didn't wait for an invitation or the light banter that usually preceded a work session.

"I need to talk about a couple of things to be sure I know what I'm doing before I go further. Got a few minutes?"

"Yes. Go."

"As it now stands, the law of self-defense probably won't let very much evidence into the record regarding Les's conduct. I mean, other than right around the time of the shooting. The judge isn't going to let us get too deep into the history of Les Carson, and he sure isn't going to let us turn the Joan Carson trial into a Les Carson trial."

"Yes. I want that profile for my own reasons, but I agree with you that except for the time frame immediately preceding the shooting, this is a Joan Carson trial. Les Carson isn't who you wanted to talk about, is it?"

"No. But what if the law *would* allow you to go into the Les Carson history? What he was before last spring, the change that began last May, the degeneration of his relationship with Joan, the downward plunge from a model husband to a raging brute in just a matter of months—would that help the defense of Joan Carson?" David's eyes were boring into Ben's.

Ben leaned forward as David concluded, suddenly intensely focused. "Dramatically. What have you found?"

"The case of State versus Wanrow, 559 Pacific Second 548. The supreme court of the state of Washington handed it down two or three years ago, and the Colorado Law Review analyzed it just a while back. Let me give you the facts, then the ruling." David raised his eyebrows, waiting, and Ben nodded his go-ahead.

"Mrs. Wanrow was a small woman with her leg in a cast, who went to visit a neighbor overnight at the neighbor's request. The neighbor was home alone with a minor daughter in the house, terrified of a good-sized bully prowling around in the neighborhood. *Both* women knew the bad reputation of the bully, so when Mrs. Wanrow left, she tucked a small pistol in her purse, just in case. In the night, the bully came to the front door drunk. He knocked and demanded entrance, stating he hadn't molested the little daughter, as the mother had alleged. Mrs. Wanrow left the neighbor and the bully in the front room talking while she hobbled back to the little girl's bedroom, just to make sure she was still safe. Mrs. Wanrow had her purse with her, her hand on the pistol. She was pretty scared. As she turned to go back out to the front room, the bully happened to be standing there in the doorway. His unexpected appearance terrified her. She impulsively jerked the pistol up and fired it. The single shot killed him."

David paused, giving Ben time to react. Ben bobbed his head and David continued.

"The trial court held the line on traditional self-defense law, and Mrs. Wanrow wasn't allowed to tell the full story of why her fear impelled her to fire the fatal shot. Just facts surrounding the incident, with a couple of innocuous statements about his reputation, were brought into the trial. She was convicted of murder. On appeal, the supreme court really ripped into it."

Ben sat quietly while David continued.

"Bottom line. You can't try a woman who claims self-defense on the same principles used to try a man. They changed the law, the same law we have in this state, that's been standing between Joan and a fair trial."

Ben was incredulous. "How? What did they change? What did they say?"

"They said our current body of knowledge concerning the female gender has left our court rules in a mess—such a mess that if we don't change the rules, we're going to be denying women equal protection under the law. We've dug our own grave with our blind dedication to the 'reasonable man' standard. We've got to start talking 'reasonable woman' right along with it.

"They said that while the 'reasonable man' standard was intended to be neutral, it has created a prejudiced position against women. It's all masculine and ignores the feminine. To correct it they made some sweeping changes."

Now David slowed his speech and put emphasis on key words.

"They stated the 'reasonable man' rule presumes that the female victim is somehow supposed to be the equal of her male attacker, just like it was two *men* engaged in the combat. That's ridiculous. A *woman* engaged in a combat with a *man* isn't going to see him as representing *brute* force. She's going to see him as a *deadly* force because she's a *woman*."

David paused. "Have I said that well enough so far, Ben?"

Ben nodded to go on, not wanting to stop the flow.

"Giving her the right to fight back with deadly force changes most of the rules. It automatically gives her the right to use *deadly force* to stop him. Under some circumstances, she can justifiably *kill* him, when the same killing would be a murder if it was done by a *man*.

"The court said the jury instructions had to be changed; no more 'reasonable man' jury instructions if the defendant is a woman. No more excluding testimony that attempts to enlighten the jury regarding her gender and the impact her gender has on how she saw things at the time of the killing.

"They also said the jury is entitled to know the entire relationship between the victim and the defendant. They suggested the purpose of the trial was to put the jury in her position as far as possible, so they could judge her fairly. They went a long way toward making it a subjective test."

Ben's eyes were boring into David's. Not a word or expression escaped his attention.

"In their summary, I think the court put the keys into our hands for most of the Carson defense." David paused and spoke his last sentences quietly. "The court said that where appropriate, the jury should take into account the relevant differences—meaning psychological differences as well as physical—between a male and a female, when those differences influence their behavior in a life-threatening situation. Furthermore, application of this standard would necessarily be somewhat subjective.

"They concluded by declaring that failure to abide by these concepts is a denial of the constitutional rights of women to equal protection under the law. A trial under the facts of the Carson case, without using the rules of the Wanrow case, is a trial without due process. We're into the foundations of the fifth and fourteenth amendments of the federal constitution."

David stopped. The air seemed charged with electricity.

Ben didn't move nor shift his eyes for several seconds. Then he put his face into his hands, elbows on the desktop, for several seconds while David waited in silence.

Finally Ben raised his head. "What's the down side?"

"Mrs. Wanrow fired only one shot, not two. On the re-trial, her conviction was reduced from murder to the lowest degree of manslaughter, which was pretty good. But she was still convicted of a felony. The law review article talked about a 'battered woman' concept that's becoming popular too, but it's not relevant to this case."

Ben leaned back in his chair and began exploring the possibilities.

"Stop me when I go wrong. That court said both physical and psy-chological differences?"

"Both."

"You mentioned a 'battered woman' issue. Help me with that."

"That has to do with women who are mentally and physically battered and abused by their husbands, or some other male, over a long period of time. They finally kill the man who has beaten them, and they see it as an acceptable act. The time frame in the Carson case is too short; we don't have that issue in this case."

Ben nodded understanding and continued with his questions.

"Under the Wanrow ruling, should we be able to get in the whole story of the radical changes in Les's behavior the last few months of his life?"

"Yes. I would say yes."

"Should we be able to get in testimony about how the events lead-ing up to the shooting put Joan in a frame of mind, a subjective frame of mind, that can be a defense against intent to commit murder?"

"I'd say yes, on the strength of the Noble case, right here in Colorado."

"Can we get a jury instruction that casts this whole thing in the feminine gender, and in addition, instructs the jury they should take into consideration the relevant differences between a male and female that influence behavior in life-threatening situations?"

"We should be able to get it."

"Can we get expert testimony defining those basic differences? Maybe from Wylie?"

"I'd say yes."

"If I understand this right, David"—he paused to check his thoughts—"you're suggesting the traditional laws of self-defense are history, in a trial where a woman claims self-defense in a murder trial like this one. We get a whole new set of rules for admission of evidence, relevance of psychological testimony, and jury instructions—the most significant parts of our whole system?" Ben's brow was knitted. He didn't move, waiting for the answer.

"I believe that's what Wanrow is suggesting."

"Okay. Now let's address the key question in the Carson case. How do we use the Wanrow rules, when the two cases can be distinguished by the prosecution on the single question of the ten-second gap between the two shots? Until we remove that roadblock, I don't think we're going to be allowed to argue the Wanrow case before Judge Boyd, and that puts us right back where we started. That time gap before the second shot gave Joan too much time to think. Woman or not, she's going to be held accountable for conduct befitting her maturity, and that leaves us back where we started. Can you get Wanrow to solve that problem?"

Ben was startled by David's reaction. He didn't speak for a moment. He rose from his chair, stepped toward the front edge of Ben's desk, and leaned forward on his outstretched arms.

"Ben, that one blew right by you. The essence of the Wanrow case isn't the number of shots. The essence is the *perception of the female*. If she is terrorized sufficiently, maybe her perceptions of a deadly force will carry her through two or three or five shots. She won't be counting the shots. She'll be killing her tormentor."

Ben's jaw dropped as the concept struck home. He sat back in his chair his arms dropping to his sides. He spoke quietly.

"Well I'll be . . ." A few seconds passed and he finally shook his head. "I don't know what Judge Boyd will do with it. It's so slim you can hardly see it, but it's the first clear chance we've found. Get your memo prepared and on my desk ASAP. David, that's good work."

David nodded and turned to leave. Ben called after him, a trace of grin tugging at the corners of his mouth.

"Hey, wasn't that a little risky, coming right over the top of my desk to tell me I missed it and to wake up? I might have just reached up and pinched your nose."

David looked back at him, thought for a second, and answered.

"Maybe. I had to get your attention somehow. Besides, when I come in and speak the pure King's English to you, and you don't get it, I've got a right to do a little nose-pinching myself, wouldn't you say?"

He waited to see how Ben was going to receive his impertinence.

Ben grinned for a split second, then his expression changed to dead serious. "Get outta here. You ain't gettin' paid to stand there and insult the boss." He heard David's chuckle just before the door closed.

Ben felt the rise of excitement at the thought they had just found a chance, however slight, to at least make an argument against the single issue that had been squarely blocking their path from the very beginning.

For just a moment he wondered when Dupree would find the Wanrow case, and what he would do with it when he did.

Ben sobered at the thought.

● ● ●

In his office building across the street from the courthouse, Dupree looked up and nodded, putting down his file and leaning back in his chair.

"Hi, Bruce. Take a seat. I got your memo. Everything was good, but I wanted to make sure of one question. It's this case—" he opened his file and quickly ran a finger down a page—"State versus Wanrow. Washington State supreme court about two, two and a half years ago. Remember it?"

Bruce nodded his head, waiting. "I caught some implications there that I wanted a better hold on. I think my question was whether or not that ruling could be construed as a mandate to open the flood-gates of testimony, psychological evidence, and revised jury instructions for every case where a female is defending herself on the claim of self-defense. Are we arguably looking at a flat rule like that, no matter what the facts are?"

Bruce thought for a moment and opened his file. He quickly thumbed a couple of sheets of paper up and folded them back over the clip. He scanned a typed sheet for a moment, then looked back at Dupree.

"I don't think so. No other state has construed it that way. It shows up a couple of times in other state supreme court decisions since it was handed down, but always in support of minor issues. No one has made the holding you're suggesting."

"Could they?"

"Yes, they could. If it caught some judge's fancy just right, he could use it to support some pretty dramatic changes in the self-defense laws."

"Are the facts in that case substantially different than our Carson case?"

"Altogether. In that case, a crippled woman shot a drunken neigh-borhood bully when she turned around and he was unexpectedly standing right behind her. She claimed the single shot was fired by reflex. In our case, Joan Carson ran the action of a slow-lever-action rifle, waited several seconds, and did it again. Factually, the two cases have little in common."

"Any real threat here that you can see?"

"I see a possibility. Slim. On a scale of one to ten, maybe a two."

"Would you write a supplemental memo and develop both argu-ments for me? And, Bruce, in the memo identify every single iota of fact that distinguishes the two cases. I can't see enough similarity in the two cases to even *suggest* the Wanrow ruling should affect the Carson case. Just be sure those differences are spelled out loud and clear. I think your memo will be included in the pre-trial brief for the judge. Maybe we can kill the Wanrow case before the trial even starts. Okay? That's the only case I saw that raised a question."

"Sure. No problem."

Dupree busied himself as Bruce left, but he couldn't quite rid him-self of a lingering thought about the Wanrow case. Was there really something there he was missing? He paused, then shook his head. It was nothing to worry about. Get the facts. In the end, facts always win.

CHAPTER ELEVEN

"PLEASE COME IN, BEN. HERE, MAY I help you with your coat?"

Wylie rapidly walked into his foyer to greet Ben. As Wylie hung his coat in the small closet in the corner of the foyer, Ben nodded to Maggie.

"How are you?"

"I'm fine, Ben. A little chilled today, but fine."

Ben glanced out the window at the dark sky, with lead-colored clouds scudding by, filled with snow. "Looks like we're going to have some winter before long."

Maggie nodded as the two men went into Wylie's office, closing the door behind them.

Wylie gestured to Ben to be seated in the overstuffed chair facing his desk, and then sat down in the chair next to him, nearly facing him. He leaned attentively toward Ben as he opened the conversation.

"Ben, I'll be leaving tomorrow on the 12:10 for the convention in Europe and won't be back until December 12th. I wanted to cover a few things with you before I go. First, what has your investigation yielded concerning Les that may be helpful?"

Ben could see in Wylie's eyes that he wanted desperately to have positive information. But he couldn't give it. He glanced at the floor, then back at Wylie. "Nothing. Absolutely nothing. I've interviewed everyone at the construction company that worked with Les and the CPA that has handled their books for ten years. We delivered a certified copy of every document the coroner had concerning the examination of Les to Bill Heyrend. I personally had them certify we had it all. Dr. Heyrend came up dry. Not a thing. The interviews proved no head injuries, no known drug abuse, no alcohol abuse, no shocking moral departures—nothing."

Wylie shook his head and broke off the conversation for just a minute, feeling a sense of failure.

"Ben, I'm sorry. I was—and still am—convinced something went wrong. Don't give it up. It may yet show itself."

"You couldn't feel worse than I do about it, Wylie. I hope something still shows up. Oh, do I hope so. But I can't go into final trial preparations waiting for it to drop into place. If it doesn't surface soon I'll have to presume we aren't going to find it and finish preparing the case without it."

Wylie's head dropped forward again and for a moment the bitter disappointment hung heavy between the two men. Wylie continued.

"I received your memo regarding the case of State versus Wanrow. The possibilities of that case are thrilling, to say the least. I understand the big question of whether or not Judge Boyd will be persuaded to follow it is yet to be decided, but it is still the first hope I've seen for this Carson case in quite a while. The implications of the Wanrow case are what prompted me to invite you here today. As I analyze it, there is one dimension that is subtle. I am convinced it has been overlooked."

He looked directly at Ben, pausing to be sure he had Ben's undivided attention before he dropped the bomb.

"Ben, you're making a mistake. I think it's serious. I believe Dupree is making the same mistake and I don't know if he has professional advice that will sense it in time to correct it."

Ben's face showed his surprise. Without a word, he waited for Wylie to continue.

"Would I offend you if I took a few minutes to talk about it?"

"Be my guest."

Speaking slowly, his eyes alive with intensity, he began.

"To support the conclusions I want to reach, I will have to give you some background. This case centers around our need to submit evidence that will persuade a jury that there are basic differences between the psyche of the female and the male. By that I mean, Joan reacted as a typical female would have reacted in shooting Les; a man in the same circumstances may have reacted differently. Okay so far?" Ben nodded to continue.

"The leading authorities in the fields of psychiatry and psychology do agree that there are differences, but past that fundamental premise, there are any number of different theories and schools of thought. The result is that any testimony I give in support of my view on those differences will be compromised by a state psychiatrist who will contradict me and have authorities to support his view. I'll probably agree that his authorities are as reliable as mine if I'm asked on the witness stand.

"So what is the mistake I see you making? Let me state it obliquely by making a proposal.

"Cut through the crap, Ben. Don't let this degenerate into a standoff between opposing psychiatrists who are both sinking rapidly into the quagmire of conflicting theories."

Ben knitted his brow, puzzled. "Don't use you? Forget the possibility of using psychiatric testimony? You just lost me, Wylie."

"No, not at all. Use me, but just to lay the foundation. Then call a female psychologist to give the testimony that sets the essence of the female psyche before the jury."

Wylie paused and waited, hoping he wouldn't have to say more.

Ben stared at him blankly for several seconds. He leaned back in his chair for a moment, then jerked himself straight again, staring at Wylie in surprise, nearly shock.

"Unbelievable. How did I . . . Wylie, that's genius. She won't be giving the jury a lecture on psychology or psychiatry; she'll be giving testimony from her own being. She will have a conviction in her statements that a man could never touch. I can't believe how simple that is. And I would have never thought of it." Ben was blinking, still feeling the impact. Wylie smiled, then sobered and paused.

"You just defined the basic difference, Ben. Male and female."

"Help me. What do you mean?"

"Any normal woman would know that instantly. Any normal man would probably never have seen it at all. A woman looks at the same world we do, Ben, and sees the same physical objects. But she sees more. She sees from within, while we're stuck with seeing with our eyes and our heads. My advice is, get a woman to tell the jury about women."

Ben was shaking his head, still trying to see past the doors Wylie had opened for him.

"Who have you got in mind?"

"Her name is Dr. Carrie Johnstone. Here's her address and phone number. While I'm gone in Europe, get Joan to her and she'll take it from there. I've briefed her on the case."

Ben took the slip of paper and studied it briefly, then folded and inserted it inside his breast pocket wallet.

"Thank you, Wylie. Take care of yourself and Mary on the trip. Be careful. Godspeed." He thrust out his hand, and the two men shook hands as their eyes locked for a moment before Ben turned and walked out of the office.

● ● ●

Dupree dropped the letter back on the top of his desk and leaned back, his brow furrowed in deep concentration, pondering the documents he had been studying for more than an hour. Slowly his hand reached for the intercom button.

"Sharon, I need you to arrange a meeting ASAP with four people: Bruce Dayley, Charlie, and two men from State Mental Health. That's right, out on Arkansas Boulevard. Their names are Chris Meadows and John Ratachek. R-A-T-A-C-H-E-K. He's a psychiatrist and Meadows is a psychologist. Let me know as soon as you can get them all here at the same time, would you?"

At 4:30 that afternoon, Dupree was waiting for the four men, piles of photocopy work prepared and waiting, one pile for each of them. Three of them arrived together and a minute later the last one rapped on the door and entered.

"John, how are you? Come in and take a seat, over there." Dupree gestured to the large chair he had brought in from the foyer. "Do you know all these men?"

"All but this young man. I am John Ratachek." He offered his hand.

"I'm Bruce Dayley. I'm an assistant to Mr. Dupree. I'm pleased to meet you." He stood, shook Ratachek's hand, then settled back into his chair. He preferred to get on with the business of the meeting.

Ratachek took his seat and turned to Dupree, expectantly.

"Gentlemen, this morning I received Ben Cooper's Rule Sixteen compliance in the Carson case. Here are the photos of Joan Carson taken by Dr. Winters at the emergency room that morning; we knew about those. They show the damage done by Les Carson. Boy, is she a mess.

"I also got the names of his witnesses. At the top are Dr. Wylie Benoit and Dr. Connie Johnstone. You all know Wylie. Connie Johnstone is a psychologist, a woman." Dupree paused and glanced at the stack of documents for emphasis.

"I got unexcised, complete copies of their reports regarding Joan Carson."

He paused and watched their eyes. The room was dead quiet, save for the faint hum of the heating system. The four professionals stared in disbelief.

"We got it all, gentlemen. The examinations of Benoit and Johnstone are verbatim. I've never seen a more complete confession of a murder. Joan Carson knew where those shots were going and she put them smack on the button. She knew they would kill him when she fired them."

The eyes of each man diverted momentarily as they leaped ahead in their thoughts and conclusions.

"Charlie, it will be of special interest to you to find out what was driving Ben that morning—when he kicked the door open."

Charlie spoke. "Bad news?"

"No, just the other way around. Les Carson was his closest buddy from birth. Joan Carson was the little sister of his other best friend, Joshua Albertson. Get the picture?"

Charlie nodded, remembering in his mind the image of Ben standing in front of his desk that evening in the old, beat-up sweatshirt, trying to make a deal to keep Joan out of jail. Charlie let his head drop for a moment, muttering to himself, "I should have known."

"Anyway, bottom line, because we haven't got time to waste: Those reports from Benoit and Johnstone reach the conclusion that Joan Carson was not able to form the intent to commit murder or any degree of homicide. The basis for the conclusion is that she's a woman, and under the circumstances of this killing, reacted as a woman would. Thus, she was unable to form the necessary intent. Meadows and Ratachek, would you get into the reports and make an evaluation as soon as you can? If you need to examine Joan Carson, she will be available any day starting tomorrow, for any amount of time—I've already arranged that. I'll be going into a pre-trial in about a week, and the trial starts just about three days later, the 29th. Can you work within that time frame?"

Meadows and Ratachek considered, then nodded. Meadows added, "Yes, I think so."

"Okay. Charlie, you'll pick up some comments in the reports from Ann Fenton and Tom Price, and I think their CPA, whose name I've forgotten—maybe Gilbert or something like that. Ben's been out there interviewing them. I don't know why. Could you find out? Maybe interview them in the next day or two?"

"Sure. Today."

"Bruce, Cooper also wrote a letter to Judge Boyd, copied to me, right there on the desktop. Take it and write me a memo covering the constitutional question. Cooper thinks the Wanrow case mandates we must allow Joan Carson to introduce evidence at the trial that runs smack across the face of law this state has honored for 150 years. They're trying to change the 'reasonable' test because Joan Carson is a woman. Under the facts of this case, I think he's wrong. Ten seconds between shots is enough time for a human being of above average intelligence and maturity to think about it, man or woman. We've covered the Wanrow case before, but don't leave a stone unturned in this memo. I'll have to give it to the judge at the pre-trial. Nail that constitutional issue down and be *sure* it lays out the facts of the Wanrow case in Technicolor. Those facts have nothing to do with the Carson case, and when all the smoke clears in one of these things, the facts win almost every time. Okay?"

He raised his head to include them all as he continued. "Have I said enough? Do you all understand where we're going?" He watched their eyes and their affirmative nods.

"Just one more thing. What in the world motivated Cooper to give me all this stuff? I never saw an unexcised report like this in my life from a defendant accused of murder. Have any of you guys seen one?"

All four men murmured negative replies.

"Charlie, you've been in this from the beginning and you've dealt with Ben longer than any of us. How do you read this crazy move?"

Charlie paused while he marshaled his thoughts as best he could.

"I don't know. I get the impression he's telling us the facts don't matter. That's all I can figure from it." His brow was drawn up in puzzlement.

"The facts don't matter? Aw, come on. Know what the judge is going to instruct the jury? 'Make your decision based on the facts; consider the facts, coolly and dispassionately.' Finally, the facts are all that *does* matter."

Dupree suddenly stood behind his desk, his forehead wrinkling, his concern turning to frustration. Softly, almost to himself, he said, "What am I missing in this case?"

He paused and settled back into his chair.

"Hey, I don't mean to dump that on you guys. If you don't have any questions, let's get at it. Give it your best shot. I want to thank you in advance for your work and your trouble. Okay? Sharon's made a copy of everything there, one for each of you. Your names are on them. Put them under a microscope, and please, if anything jumps out at you and tells you what Cooper's doing, call me anytime, day or night."

They all rose and picked up their copies, glancing through them and making small comments to each other as they left. Only Charlie remained. He waited until the door closed before addressing Dupree.

"I got a report back from Don Qualls. He's known Joan Carson most of her life and he tells me she could do the shooting as I described it. She grew up with the rifle that killed Les Carson."

He paused, then continued thoughtfully.

"Al, maybe Cooper's accomplishing just what he intended. Maybe he's trying to tip you off balance. Try your own case. Don't get too far from the facts. Do what you do best."

Dupree looked at him for a few seconds, then his head dropped forward and he glanced back up.

"Yeah, I—maybe you're right, Charlie. I think you're right."

CHAPTER TWELVE

BEN HUNG HIS OVERCOAT IN THE corner closet of his office and turned toward his desk, tugging at the bottom of his vest. He sat down in his chair, scanned his daily appointment log, and picked up his phone slips, idly spreading them on the glass desktop with one hand while he pressed the intercom button with the other.

"David, would you come in here for a minute or two, please?" David soon rapped on the door and walked in.

"Hi. Come on in and have a seat. Yesterday I had a visit with Wylie and I told him we had given everything from the coroner's office to Dr. Heyrend—Bill Heyrend. You hand-carried that, as I remember it." David nodded. "Just want to be sure. Did the coroner's office include everything in what they gave you?"

"Yes, they did. I was there while they went through the file, and I saw them copy every sheet, including the scratch notes with doodles and trivia. The record included every test they made, including the one on the shreds of tissue picked up off the floor. The tests were all there in the record. They certified it and I delivered it to Dr. Heyrend. He has everything they have."

"That's what I told Wylie. I had to be sure. It's important." Ben paused a second to break the thought, then continued.

"David, a while back I interviewed some of the people at the construction office. A little thing Ann Fenton mentioned kind of hung in my mind for a day or two, but it didn't mean much at the time so I passed it over. Then I got to thinking about it again last night, after my visit with Wylie. So I called Mrs. Fenton for closer detail on it and what she said is really nagging me.

"Glenn Tolboy died of a heart attack just before Les was killed, which wasn't remarkable because he was struggling to recover from a heart attack he suffered last May. Yesterday on my follow up call I got the details. Ann Fenton said the afternoon before he died he felt a heart flutter, so she got him one of his quinidine capsules, and he took it and laid down. Just a few minutes later she and the crew left, but he stayed there, which wasn't unusual for him. Then a day or two after his death, she saw the same bottle, and about six or eight more of the capsules were missing. She's sure of it because she remembers the missing amount being almost a third of the bottle. Though it surprised her, she figured he must have felt more flutters and taken the additional capsules. Ann's information was unsettling to me so I called forensics to find out what side effects quinidine has, wondering if Les had been stealing them from Glenn and using them. They said they couldn't make a decision about that without knowing more about Les, but ordinarily the side effects of quinidine are pretty minimal. However, the direct effects are dramatic. Six of them in a single evening would have stopped Glenn's heart and killed him."

Ben paused to give emphasis.

"See the problem? I need to know what happened to those six capsules. I've got Les under allegations he was doing brutal things to Joan and had just recently had an unprecedented shouting match with his partner. I've got six missing capsules that could stop a man's heart. And Glenn Tolboy is dead. All these events occurred in the same place in a limited time frame. This is exactly the kind of setup Wylie advised me to look for weeks ago and I've got to get some answers.

"So, would you take a few minutes and go to the coroner's office or the public records office and find out what the official cause of death was for Glenn Tolboy?" David saw the strain, the near desperate hope, in Ben's face that he was wrong.

"You bet I will." David nodded and left.

Within the hour, David rapped on the partly open door and walked in. Ben glanced at David, startled at the grave look on his face.

"What's the result?"

"The listed cause of death was coronary failure following massive angina attack. The severe heart attack had been preceded by premature ventricular contractions and arrhythmia. There were no traces of quinidine in the blood."

Ben's head jerked forward in surprise.

"Are you sure, David? No trace at all?"

"I am certain. The official record shows no trace at all."

"Impossible. Impossible. Come on, David."

"I was at the office and looked at the records myself."

"Can you get that office on the phone and let me talk to the person who helped you?"

In a moment David turned the phone over to Ben.

Ben's voice was rising.

"David tells me your records show no quinidine in the blood of Glenn Tolboy on the night he died. We had been led to believe he might have taken six to eight capsules, four-hundred-milligram strength, within about six or seven hours of his death. In your opinion, if he had, would it have shown up in the blood analysis?"

"Six to eight standard-size capsules of quinidine, four-hundred-milligram strength? Yes, we would have picked that up easily. I can tell you right now it isn't there."

Ben's expression went blank in disbelief. He mechanically said thanks and hung up the phone slowly, his mind groping.

"I thought Les might have somehow got those capsules down Glenn and stopped his heart. I'm glad that I was wrong, but I'm losing my patience fast with something in this case and I don't even know what it is. I only know we've got six missing quinidine capsules and I *have* to know their disappearance had nothing to do with Les Carson. I need you to go to his office and spend one whole day there, from nine to five. Start at the light bulbs and finish below the carpet pad. Examine everything in the room. Get down on your hands and knees and part the nap of the rug in a few places. Go through every book, every note, everything in the desk and bookcases. Presume nothing. I want to know everything there is in that desk of his. Take everything out of each drawer, one drawer at a time, and lay it out. Take out every paper clip, broken pencil lead, pencil sharpener shaving, dust, dirt—anything. If you don't know what it is, put it in a plastic bag and identify where it came from. I will have forensics analyze it. When you leave, have everything back where you found it, except those items you have questions about. Can you handle that?"

David nodded yes and asked, "Is there anything in particular I'm looking for?"

"I wish I knew, David. I'm hoping you can find something to help us turn a corner in this case. Would you like some help? I can have Laura there from nine until five in the afternoon. She has handled this kind of thing for me before and she does pretty good work."

"I'd be glad to have the help. Shall I meet her there?"

"I'll have her there by 9 o'clock sharp."

Throughout the next day, Ben worked at the office, but in his mind was the ever-present question of what David and Laura were finding.

When the knock came at his door, Ben glanced at his watch. It was 5:35 P.M.

David walked in, carrying a small, thin, black attaché case. His tie was loosened and his eyes were slightly bloodshot. He walked to Ben's desk and laid the case down, then sat down in the overstuffed chair without taking off his overcoat. Ben looked at him, waiting.

"Laura and I finished half an hour ago. Want the bottom line?" David leaned forward, popped open the two locks on the case, and withdrew five small, sealed plastic bags. They appeared to have almost nothing in them.

"This is all we found that we couldn't identify. The first three bags don't have much that's of interest. The last two might. Number four has a lot of dust and debris from the top right desk drawer in Les's desk, which includes a lot of white powder. We think number five has one of the six missing capsules you're looking for. On her hands and knees, Laura found it wedged between the carpet and the metal housing where the telephone cable comes up through the floor to the phone on Les's desk. Ann says it is one of Glenn's capsules and it probably just got dropped, stepped on, or kicked against the telephone connection and mashed down into the carpet. It's leaking a little of the quinidine."

Ben immediately picked up the bags numbered four and five.

"Tell me about the white powder. Exactly where was it located in the drawer? Upper right drawer?"

"Yeah. Toward the front, on the left side. It was somewhat mixed with the other debris in the drawer. If you're thinking what I'm thinking, number four—the white powder—is the one forensics ought to see first."

"I'll go to forensics first thing in the morning. Want to come along?"

● ● ●

En route the next morning, Ben and David sat silent in the car, deep in their own thoughts. As they pulled into the forensics parking lot, Ben spoke.

"Which side of the telephone cable housing was the capsule on?"

David thought for just a second. "On the side nearest Les's chair.

"Ben nodded as they stepped out of the car into the cold air, both hurrying to the large double glass doors. They walked a few steps down the corridor and entered a door marked LABORATORY. A man wearing a white, knee-length smock glanced up and approached the counter.

"Ben, how are you?" He extended his hand and Ben shook it warmly.

"Fine, Owen. Meet my associate, David Ballantine. David, this is Owen Wahl. He is the chief chemist here."

They shook hands.

"What can I do for you, Ben?" Owen had his eyes locked on the attaché case David had laid on the countertop.

"We have some plastic bags and we just need to know what is in them. We are probably most interested in numbers four and five. Any idea how long we should wait for results?"

Owen looked at the men over the tops of his half glasses, then back at the case. Ben opened it, showing the five plastic bags.

"That will depend on what is in them." Owen picked up the bags and looked at their meager contents.

"From what I'm seeing, I can probably be finished before noon." He was smiling.

"If you run into anything that needs explaining, let me know. Otherwise I'll have David pick them up at noon."

"Done. Nice meeting you, David. And nice seeing you again, Ben."

Ben drove back to the office and both men busied themselves for three hours. At 11:40, David left for the laboratory. When he arrived, the report was waiting. David opened and read it, his eyes growing wide in disbelief. He turned to Owen.

"Any possibility of error?"

"None whatsoever."

David thanked Owen for his work, inserted the report back into its envelope, and drove back to the office.

Unannounced, he entered Ben's office and laid the report on his desk. Ben stood facing David, knowing from his expression that something was wildly wrong.

"Owen said bag number five contains powdered sugar in a quinidine capsule. Bag number four contains powdered sugar." For ten seconds, neither of them spoke. Then Ben reached for the phone.

"Mrs. Fenton? Ben Cooper. We have a severe problem. Do you think you can find the bottle of quinidine capsules Glenn had remaining in his office? Is it still there? And do you happen to know where the bottle is that he carried in his coat pocket?"

"I have the office bottle right here, in his desk. I imagine the one he carried in his coat is still there, and Merva, Glenn's wife, has the coat."

"Good. If I send David down, would you turn it over to him? We want to have the contents examined by the state forensics lab. Good. I'll have David out there within half an hour. Thanks."

Ben dialed the phone again. "Mrs. Tolboy? This is Ben Cooper speaking. We have a question and I think you can help us. Do you happen to know where to find the bottle of quinidine capsules Glenn kept in his coat pocket? Yes, I'll hold." As the seconds ticked by, Ben didn't move.

"You have them right there? If I send my associate by in the next hour, would you be willing to let us take them to the state forensics lab for examination? No, nothing serious. We are just finishing a lot of details in our investigation. Will that be all right? Good. David will be there in about forty-five minutes."

He looked at David. "Deliver the bottles to Owen and wait for him to make the tests. I'll call ahead and tell him what he needs to know. He will give you a verbal report, and when he does, get in your car and come right here."

David left without a word. Ben immediately dialed the number for the lab. "Owen, we have something of an emergency here. Your findings were undoubtedly correct, but they left some pretty ragged holes in our preparation of a murder case. David is on his way there with two bottles of bag number five. Is there some test you can quickly run to see if they are quinidine or sucrose?"

"Yes. Easily. How many will there be?"

"About twenty-five capsules, I would guess. One bottle is full and one about three-quarters empty."

"Should take not more than half an hour."

"Could David wait for a verbal report, with your usual written report to follow?"

"When should I expect him?"

"About an hour."

"No problem. I can handle that."

They said their goodbyes and as Ben hung up the phone, he punched the intercom and asked Marie to hold all his calls except for emergencies, and move all his afternoon appointments to the next day.

He slowly took off his suit coat, unbuttoned his vest, rolled up his shirtsleeves, and laid out the Carson files. He was deep into a word-by-word review when he was startled by the knock on his door. David entered without invitation.

Ben looked up at him and spoke.

"Quinidine in every last one of them."

"All twenty-six. Four-hundred-milligram quinidine. How did you know?"

"I'll be here past closing time. Can you be here at 7:30 in the morning? I think I'll have something to tell you."

David sensed that now wasn't the time to pry.

"I'll be here."

Ben followed David to the door and stepped out to the receptionist. "Marie, I am not available to anyone for any reason. When you leave the office, come tell me, please."

At 8:10, Ben stopped. The big erasable board was nearly filled with small writing. He leaned back in his chair and rubbed his eyes with the heels of his hands. As he did, he felt that strange, electric feeling that comes with being deep into the truth, poised on the brink of stepping into the full light. He knew he needed one more bit of information to pull his unbelievable, shattering conclusion together.

Hesitantly, fervently hoping he was wrong, he reached for the phone and dialed the home number of Ann Fenton.

"Mrs. Fenton, Ben Cooper speaking."

There was a pause. "Hello, Ben. This is a surprise."

"Mrs. Fenton—Ann—I apologize for calling this late, but I need just a minute of your time to put the last few pieces of a puzzle into place and I think you can help. Do you mind? Have I caught you at a bad time?"

"Not at all. What can I help you with?"

"Do you recall our conversation about Les and Glenn, and the events surrounding the day Glenn died?"

"Yes, I do."

"I have just a couple of questions about that to make my file complete. Going back to the morning you walked in, about 6:30, and interrupted Les in his office as he was closing the drawers to his desk, do you remember the details?"

"Sure. Very well. Why?"

"I need to start there and track from that event until the next morning. Can you recall the sequence of events?"

For ten minutes Ben asked short, direct questions, and Ann answered them with precise, complete answers. When he had what he needed, Ben thanked her for her trouble, assured her nothing was wrong, and said good-bye.

Ben leaned back from his desk for a moment, his mind working. Suddenly he glanced at the clock and grabbed the phone, dialing the home telephone number of Wylie. The recorded message referred him to Wylie's professional answering service, which in turn informed him that Wylie had left for Europe at noon and would not be returning until December 12th—in dire emergency his cases would be handled by Dr. Frank Zabriskie.

Ben banged the phone on its cradle and slammed the flat of his hand down on the desktop in an anger he could hardly control. He shoved the Carson file away from him to a corner of his desk. Then, alone in the silence, he folded his arms, closed his eyes, and leaned forward to bury his face on his desk, letting the hot, searing truth wash over him. Sorrow and dread filled him, pushing every other thought and emotion out of him.

Chapter Thirteen

....

"COME IN AND SIT DOWN, DAVID."

Ben glanced at the clock. It was 7:25 A.M. The office was vacant and silent, except for the two men and the quiet, nearly inaudible hum of the heating system.

"David, what I am about to tell you must remain between you and me until I am able to understand what significance it has in the Carson case. It can't leave this room. I'll tell Wylie, but this must not reach Joan, Laura, or anyone else. Do you understand?"

"Yes." David waited. He hadn't seen the expression that was now on Ben's face since the morning of September 18th, the morning of the killing. Something was terribly wrong.

"Wipe your mind clean of all conclusions you have reached in the Carson case, at least regarding Les. You have to start from zero. Now track with me."

Ben gestured to the erasable board, inviting David to follow the facts while he spoke.

"For some reason that had no basis in fact, Les somehow concluded Glenn Tolboy was taking advantage of the company income and stealing money from him. He had a loud, abusive argument with him about it, which Ann Fenton overheard. The following morning, she came early and found Les closing drawers on the right side of his desk. All three of them, which was a little unusual. She didn't know what was going on and he never explained it. He simply closed them and walked out without one word to her. Later that day, Glenn came to the office and did a few things. In the late afternoon, he felt his heart flutter, so Ann got him a quinidine capsule and he took it and laid down to rest. She remembers that the bottle was over half full when she got the capsule. The office closed a little later, but Glenn stayed there, which wasn't unusual. However, he didn't show up at home at the expected time. Finally Merva, his wife, got nervous and called down there to see if he was all right. There was no answer, so after a few tries she went down to see what was wrong. She found him there, nearly dead. He died that night from a massive heart attack. Ann saw the capsule bottle sometime a day or two later and it was nowhere near half-filled. She later estimated Glenn must have taken about six to eight of those capsules. If he did, the quinidine content in his blood would have been obvious. The medical report you read said there was no trace of quinidine in his system. Six capsules of that size, filled with four-hundred-milligram-strength quinidine, would have probably stopped his heart and killed him. It would never have resulted in a massive heart attack. It would have had just the opposite effect.

"So I sent you out to search Les's office. In the upper right drawer of Les's desk you found some grains of a white substance we both thought would be heroin or cocaine and maybe the answer to what went wrong with Les. It was powdered sugar. Joan confirmed she kept a little powdered sugar in the apartment to bake with. The one quinidine capsule you found jammed against the telephone connection housing under his desk also contained powdered sugar. Following Glenn's death, the office crew went to the hospital and Les just showed up there with them. The question is, how did Les find out? Tolboy's wife Merva didn't tell him where Glenn was, what had happened, because she couldn't find him. Joan never saw him all night and doesn't know how he found out. Ann Fenton didn't see him until he got to the hospital. I've talked with all of them and none of them told Les. No one can account for how Les knew Glenn was dead at the hospital. The hospital and the coroner didn't ask about the quinidine capsules because they didn't know Glenn was even on quinidine. Ann answered all their questions, but that one wasn't asked, and she didn't know enough about quinidine to volunteer it. She didn't know six of them would have killed him, nor did she know about the missing ones for a day or two afterward, so the six missing capsules didn't draw any special attention at the time."

Ben paused and looked at David. "Do you have any questions on the facts so far?" David shook his head and Ben continued. "Those are the facts. Now let me tell you what I think. Brace yourself.

"Les came to the office the day before Glenn died and was responsible for a terrible argument in which he accused Glenn of stealing company money. I think Les spent part of that night in the office. He took the bottle of quinidine from Glenn's desk and removed six to eight of the capsules, and pulled the halves apart. He dumped the quinidine and refilled them with powdered sugar from the apartment. He used a paper clip or a matchstick or something like that from his desk drawer to tamp it in. Then he pushed the halves of the capsules back together and put them back in the bottle. He had to take the top six to eight so that no matter which of the first several capsules Glenn took, he would get one filled with powdered sugar, not quinidine. It's possible he marked the fake capsules with a small scratch or something, although it wouldn't have been necessary to do what he wanted. When he finished, he brushed the rest of the powdered sugar off the desktop and some of it got into his top right desk drawer, which was just partly open when he looked for something to tamp it in with. You found the few grains in your search.

"He did the job sitting at his desk, at night, with the doors closed. I think he counted the capsules back into the bottle and concluded he was one short. He looked for that missing capsule all through his desk, on his lap, and even on the floor. He didn't know it had fallen, and it either bounced against the telephone housing connection under his desk or it was pushed there by his foot and partly jammed down below the level of the carpet. In any event, he didn't find it. I think he then figured he had made a miscount one way or the other and he put the bottle back into Glenn's office. From all appearances, the bottle looked perfectly normal and no one was the wiser regarding the six to eight fake quinidine capsules.

"I think he probably spent the remainder of the night in the apartment. By morning the missing capsule was bothering him and he went to the desk for a last search before anyone got there. He went through all the drawers on the right side of his desk. That's when Ann Fenton interrupted him and he quickly closed all three drawers and left without a word. I imagine he was pretty flustered. Later that afternoon, Ann Fenton got the bottle of capsules and gave one to Glenn because he felt his heart begin to flutter. He got powdered sugar, not quinidine. Ann left, and the office closed down. Glenn stayed a few minutes there at the office after they left and no one thought anything of that because it was normal. There alone, he felt his heart flutter getting more severe and he took another capsule. Minutes went by and nothing was correcting the flutter. I think Glenn had been told by the doctors to not take more than two or three in a short time span, and by that time, he was starting to feel real pain and lose consciousness. So he tried to get to the phone to call his wife, or someone, and that's as far as he got. He went down and pulled the phone over on top of him as he went. A little later his wife got nervous at him being late, so she tried to call the office but got an unanswered ring on one of the other lines. He was already unconscious and dying. After a few tries, Merva got concerned and came down. She found him on the floor with the phone receiver in his hand, the cradle pulled over on top of him. The examination showed the heart had been destroyed by a massive attack. It was not a heart stopped by six quinidine capsules.

"I think Les was in the building the whole night when Glenn died. After they took Glenn to the hospital, I think he went back into Glenn's office and got the bottle, removing enough of the capsules to be sure he got all the ones he had loaded with powdered sugar—or checked them by some little mark he might have put on them—but either way, he got enough of them to know he had all the fake ones and flushed them down the toilet. He put the bottle back on Glenn's desk and then got out of sight for a while. Neither Merva nor Joan could find him to tell him about Glenn because he was there all the time, hidden. He later just sort of appeared with the rest of the crowd and no one much noticed because it was normal to have Les around. A couple of days later, when Ann took a look at the bottle on Glenn's desk, she thought he had tried to avoid the heart attack by taking six to eight capsules. He might have taken two.

"The result was, Glenn died taking capsules he thought would save him, but which were useless because they were powdered sugar, not quinidine."

Ben paused and his eyes lowered. David saw the pain and torment in his eyes as he spoke his last sentence. "That's what I think happened. I think Les killed Glenn."

For several seconds, David simply stared at Ben, not knowing what to say to relieve the crushing truth Ben had reached.

"That's incredible. It's unbelievable."

Ben raised his head and squared his shoulders, and David could see him take control of himself. "Can you take all the facts we have and make it come out different?"

David couldn't answer. He shook his head.

Ben continued. "I think it's true, but I'm sure I would never be able to prove it legally. It answers every question except two. If Les did it, why, and more important, what difference does it make in the defense of Joan Carson? I swear, the Les Carson that would do that is a total, absolute stranger to the Les Carson I knew. I can hardly let my mind think about it."

David was still staring in disbelief, trying to grasp what Ben had just told him.

Ben suddenly threw his pencil forcefully on his desktop and stood, again struggling to control his anger.

"It's not fair! I figured it out eight hours too late. Wylie wanted an act of violence unrelated to Joan and I found it eight hours after he left for Europe. I have to start the trial without knowing what happened to Les. I only believe it *is* the key, or will *lead us* to the key, to this whole heart-breaking mess."

He paused and brought his frustration under control. With a pained expression, he turned to David.

"David, I hope you'll understand. I don't mean to embarrass you. I can accept losing Les—we've all got to go sometime—but I *can't* accept the destruction of the memory of what the man was. I've got to go over everything again. I've missed something. It's right there somewhere, either so obvious we can't see it, or still hidden. But it's there."

He opened the files and for nearly an hour they went over the psychological reports, the notes from Ben's interviews, the copies of the coroner's records, the forensic reports, even back to the diagrams they had drawn of the room and the details surrounding the shots that were fired. As they continued, it became apparent to Ben he was forcing things, reacting to his personal feelings at the expense of good sense. He slowed, then stopped.

"David, thanks. I think I've pushed it enough today, probably too much. I need to get out of here and get a fresh look at this.

"Would you ask Marie to try to get Richard Frazier on the line? You know Richard? The criminal lawyer in downtown Denver? I need to run this past him for an hour or two. Maybe he can see something I'm missing."

CHAPTER FOURTEEN

"MARGE, YOU READY?"

"Yes, your honor." The court reporter ran four or five sets of impressions on the paper tape feeding past the keys on the stenograph, checked to be sure they read correctly, and sat with hands poised, looking at Judge Boyd.

They were seated at the table ordinarily used for defense counsel during trials, in room 414, Judge Boyd's courtroom. For the close give-and-take of a pre-trial conference, Judge Boyd preferred to be off the bench, down with the attorneys. He was still wearing his black robe from the arraignments he had just finished, but had unzipped it, lending an informal feel to the proceeding. He sat facing Ben and Dupree, his thin, small, wiry frame topped by his straight, thinning, sandy-colored hair. His face, dominated by a hawkish nose and gold-rimmed bifocals, was tipped forward, examining the contents of the file. Ben and Dupree were busy laying out their briefs and exhibits on the old, scarred table that had been cleared.

In his slightly high-pitched, raspy voice, the judge began. His pace suggested he would move along without much nonsense.

"Okay, Marge, for the record, this is the time set for the pretrial conference in the case of State versus Joan Carson, on a charge of first-degree murder. Criminal number CR 2127. Are both counsel present and ready to proceed?"

"Counsel for the state is present and prepared."

"Counsel for the defense is present and prepared."

"Okay. I've called for this conference under Rule Sixteen (e)(1) because I think we're going to get into some unusually complicated matters in this trial and I want everything that's possible to be cut and dried going in. I think we'd better start with the easy stuff first and then address the tough issues. Any objections to that?"

Neither counsel spoke.

"No objections? Then let's get to it. Any objections to the usual arrangements of who sits at which table? Prosecutor nearest the jury, defense farthest?"

Both counsel nodded in the affirmative and for fifteen minutes the judge proceeded through the usual list of items to be handled on the record. The attorneys responded by affirmative nods to the standard procedures of who would sit where in the courtroom, where the lectern would be located, how the voir dire examination of the jury would be handled, the use of the jury questionnaires, the number of peremptory challenges given to each lawyer—ten each in this case—by which they could bump a juror off the jury without giving any reason, and the order of case presentations—prosecution, then defense, then rebuttal. Then the judge slowed.

"Okay. Witnesses. Have each of you sent your Rule Sixteen compliance to the other?"

Both men nodded.

"Any changes or amendments at this time?"

Dupree responded, "None." Ben nodded agreement.

"I have one question I have to get answered. Al, you've listed Ben as a possible state's witness. What's that all about?"

"I intend to have him testify no one was seen leaving when he drove up. He was the first to arrive after the killing."

Judge Boyd looked at Ben, his surprise apparent.

"Al, are you setting this up for a disqualification? Will his testimony reach the heart of the issues?"

"No, your honor. Just that he was the first to arrive and that he neither saw nor heard anyone leaving the scene of the crime. I presume that is what his testimony will be."

"Can't you stipulate to that?"

"I can't, your honor. It will be necessary to close loopholes at the beginning of the state's case. I'll have to call him."

"Okay. I'll let you call him. But I will limit your questions to exactly what you just told me and I am ruling now against any motions for disqualification. That will be part of the pretrial order. Understood?"

Dupree nodded.

"Each of you intends on using a psychologist and a psychiatrist. I have copies of their reports and it brings me to my first real question."

The judge paused, wording his next statement carefully in his mind before speaking.

"Ben, I have an unexcised copy of the reports from your experts. There are some incriminating statements there that are attributed to your client. In fact, they make a case for the prosecution. Do you intend to make that available to the prosecution?"

"I already have, your honor."

Judge Boyd stopped and looked directly at Ben in near disbelief. "You're sure you don't want to withdraw that and move to substitute an excised copy?"

"No, your honor. The defense wants it to stand in the record as you have it."

Judge Boyd looked at Ben, skeptical and questioning.

"Sure? Okay. It's in the record." He was shaking his head slightly.

Dupree's eyes narrowed, still showing the surprise from reading the reports days ago, the surprise now compounded with the reading he was getting from both the judge and Ben. The judge continued.

"Can I lock you both in to your witness lists? Anyone you want to add before I move on?"

Ben spoke. "No one, your honor." Ben looked casually at his list, then at Dupree's, waiting to see if Dupree had caught the significance of using a female psychologist and wondering if he had prepared one, in turn, for the state.

"Our witness list will stand as it is, your honor." The only psychological experts on his list were Ratachek and Meadows.

Unnoticed by either Dupree or the judge, Ben quietly sighed in relief. The judge moved on.

"Exhibits. What have you got for exhibits?"

Dupree handed the judge a list.

"Where are all these items? The rifle, the bullet, and the other things?"

"I will produce them at trial, if that's agreeable, your honor. I have the photographs and the reports of the experts here."

"Hand them to Marge for identification. Ben, any objections to the rifle, casings, and bullet being introduced at trial without being here for your inspection?"

"None, your honor."

"Okay. Ben, what have you got?"

"Here are my photographs and my reports."

The judge handed them to the reporter, who placed the exhibits from both sides in boxes marked "Prosecution Exhibits" and "Defense Exhibits." The prosecution exhibits were lettered, the defense exhibits numbered.

"These exhibits seem pretty cut and dried. Can we agree to put them into evidence without the usual folderol of proving who made them and their authenticity and all that? Can we just stipulate them into evidence and save some time?"

Dupree spoke. "I can't waive foundation for any of the exhibits, your honor."

Judge Boyd looked at him inquiringly, then continued making notes for a moment.

Ben responded. "I'll waive foundation for prosecution photographs and the rifle and—"

"Dupree cut him off. "No waiver, no stipulations."

Judge Boyd paused and leaned back, dropping his pencil on his pad.

"Al, you're going to require foundation for everything? Even the stuff that's obvious? Even the stuff Ben is giving away up front?"

"The state wants the right to present its case, your honor. All of it." He paused and waited.

Ben didn't change expression. Judge Boyd paused momentarily, then picked up his pencil and continued writing, his eyebrows raised. "All right. You've got the right to do it, if you insist." He finished writing and looked at Marge to be sure she was caught up.

Judge Boyd leaned back again in his chair, removed his gold-rimmed bifocals, and absentmindedly began wiping the lenses with the tail of his black robe.

"I got your notice on the constitutional issues raised in the Wanrow case, Ben. Al, did you get it?"

"Yes, your honor."

"I've read the case. I agree with some of it, and I have a question about some of it."

He paused. Neither Ben nor Dupree were moving. Both were waiting to see if the judge would indicate his acceptance or rejection of the Wanrow case, knowing that single decision would instantly and dramatically change the course of the case. The judge continued, noncommittal. Ben and Dupree relaxed.

"Could you submit simultaneous briefs on a couple of issues within two days?"

Ben and Dupree nodded and prepared to write.

"First thing, I want opposing arguments on jury instructions. I need your ideas on casting the pertinent jury instructions in the feminine gender. Right now, what we've thought were pretty neutral instructions are in question as being slanted in favor of males. I don't know if we'll need the new ones, but I don't want to have to invent them at the end of the trial if we find out we do.

"Next thing, I want opposing arguments regarding how far we go with the use of experts. If we wind up using them, I want to know what limitations, if any, you two think should apply.

"Last thing, let's hear what you've got to say about how far a court should go to be sure it provides due process and equal protection to the defendant in these circumstances."

He paused. "I can't make any advance rulings on the issues or the evidence now. I'll just have to handle it when you make your offers during the trial. Any questions?"

Neither Ben nor Dupree changed expression.

"Defense has no questions, your honor."

"Prosecution will have the brief prepared, your honor."

"Good. Anything we missed? Anything we need to add?"

Ben and Dupree started assembling their papers.

"Thank you, gentlemen. Marge, can you get all this transcribed by morning?"

"Yes, your honor."

"Can you two come back before noon and sign this? Section (e)(2) says you should. You'll be bound by it when you do, so read it before you sign it. You don't need to come together. I'll be here most of the morning if there is anything you disagree with. All right?"

Both men nodded. Marge made the last few impressions on her tape, tore it free from the stenograph, and began putting the rubber bands around the inch-high stack of folded tape.

"We're off the record. Ben, with the expert reports you left in the record, I wonder if you haven't made this into a one-issue case.

"I think that's probably right. At least one *major* issue. How would you characterize it, judge? If you'd care to verbalize it."

Both Dupree and Ben stopped gathering their papers, waiting.

Judge Boyd held a steady gaze at Ben.

"Sure. 'Under the facts of this case, does this woman have a constitutional right to a trial on rules different than those by which a man would be tried on the same facts?' Is that close?"

Ben reached up and rubbed his jaw, thoughtfully.

"I think that covers it. Most of it anyway."

Judge Boyd turned his eyes directly to Dupree.

"What about it, Al? How do you see it?"

"Probably the same way, but a little different wording. I think the issue is, 'Do the facts in this case justify a substantial departure from established law?'"

Judge Boyd waited a few seconds, then broke off the conversation and turned toward his desk.

"Thank you for your time and cooperation. See you Monday morning, November 29th."

Dupree walked across the street to his office building, took the elevator to the thirteenth floor, and just after he entered his office Bruce rapped on the door and walked in.

"How did it go?"

"Just like clockwork. Not a hitch in the game plan we've worked out. No surprises from Cooper. I keep waiting for the other shoe to drop and I still have the uncomfortable feeling it's about to, but so help me I can't see it coming. Cooper's locked in by the pre-trial order and there wasn't one thing new or unexpected. We'll present our witnesses just like we've rehearsed it, with all the exhibits.

"We do have some documents to prepare. I've got some notes for you in the file and I'll dig them out. But they're just what we expected—no problems I can see.

"The judge didn't give an indication about where he stands on Wanrow. But the more I think about it, the more it seems to me our case doesn't really stand to get hurt, no matter which way that goes. The facts are so one-sided and Joan Carson is of such maturity and intelligence that—woman or not—I can't see a Colorado jury giving her the benefit of ten seconds with a smoking rifle in her hands before she pops off a second shot that kills her husband. I think our case argues just as well, male or female. Anyway, let's get out the file and get you started on your drafting."

CHAPTER FIFTEEN

••

"HI, BEN, COME IN AND HAVE A SEAT. Sharon, hold all calls until I come out."

Dupree stood to one side of the door to his office and Ben walked in. Dupree followed, closing the door behind him. Ben was still standing, waiting.

"Take off your overcoat and have a seat." Ben folded it over the back of a chair as he sat down in front of Dupree's large desk.

"I appreciate you taking the time to come over. Has the cold front moved in yet?"

"No, but it's coming. The wind just began to stir from the north as I parked. I'll bet the temperature dropped five degrees during the drive from my office to here. It's coming."

Ben waited.

Dupree was leaning back in his chair, fondling a bronze letter opener as he continued through the accepted process of word-stancing by which each man was feeling out the other.

"We got top billing on the front page of the *Globe* this morning for show of the month. With the buildup they gave this trial, someone should sell tickets."

"I think the chances of a fair trial and verdict are inversely related to the media's efforts to fulfill their self-appointed, sacred duty to keep their public impartially informed." Ben smiled. Dupree chuckled briefly.

"They must have lifted most of it from the minutes of the pretrial conference. Judge Boyd doesn't mince words, does he?"

"I think he runs his own court. And I think he has a handle on the Carson case." Ben had offered the first opening.

Dupree looked up at him, gauging. "I think he does. It looks like we're heading into some uncharted seas in this one."

"Oh, there are some reference points here and there, I think. But you're right. How they apply to this case—well, that ought to be interesting."

"I took a little time to lay this all out since the conference and it appeared it might be in the interests of both sides if we at least discuss where we are. There's a chance our conclusions might overlap."

"Possible. What have you got in mind?" Ben waited.

"I think Judge Boyd is prepared to instruct the jury on all possible offenses, first-degree murder to justifiable self-defense. We were prepared to go after first-degree murder. Still are. But with what we've developed, I don't feel good about it. I don't think a jury will go with it. I think the worst they will find is second degree. Maybe manslaughter."

"That's possible. I know it won't be murder, either degree. I think they might go with a total acquittal."

"I think your client got caught in a tough spot. I can understand where she was coming from when she got her hands on the rifle. If she had fired just the first shot, I doubt there would have been much of a case. But she fired the second one. More than eight seconds later. That poses a problem this office can't ignore."

"How have you established that it was more than eight seconds between shots?"

"We took two of our best out there and ran five timed tests under circumstances as close to identical with the Carson facts as we could make them. The average was eight point four seconds. The slowest time was eight point eight seconds. The fastest was seven point nine. Giving her every advantage, she couldn't have delivered those bullets in much less than eight seconds. More like ten."

Ben remained silent, his face immobile. Dupree continued.

"In my view, a jury isn't going to buy the time element. Man or woman, eight or ten seconds is too much time. I think she's looking at a manslaughter conviction. I don't see an acquittal."

Dupree waited. Ben finally responded.

"I think the worst she can get with a jury is criminally negligent homicide. I think there is a better than fifty-fifty chance of an out-and-out acquittal."

"Second-degree murder is eight to twenty-four years. Manslaughter is two to eight. Criminally negligent is one to four. You willing to gamble with Joan Carson's life?" Dupree looked intently at Ben.

Ben responded. "Where are you?"

"Manslaughter. We cooperate in a plea for leniency."

Ben stood and walked away from the desk, toward the windows, looking out at the mountains for a minute.

"I don't think so. I think the worst a jury will do is criminally negligent. The best, total acquittal."

Dupree tossed the letter opener on the desk and rocked forward.

"Aw, come on, Cooper. No Denver jury is going to let anyone— man or woman—blow a man's head half away with a shot that wasn't necessary. She could get second degree as easy as not. Eight to twenty-four. That doesn't make any difference?"

Ben considered.

"Yes, it makes a difference. *Any* felony conviction makes a difference. But the unknown quantity is, what will a jury do with the Wanrow doctrine? If they buy *any* of it, it's going to help Joan."

"That's a roll of the dice, Cooper. You want to roll dice with your client's life?"

"No. But I don't want her living with a felony record either."

"She's going to wind up with one, as sure as she goes through a trial. You can at least control some of it if you hammer out some middle-ground deal, now."

"No felony. I can't get into a deal that includes a felony."

"You can't get into a deal that *doesn't* include a felony, Cooper. Come on, man, she *killed* him. Two shots. The second one slams the door on her. Face it."

"Assault in the third degree. I'll consider that."

"That's a misdemeanor. No deal. She killed him."

"Criminally negligent homicide with a withheld judgment, one year probation. If she abides the probation, dismiss the charge."

"I can't. This is too high profile. We *have* to get into a felony—"

Ben cut him off. "I don't care about too high profile. Forget about everybody else. When do we get down to letting the *law* settle this with *Joan Carson*? When do we get there?"

"Manslaughter, with no prison time?"

"No. And how would you plan to commit Judge Boyd if I did agree?"

"Tentative. If he won't agree, the deal's off."

Ben walked back toward Dupree.

"No. No. No felony record. Have we reached the impasse?"

"Yes, I think we have. I've offered you the best deal I can offer and still discharge my duties to this office. I can't let a killing like that one set the precedent you're suggesting. You know that, Cooper. I can't believe what you're doing to your client."

"I see Joan in about an hour and I'll tell her every offer we've made to each other. If she sees it differently, I'll be back to you within forty-eight hours. Otherwise, I guess it's next Monday morning." Ben stood still, eyes searching Dupree's.

"Next Monday. Thanks for coming over."

Ben put on his overcoat, then paused and extended his hand. Both men's eyes locked for just a few moments as they shook hands. An odd, unexpected, silent moment of mutual respect passed between them before Ben turned to walk to the office door, Dupree beside him.

CHAPTER SIXTEEN

"COME IN, JOAN. LET ME HELP YOU with your coat. How was the traffic?"

"Not bad. The boulevard wasn't plugged up yet with the 5 o'clock commute."

Ben elected not to get into small talk. He came straight to the point.

"I spent half an hour with Al Dupree this morning. We opened a discussion about a plea bargain. You should know about it." He leaned back in his chair a moment, while Joan's forehead wrinkled as she grasped the significance of what she would be hearing. Ben continued.

"He is offering you an opportunity to enter a plea of guilty to manslaughter, on terms that will not require you to spend any time in prison. It will give you a felony conviction record, with no opportunity to have it dismissed. You might want to think about it."

Joan leaned slightly forward, her mind working. Then she spoke.

"That's it? I plead guilty to manslaughter and accept a felony record and it's over?"

"Yes." He waited.

"Did you make an offer to him?"

"Yes. A guilty plea to misdemeanor assault or criminally negligent homicide with a year's probation followed by a dismissal of the entire case. He rejected it. He insists on a felony conviction in some degree."

"How do you see it, Ben? What will the law do with it if we go through a trial?"

Ben lowered his eyes for a moment, the question obviously pulling him into a personal quandary that left him uncomfortable.

"I had to face that a few days ago. I thought I couldn't trust my own judgment because of the stakes involving you and Les, so I spent a couple of hours with a very fine criminal lawyer that I work with from time to time, Richard Frazier. I laid it all out and asked his advice." Ben paused, struggling for the right words. Joan waited with a sense of dread.

"He thinks the best a jury trial can give you is a hung jury. That means Dupree will have the option to bring it to trial a second time. He suggested we work out the best deal we can and live with it."

Joan stared at her hands while she thought everything through.

"What was his thought about the worst that can happen if we go to a jury trial?"

Ben hesitated until the silence hung thick. Then he looked at Joan directly. "First-degree murder."

"Do you think Dupree will bring it to a second trial if you get a hung jury?"

"That would depend on what evidentiary rulings Judge Boyd makes during the first trial. There's no way to know that now. Dupree might force a second trial. There's a good chance of it."

"What would the second jury do that the first one wouldn't?"

"That's a pure guess, Joan. No one knows."

"What's your best judgment, Ben?"

Ben's expression changed slightly, as the pain of his personal dilemma surfaced.

"Professional judgment or personal judgment?"

"Both,"

"I have to sit down every time I come to that fine line and sort it out all over again, Joan. Professionally, the odds are against getting the law changed so you can tell your entire story and then swinging the jury far enough to get them past the facts. I would be foolish to let you go to trial thinking it will happen easily. All I can say is that it *might* happen. If you *aren't* allowed to tell it all, your chances of winning a jury trial are poor. You see, all the testimony we've prepared with Dr. Benoit and Dr. Johnstone might be disallowed. You might be limited to telling just a little bit about you and Les, except for the time period just before the killing. The jury might go to their jury room with only enough information to know he beat you and you shot him dead with two shots spaced ten seconds apart. If that happens, you run the strong risk of a serious conviction—maybe murder. I've told you all this before.

"Personally, I can't stand the thought of what's going to happen, either way. My instinct is to fight it. I know that when you had the rifle in your hands, there wasn't the slightest thought that what you did was wrong. I want in the worst way to have you tell that to a jury, as only you can, and make them understand it."

He paused. "Joan, there's a third way. Maybe you should take it."

She looked up, startled. "What is it?"

"Fire me and hire someone else. Maybe Richard Frazier. He'll make a purely professional decision. I don't know if—I don't think I can."

Joan thought for a moment, then responded.

"No, I think that would be a mistake." Then she continued, changing the course of the conversation slightly.

"Did you find anything to help explain Les?"

"No. Nothing. We exhausted everything we could think of and came up empty. It may yet develop, but I've had to finish trial preparations without it. You understand, even if we had it, Judge Boyd might not let us put it in evidence. He wouldn't let the trial become diverted into judging Les's misconduct because it would tend to pull the jury away from the real issue of his death. But if we found it, and he let it in, it would tend to corroborate your testimony—make the jury believe you."

Joan stood and walked over to the windows, looking out for a long time. Ben let the silence run. Then she turned and walked slowly back to her chair.

"Go on with the trial, Ben. I can accept a felony conviction a lot easier than I can accept not knowing what twelve people would have decided about what I did. I have to know."

They looked at each other long and hard, their eyes fixed. Ben broke it off.

"Please listen carefully to the few things you must remember during the trial. Wear modest, subdued clothing. I can't think of anything I've seen you wearing lately that's otherwise, but remember what I just said. Don't wear slacks. Also, wear a normal, pleasant expression at all times. Don't try to be an actress; just be your usual self. No matter what you hear from the witness stand, don't change your expression. So far as you're concerned, everything that happens—everything that goes on—is exactly what you expected, and you're prepared for it and it doesn't disturb you. Do you think you can handle that?"

Joan nodded, her intense concentration apparent.

"Don't solicit or patronize or romance the jury. Don't even look at them. Don't be obvious in ignoring them, but just don't let them get the feeling you're trying to silently charm them.

"Now, listen carefully to this next part. You're going to be absolutely certain I've lost my mind while Dupree is putting on the state's case because I won't be objecting to anything. You'll be thinking I should be stomping and storming and giving him fits. It won't happen. You'll just have to trust me. I might even stipulate to a few things, to make it easier for him. So no matter what happens in that courtroom, decide right now that I am doing my job, that you trust me, and that there will be no questions on your part. I won't tell you anything more important than that. You've *got* to accept that." He paused for emphasis. "Do you understand?"

"Yes, I understand what you're saying, but I don't know why. Can you tell me?"

"No, not all of it, because it will tend to make you want to react differently than you would otherwise and I don't want the jury to get the feeling they are seeing a Joan Carson that is being anything other than the real Joan Carson. Part of the key to this trial is having the jury *know* they're seeing *you*. Now, as badly as I worded that, do you catch what I'm trying to get across to you?"

"Yes, I guess I do. You have a game plan that requires me to just be me and you're worried that if I get too deep into the why of it, I'll tend to try to promote it and it might affect the jury."

"Right on. Can you accept that and live with it?"

She looked at Ben a moment while making her decision.

"Yes, I can."

"You understand you won't take the witness stand until after Dupree finishes the state's case? That means we'll be about two weeks into the trial before you testify. I'll brief you again before that. For now, just go home and repeat everything I've told you over and over again until it gets down inside you. Okay?"

"Yes. That's okay."

Ben looked at the file for a minute, then raised his eyes to Joan.

"I think that's all for now." He started to rise and she leaned forward to rise with him. Then he settled back and she stopped, waiting.

"No, Joan, that isn't all. I need to—what's going on inside you right now, Joan? Really. Your heaviest thoughts."

She was caught unprepared for the turn in conversation. She leaned back into her chair and spent a moment organizing her thoughts.

"I guess the worst problem I have is the law, Ben. I won't know how to respect the law anymore, if it won't let me tell my whole story. How is it that anyone, *particularly* a judge or jury that has to decide whether I go to prison—or maybe die—could ever *think* of judging me without knowing the whole story? How can that be? How—why would they limit the testimony and the evidence? It seems to me their attitude should be just the opposite—they'd want—*demand* all of it, if for no other reason than to protect their own conscience when they make the judgment."

Ben looked at her, caught by the purity of her wisdom. The thought came to his mind, "There it is—the essence of this whole case: the female psyche in conflict with an unjust, man's world."

"Joan, I can't defend the system in this case other than to tell you that its only justification is that humans can't do it any better. We try. We struggle. But in the end, we know that flawed people create flawed systems. God only knows how I wish it were different. I hope you understand."

Her head slowly nodded. "I understand." Then, as though having taken her final position, she turned her face to Ben and continued.

"Let's get on with it. Monday morning?"

She rose with a firm smile on her face and reached for her coat. Ben came around the desk to help her.

"Monday morning. Be here about 8 o'clock and you'll ride over with me. Okay? And keep your spirits up. Hey, we faced worse than this when Jesse broke his back, remember?"

Joan broke into a grin at the remembrance of her father spending five months in bed with his cracked spine mending, growing irritable, then obnoxious, and finally intolerable, as Ben and Les and the others in the valley came to help keep up the work he figured was properly his.

"Do I remember? After nursing that broken back for about four months he got cabin fever so bad that Mom about broke his neck too, just to get ten minutes of peace." They both laughed.

"Oh, one more thing. I'll need you in my office every morning around 8 o'clock so that you can ride with me to the courthouse. Will it be all right if the twins take their own car directly to the courthouse at 9 o'clock for the trial?"

She sobered as her thoughts returned to the realities they were facing.

"Sure. They'll understand. Thanks, Ben. I'll see you Monday morning." He walked her through the foyer and watched as she backed her Buick out of the parking lot. His face was drawn as he contemplated what she would be facing in the next three weeks.

PART TWO

THE TRIAL
November 29th–December 17th

PROLOGUE

....

COMMON SENSE WOULD SUGGEST that he who comes to the courtroom most skilled in the law and the facts should win the case. Indeed, thorough and exhaustive preparation is one of the necessities if one is to succeed in the practice of law (presuming there is some generally accepted definition of what that means).

However, any lawyer who has tried enough cases finally understands that "best prepared" doesn't always mean "the winner." For mysterious reasons not understood fully by anyone, and at a rate of occurrence that is at least unsettling to dedicated attorneys, the "best prepared" case sometimes loses. This phenomenon is best understood by referring to the little old lady who sat in the middle of the back row of the jury, listening intently. After the trial, she responded to inquiries about why she voted as she did for the verdict. "I don't know why; I just felt that way."

Seasoned lawyers know. Prepare the best case you can and present it as simply as you can. When you're through, close your file and sit down and forget it. You will win or you will lose, but never let the vagaries of the minds of twelve strangers become the measuring stick of your performance.

At the approach of the Carson trial, two seasoned, legal heavyweights were girding for the severely lopsided battle over whether one of them could sway a court and jury forcefully enough to change existing law. Neither had any illusions regarding the staggering odds against it. And neither had any illusions that the odds meant almost nothing to the little old lady in the middle of the back row.

The stakes? The life of Joan Carson.

November 29th–December 3rd

"GOOD MORNING, LADIES AND gentlemen. I am judge Randolph Boyd and this is the Second District Court of Colorado, in and for Denver County. This is room 450 of the county courthouse. We are meeting in the city council chambers because of space limitations in my courtroom. Each of you should have received a *venire facia*, or a notice to be at this place at this time, for selection of a jury to try the case of State versus Carson, which is a first-degree murder case. Is anyone here that did not receive such a notice?"

The judge's voice echoed slightly in the square, high-ceilinged auditorium. He moved his head away from the microphone to avoid feedback. No one stood.

"You are the *venire persons* selected at random by a computer, through driver's license records, tax records, and other public records, to give us a fair and representative selection of the county's population.

"From among this *venire*, thirteen persons will finally be selected to sit on a jury panel to try the case I mentioned. Twelve jurors and an alternate."

Judge Boyd took a deep breath and patiently began the tedious, detailed, and at times monotonous process of selecting thirteen acceptable persons from the 137 anxious candidates. The law required him to put them through a lengthy process of completing an extensive questionnaire, which then had to be delivered to Sam Everett, the jury commissioner.

The completed questionnaires revealed fifty-five persons who had obvious disqualifications to sit as a juror, such as age, physical handicaps, family circumstances, and biases. The eighty-two who survived the first elimination were invited back to judge Boyd's courtroom, room 414, at 1:30.

At exactly 1:30, Judge Boyd faced the courtroom, every seat filled, with ten or twelve persons standing in the rear. All were silent, their feeling of being in an alien world evident by their stares and their motionless attention.

The judge briefly surveyed the room and opened his file. With a sense of resignation to the drudgery of his duty, he began his procedure of filtering out thirteen acceptable people.

"Good afternoon, ladies and gentlemen. This is courtroom 414 and I am Judge Randolph Boyd. This is the continuation of our meeting this morning. We are now going to begin the process of selecting the final thirteen who will act as jurors, twelve regular, and one alternate. From this point on, all proceedings will occur in this courtroom."

Then, moving as rapidly as he could without confusing the eighty-two *venire persons,* he introduced the parties and the attorneys, explaining the purpose and procedure of a *voir dire* examination. Then he began the questioning process.

"I will now ask you as a group certain general questions which you can answer yes or no. If your answer is yes, please stand and remain standing until I can inquire of you individually."

He read through three pages of general questions, soon settling into a colorless monotone that caused the *venire persons* to lean forward and concentrate to understand both his words and their meaning. From time to time, persons were excused as they responded with answers that revealed good cause to be dismissed.

At 3:50 P.M. following the first brief recess, the judge looked at Dupree and addressed the remaining *venire.*

"The attorneys for each party will now conduct their portion of the *voir dire* examination. Mr. Dupree, you may examine the first *venire person.*"

Dupree chose to remain seated, and beginning with the first person called, he read from a lengthy list of prepared questions. As he finished with each one, judge Boyd nodded to Ben, who then began his questioning. The repeating of the same fifty or sixty questions to each *venire person* by each attorney soon developed into a monotonous, nearly ridiculous exercise in boredom.

Through the week the process ground on and on, relentlessly, steadily. The number of *venire person* decreased one at a time as some were dismissed for cause, and finally by peremptory challenge.

At 3:20 P.M., on Friday, December 3rd, judge Boyd heaved a sigh of relief and looked down at Dupree and Ben.

"Counsel, it appears we have thirteen jurors who are acceptable to both sides. Mr. Dupree, do you accept the twelve jurors and the alternate as they are now constituted?"

"Prosecution accepts the jury, your honor."

"Mr. Cooper, does the defense accept the jury and the alternate as they are now constituted?"

"Defense accepts the jury, your honor."

"Ladies and gentlemen, the thirteen persons now sitting in the jury box have been accepted by both parties. It appears we have our jury. All other persons are excused. Please check with Mr. Everett before you leave the building for the next jury call. I note it is 3:25 P.M. I don't think it would be wise to begin this trial at this hour on a Friday afternoon. This court will be in recess until Monday morning, December 6th, at 9 o'clock.

"Sam, swear the jury in and give them the usual admonition. Be sure the others know when to report to you next. Any questions? We stand in recess."

Judge Boyd banged his gavel and began gathering up his papers.

Of the twelve regular jurors, eight were men and four were women. The alternate was a man.

Ben and Dupree briefly scanned their notes, confirming that the pattern that emerged was exactly what they had expected. Dupree had tried to seat the most as many jurors as possible whom he thought were fact-oriented; Ben tried to seat those whom he felt were gender-oriented.

The battle lines were drawn.

Monday, December 6th

"MR. DUPREE, ARE YOU PREPARED with your opening statement?"

Judge Boyd was peering over his bifocals at Dupree, looking slightly dwarfed in the large, stuffed leather chair behind the elevated bench that dominated the courtroom. He had finished the introduction of the parties and their attorneys, the description of the case, and the preliminary instructions to the jury. He had cautioned the spectators and the news media representatives to remain quiet and orderly, despite the fact they were jammed wall to wall in the courtroom.

Dupree rose, picked up his file, and walked to the lectern, facing the jury.

"Yes, your honor."

"Very well, you may proceed."

"Thank you, your honor,"

Dupree paused, bringing his eyes to meet those of each juror, taking time to let his mind adjust to the moment.

The courtroom was divided into square halves by a banister; one half with twelve benches arranged with an aisle between them for those who came to watch the proceedings, the other for the affairs of the court.

The half of the room prepared for court proceedings was arranged so that the participating parties each took a position, which in turn, formed a square. The jury box formed one side of it, backed up against the tall windows, and opposite the jury box was the defense table, where Ben and Joan were sitting. The two remaining sides were formed by the prosecution's table, which was to Ben's left, and the judge's massive bench. Seated to the judge's right was his reporter, Marge, and just beyond her, the bailiff, Roy Durfee. To the judge's left was the court clerk, Phil Jessup, who was responsible for the exhibits. The lectern was sandwiched in at an angle between the end of Dupree's counsel table and the jury box. The center of the square was

left open for easy movement of the court personnel in obtaining
exhibits and assisting witnesses to the witness stand, located just to
the left of the judge. This gave him full view of each witness. The banister dividing the room was behind Dupree's counsel table.

The plain, white plastered walls and the scarred, worn tables and
benches showed the wear of fifty-one years. The room seemed totally
in harmony with the proceedings it accommodated: adequate, effec-
tive, no-nonsense, with a sense of earned dignity.

Ben glanced at Joan seated next to him. Dressed in a navy-blue
suit with white blouse, Joan appeared comfortable, though tired. She
was watching Dupree, her expression one of interest and respect. Ben
turned and glanced to his left, past the banister to the spectator section, where David was sitting near Chad and Sharlene.

Nothing was especially remarkable in the appearance or manner
of either attorney. Dupree looked pleasant, but not patronizing. Ben
appeared interested, but not anxious.

Dupree began his opening statement in even, firm tones. He did
not become solicitous or animated, but spoke the facts conversationally. He was simply making information available to the jury.

"Ladies and gentlemen, on behalf of the state, I wish to first
express respect and gratitude to you for being willing to take upon
yourselves the very onerous task of hearing this case. It can hardly be
a source of happy anticipation for you to know you will be required
to hear and see graphic and shocking details surrounding the shooting to death of one human being by another. It must be with some
feelings of fear that you face the sobering duty of deciding if a woman
shall spend some, perhaps all, of her remaining life in a prison, or
perhaps face death. I respect you and thank you for accepting this
burden.

"By oral testimony and documentary exhibits from various persons, most of whom are expertly trained detectives and county officials, the state will prove beyond a reasonable doubt that on the
morning of September 18th of this year, Leslie Carson was shot to
death and that the shooting occurred in the city and county of
Denver, Colorado.

"The shooting occurred in the dark, early hours of the morning,
about 5:15, in an apartment which is part of the building structure of
the Tolboy Construction Company, west of downtown Denver, on
State Highway 6, near Sheridan Boulevard.

"The state will prove that the shots which took the life of Mr.
Carson were fired at close range, ten feet or less. The first shot struck

Mr. Carson on the lower left side of his rib cage, above his belt, and passed through his body at an upward angle, leaving his body in the upper right portion of his back, through his shoulder blade.

"The second shot passed directly through his head. It entered from the left side, penetrating the temporal bone at about where it joins the sphenoid bone. It left his head on the opposite side at about the same place.

"The weapon used to fire these shots was a Savage .300 rifle. The rifle is a high-powered weapon, designed for use on large game such as deer and elk. The bullets were standard, factory-loaded Remingtons, firing a 150-grain bullet at about 2200-feet-per-second muzzle velocity. The points of the bullets are commonly referred to as 'soft-nosed' or 'silver-tipped.' They are designed to deliver maximum impact and shocking power.

"The rifle is known as a lever-action weapon, which requires the operator to work a lever down, then upward to eject a spent bullet and put a new one into firing position.

"The state will prove that the rifle was owned by defendant Joan Carson. Further, the proof will show that Joan Carson is the wife of the victim, Leslie Carson. She is the person who fired the fatal shots in the dark apartment that Saturday morning.

"The state will prove that there was a time lag between the shots. The time lag was about ten seconds.

"The proof will establish, beyond a reasonable doubt, that the defendant is an expert with the weapon used. She placed both shots precisely where she intended, knowing they would be fatal, and more importantly, *intending* that they would be fatal.

"The proof will also show that sometime prior to the shooting that morning, a dispute had erupted between Mr. Carson and the defendant. Mr. Carson, for reasons unknown, had lashed out at Mrs. Carson and struck and abused her physically. It is probable that it was during the dispute that Mrs. Carson acquired the rifle and fired the first shot, possibly in anger, possibly to defend herself against the abuse of Mr. Carson.

"The proof will show that the first shot was instantly disabling. It knocked Mr. Carson completely off his feet, into a sitting position, from which he was never to rise. He was dying. It was then that the defendant worked the action on the rifle and chambered a second bullet. Knowing that the victim was down, past any possibility of presenting a threat of further harm or violence to her, the defendant nonetheless located his head in the dark, some ten feet away, and with precision and deliberation and intent, blew his life away with the second shot.

"The state will demonstrate, beyond any reasonable doubt, that the firing of the two shots, particularly the second shot, was a homicide. It was needless. It was a murder."

Dupree closed his file and returned to his chair. He neither looked at the jury nor ignored them, but prepared for his first witness, which was to be Ben.

Judge Boyd turned slightly in his chair and brought his gaze directly toward Ben.

"Mr. Cooper, do you wish to make your opening statement now, or reserve?"

"Defense reserves, your honor."

"Very well. Mr. Dupree, you may call your first witness. Will it be Mr. Cooper?"

The jurors looked at the judge, then at Ben. Their expressions of surprise and puzzlement were evident.

"Yes, your honor. The state calls J. Benjamin Cooper."

Judge Boyd leaned forward and spoke directly to the jury.

"Ladies and gentlemen, because of events that will soon become clear to you, the state has requested, and I have granted them permission, to call defense counsel as the first witness. You must not be alarmed nor think it in any way strengthens the prosecution or weakens the defense. Wait until you have heard all the testimony before deciding what significance it has in the case. Now, Mr. Dupree, you may proceed. Mr. Cooper, rise and be sworn."

Ben rose and glanced at David, who nodded instantly, confirming his readiness to walk to the defense table and make a motion for a continuance of the trial, in the extreme event something went wrong and Ben was disqualified while on the witness stand. Without hesitating, Ben walked rapidly to the witness stand and sat down, turning directly to Dupree.

"Mr. Cooper, please state your full name."

"Joseph Benjamin Cooper."

"For the record, what is your profession?"

I am an attorney at law, licensed to practice law in all courts in the state of Colorado and federal courts outside this jurisdiction."

Calmly and conversationally, Dupree continued the questions. Did Ben go to the apartment at the construction offices the morning of September 18th, very early? Why? When he got there, was the apartment open? Did he gain entrance? How? Did he enter the room or disturb it in any way? What did he observe inside? To his knowledge, was Leslie Carson dead at that time? Did he observe what caused his death? Did he see the rifle? Did he see anyone leaving as he drove up? Who, if anyone, arrived before he left?

Ben answered every question readily and as truthfully as he could, his manner one of full cooperation. He did not look at the jury, but he knew they were reacting with deepening interest when he related kicking the apartment door open. He could also feel their revulsion as he described seeing Les's shattered skull surrounded by pools of blood on the carpet and shreds of brain tissue on the walls. When Ben left the witness stand, both he and Dupree knew he had paid a price for not waiting for Reed Jenkins that morning.

"Thank you, Mr. Cooper. I have no more questions, your honor."

"Will there be cross-examination?"

Ben walked to his counsel table and answered. "No cross-examination, your honor."

"Mr. Dupree, you may call your next witness."

"The state calls Reed Jenkins."

Reed was sworn and took the stand.

"State your name and address, please."

"I am Reed Jenkins. I live at 2521 Juniper, Denver."

"What is your occupation?"

"I am an assistant investigator with the Denver City Department of Law Enforcement."

Methodically, Dupree moved him through his qualifications as an expert, then his testimony concerning his participation in the events of the morning of September 18th. Why did he go to the Tolboy Construction Company offices? Whom, if anyone, did he see there? How would he describe Mr. Cooper's clothing and personal appearance at the time? What did Mr. Cooper do after his arrival? Generally, what was the nature of the conversation? When did Mr. Cooper leave? What if anything did he do regarding the interior of the apartment? What did he discover there? Was Mr. Carson dead? What, if he could determine it, was the cause of death? What did be then do? Did the coroner's representative arrive and did Chief Fawcett arrive?

Reed Jenkins' testimony was only a bridge between Ben and Pinnock, who was to be the next witness. Dupree questioned Jenkins no longer than necessary to put the case in proper frame and context, so that when he finished presenting, there would be absolutely no holes, nothing left to conjecture. He finished and turned to the judge.

"No more questions. Counsel may cross-examine."

Ben did not rise. "No questions, your honor."

"Mr. Dupree, you may call your next witness."

"The state calls Alfred Pinnock."

Dressed conservatively, his tie centered in a starched white shirt collar, his hair combed perfectly, Pinnock was sworn and took the witness stand. He carried his briefcase with him.

"Please state your full name and address."

"I am Alfred C. Pinnock. I reside at 221 Wallingford Drive, Denver, Colorado."

"What is your profession, please?"

"I am a medical doctor. I am presently employed with the Denver County Coroner's office as a forensic pathologist."

Pacing his carefully chosen questions to most effectively draw the precise, exacting nature of Pinnock out before the jury, Dupree moved him through his impressive qualifications, then on into the investigation of the death of Leslie Carson. He didn't ask him if he received a telephone call on September 18th; he asked him *what time* he received it and then what time he arrived at the apartment. Pinnock referred to his neat, leatherbound notebook notes and instantly gave the answers. His testimony was precise, simple, and persuasive, yet with no hint of arrogance or superiority. Pinnock's factual statements were completely rehearsed and he impressed the jury just as Dupree knew he would.

Dupree continued the questioning. Did he examine the body at the murder scene? Did the body remain at the apartment? What was the purpose of taking it to the county coroner's office? Did he conduct the examination of the body there? Did he fill out the complete report required by law? Is it in the coroner's file? To his knowledge, were photographs taken of the body?

Without a move or change of expression, Ben quietly said to himself, "Here it comes."

Pinnock answered with a nod. "Yes, there were."

"Were you present at their taking?" Dupree looked intent.

"Yes, I was."

"Where was the body when they were taken?"

"Some were taken at the death scene, others at the coroner's office."

"Mr. Bailiff, would you please hand state's exhibits A through L to this witness?

"Thank you. Mr. Pinnock, referring you to what have been marked exhibits A through L, can you identify them, please?"

Pinnock took the large, colored photographs and separated them into three piles on the sideboard in the witness stand. Then, in objective, dispassionate terms, he described them. They were photos of Les, lying on the apartment floor in the stains of his own blood, and at the coroner's office, propped up on the coroner's stainless steel autopsy table. Some were close-ups of the gaping wound in his right shoulder blade. The last two photos were triple enlargements of the crater in the right side of his head. Exhibit L was an exact copy of the coroner's entire file on the Leslie Carson case. Dupree continued.

"State moves their admission."

The bailiff started to gather them to bring to Ben for his possible objections, when Ben spoke.

"The defense has examined the exhibits and has no objections." Ben spoke in a conversational tone, much like Dupree and Pinnock.

"Hearing no objection, they are admitted. Counsel, it is 12:05. Would this be a convenient time to interrupt for the noon recess?"

• • •

With lunch finished, the jury filed back in and the judge turned to Dupree.

"Mr. Dupree, you may continue your examination of Dr. Pinnock."

"Thank you, your honor. The state requests that the photographs and coroner's file now admitted into evidence be passed among the jurors at this time for their examination."

Ben stood in one easy movement, facial, expression neutral, waiting.

Judge Boyd looked at the photographs, then Dupree.

"What's the purpose of the request at this time, Mr. Dupree?"

"The witness is going to make some explanations that will be greatly simplified for the jury if they are allowed to view the photographs and the file, your honor."

The judge bobbed his head once, then turned toward Ben.

"Mr. Cooper?"

"No objection, your honor, if the jury is instructed to keep an open mind until all the evidence is in. Some of those photographs are very shocking."

Judge Boyd nodded.

"Mr. Bailiff, deliver the exhibits to the first juror so he can pass them along. The jury is instructed to keep an open mind until all the evidence is in. Don't make conclusions based on these exhibits alone. Mr. Dupree, you may proceed.

The bailiff took the exhibits to the first juror and returned to his chair.

Without staring, Ben watched as the jury's look of innocent interest settled into shock, then revulsion as they saw the sickening, detailed destruction of Les's cranium. The women passed the last two photos along without looking at them.

Dupree waited until all their eyes returned to him, then continued.

"Now would you please explain to the jury the papers in exhibit M, the coroner's file, so they will understand what they are when they examine them? And would you please relate them to the photographs to give the jury a complete record of the examination and conclusions?"

Patiently, carefully pointing out the details as he went, Pinnock took the forms and went through all nine of the major divisions, beginning with the preliminary autopsy report and ending with the clothing and valuables list. Then he took the several pages of drawings, explaining they were his, showing the damage sustained by the body of Les Carson, and how they compared with the photographs, exhibits A through M.

"Thank you, Mr. Pinnock. Now, could you tell us which of the internal organs were damaged by the first bullet that struck Mr. Carson?"

"Yes. It penetrated the muscle structure on the lower left side, passed through the liver, the spleen, the diaphragm, part of the left lung, the right lung, and out through the right scapula and musculature covering it. It nearly destroyed every organ it hit."

"Was that shot fatal?"

"Yes, it was fatal, but it was not the one that killed him."

"What was the official cause of death appearing in the coroner's report on the autopsy data sheet?"

"Death from gunshot to the cranium."

"Could you explain to the jury, please, how both shots were fatal, but the second one actually killed Mr. Carson?"

"Yes. The torso shot was fatal and Mr. Carson was dying. However, the shot through the head followed quickly enough that he was still alive. The second shot, the head shot, killed him instantly."

"Thank you, Doctor. Now, do you have an opinion, within a reasonable degree of medical probability, whether or not the torso shot was of sufficient severity to disable Mr. Carson?"

"Yes, I do."

"What is that opinion, please?"

"It was totally disabling."

"In your opinion, could Mr. Carson have delivered physical punishment, or been a physical threat to anyone, after the first shot?"

"Absolutely not."

Ben slowly leaned forward, controlling his urge to interrupt the devastating flow of testimony. He knew that if he made objections, many of them would be sustained. But he also knew that in the long run, Dupree would have all such testimony heard. Ben waited.

Dupree continued with his machine-like precision, establishing the time of day the killing took place and finally moving into the critical question of the time lag between the two shots.

Ben's eyes narrowed. The time lag was critical. If Pinnock got it wrong, it would be nearly impossible to correct his opinion during cross-examination. Dupree put the question to Pinnock.

"Based upon the facts revealed in exhibit M, the coroner's records, and your personal observations, do you have an opinion, within a reasonable degree of medical probability, regarding the amount of time that elapsed between the first shot and the second shot?"

"Yes, I do."

"What is that opinion, please?"

Pinnock looked steadily at Dupree. "About ten seconds."

Ben quietly exhaled and started to breathe again. Ten seconds was close enough.

Dupree closed his file. "No further questions of this witness. Defense may cross-examine." He started for his chair.

Judge Boyd looked at Ben. "Mr. Cooper, cross-examination."

Ben rose, but did not leave his place.

"Thank you, your honor. Defense has no questions of this witness at this time."

Dupree stopped before he reached his chair, startled but showing no reaction of surprise, and walked back to the lectern.

"State calls Charles Fawcett."

Charlie walked up to the clerk, was sworn in, and took the witness stand, adjusting his tweed jacket until he was comfortable. The jacket fit him well, somewhat masking his usually massive appearance.

"What is your name and profession, please?"

"I am Charles Fawcett. I am the chief of criminal investigations with the Denver City-County Department of Law Enforcement."

Continuing his questions, Dupree established Charlie as a highly educated, qualified professional with twenty-two years of experience. He then moved into the substance of his testimony.

"On the morning of September 18th, did you have occasion to visit the premises of the Tolboy Construction Company on State Highway 6, near Sheridan?"

"Yes, I did."

"Are those premises within the jurisdiction of Denver City and Denver County?"

"Yes, they are."

Dupree moved into the foundations of the investigation. What triggered his visit? Who was there when he arrived? Upon his arrival, did he enter the apartment in question? What were his observations? Were photographs taken? Did he supervise the taking of them?

Charlie's answers were professional, complete, convincing. Dupree continued.

"Mr. Bailiff, would you please deliver state's exhibits N through S to the witness?"

Charlie looked at the photographs summarily, familiar with each of them.

"Mr. Fawcett, would you please identify the exhibits?"

Charlie explained exhibits N through R were photos of the interior of the apartment; exhibit S was a photo of the rifle, leaned against the wall inside the apartment, just as the officials found it.

"Thank you. The state moves their admission into evidence."

The judge interrupted, in an effort to save time.

"Mr. Cooper, any objections?"

"None, your honor. For the record, the defense has examined the photos."

The bailiff delivered them directly to the clerk and waited while each exhibit was stamped "Admitted" and then he returned them to Charlie.

The judge again interrupted.

"Counsel, it is almost 5 o'clock. Would this be a convenient time to take the evening recess?"

Leaving the building and walking toward his car, Ben spoke quietly with Joan.

"What are you feeling after the first day?"

"All right. It isn't what I expected. It really gets pretty cut and dried after a while. Are we doing all right? What you expected?"

"Pretty much. This part is the monotonous part. Nothing like TV shows, huh?"

She smiled. "No."

Ben said no more but thought to himself, "Just give it a few days, Joan. I think you'll see all the excitement you can handle."

Tuesday, December 7th

"COUNSEL, YOU WERE EXAMINING Chief Fawcett. You may continue." Judge Boyd had finished roll call of the jury and settled back in his chair as Dupree began.

"Thank you, your honor. Chief Fawcett, at the conclusion of yesterday's examination, certain exhibits had just been admitted. Handing you the photo that has been admitted as exhibit Q, I notice several boxes stacked mainly to the right of the archway to the kitchenette. Did you examine those boxes?"

"Yes, I did."

"What was in them?"

"Of the thirteen boxes, nine contained women's clothing. The others contained knickknacks and sundry items of cooking utensils, plates, and silverware. There were a few family photographs."

"In exhibit S, you identified a rifle leaning against the wall, within about three feet of the entry door, is that correct?"

"Yes. The picture shows it just as we found it."

"Is there a connection between the rifle and the deceased? And if there is, what is it?"

With terse, precise, impersonal answers, Charlie led the jury through the scene he and his detectives had developed. Yes, the rifle leaning against the wall is believed to be the murder weapon; it was not fired from the wall where it was found, but from the kitchen archway, from a low position, suggesting the gunman had been sitting or crouched. This was determined by the place the spent bullet casings were found and the angle of entry of the one bullet into the wall and the pinewood stud behind it. Mr. Carson had been standing about eight or ten feet away at the time he was hit with the first bullet, then sat down backward and took the second bullet through his head. It couldn't be determined how the rifle was transported from the place of the shooting to the place where it leaned against the wall with the safety on and two bullets left in it, one in the chamber. Yes, the photographs showed the massive bloodstains on the carpet, from the two wounds inflicted on Mr. Carson by the bullets. Yes, there were shreds of tissue, bone, and organs of Mr. Carson carried out into the room by the rifle bullets, and they appear at random on the floor, walls, and ceiling of the room on the side where they left Mr. Carson's body. No, the first bullet could not be found; officials are convinced the door was open and it exited the room through the open door. Yes, the time of death was about 5:30; it was nearly totally dark inside the room, with the drapes drawn and probably the lights off.

Dupree continued.

"Mr. Bailiff, would you hand the witness state's exhibits T and U, please?"

Ben quickly glanced at his chart of exhibits; these were the two scale drawings of the room showing the trajectory of each of the two bullets, which by being represented on two separate pieces of poster board conveyed the psychological impression of being two separate, distinct acts.

"What is portrayed in these two exhibits, please?"

Charlie continued with his responses, sounding as if he was reading from a script. They were scale drawings of the scene of the shooting, prepared by experts in his office. The heavy red line on exhibit T shows the trajectory of the first bullet, from point of origin, through the body of Mr. Carson, on out the door. Exhibit U, the second bullet, from point of origin, through the head of Mr. Carson, then into the wall.

"Thank you. State moves their admission."

Judge Boyd dropped his chin and looked at Ben over his glasses, expecting an objection. The drawings were repetitious of the photographs and not the best evidence.

"No objection, your honor."

The judge didn't move for a second, then raised his eyebrows.

"Hearing no objection, they are admitted."

Dupree moved his file on the lectern, puzzled that Ben had failed to object.

"Now, Mr. Bailiff, would you give state's exhibits V, W, X, Y, Z, and AA to the witness, please?"

He waited while Charlie glanced at each of them, then continued.

"Chief Fawcett, would you please identify exhibits V, W, X, Y, Z, and AA?"

"Yes. Exhibit V is the rifle that appeared in the photographs, the weapon used to shoot Mr. Carson. W is the bullet we removed from the wall, the one that passed through Mr. Carson's head. X is a plastic bag containing the two spent cartridge casings we found on the floor to the right of the archway. Y is a test bullet we fired from the rifle for comparison with exhibit W. Z is a photograph of exhibit W, enlarged ten times to show the rifling striations on the butt of the bullet. AA is a photograph of Y, the test bullet, enlarged ten times for comparison."

Ben maintained his self-imposed silence and control, not looking at the jury, just observing the testimony with an expression that he hoped conveyed a sense of confidence. He glanced at Joan to be certain she wasn't watching the jury; she was looking at the exhibits.

Ben knew it was just his own overreaction, but somehow the old Savage rifle loomed out like an ominous, evil, black cannon in the setting of the courtroom. He knew the jury was going to be entranced and repulsed at the same time by the bullet that went through Les's head.

"Mr. Fawcett, what did you discover when you compared the bullet that passed through the head of Mr. Carson and the test bullet you fired for comparison, exhibits W and Y?"

"They are identical. This rifle is eighty years old and well worn. It makes very distinctive markings on the bullets as they pass down the barrel. May I draw upon the photos to illustrate?"

The judge nodded and Charlie moved from the witness stand to the large corkboard, mounted on a tripod at the very end of the jury box. He pinned the photographs of the bullets on the board and with patience he compared the markings, verifying they were identical.

When he returned to the witness stand, judge Boyd interrupted. "Mr. Dupree, would this be a convenient time to break for the noon recess?"

After the noon recess was over and roll call of the jury concluded, Judge Boyd looked up.

"Mr. Dupree, you may continue your examination."

"Chief Fawcett, referring again to the rifle, what was your previous statement regarding whether the rifle fired the shots that killed Mr. Carson?"

"This is the rifle used to kill Mr. Carson."

"State moves the admission of exhibits V, W, X, Y, Z, and AA into evidence, your honor."

"Defense has no objections." Ben maintained a pleasant expression. Dupree continued.

"Chief Fawcett, would you describe how this rifle functions, and its capabilities?"

Charlie held the rifle up at his shoulder height, making it visible to the entire jury and courtroom. He drew the lever down while he described it, then closed it while he explained the ejection of a spent bullet and the chambering of a fresh one by the completed lever stroke.

"It fires a 150-grain bullet with a muzzle velocity of 2,270 feet per second, designed to kill big game such as elk, wolves, coyotes, and bears if necessary."

"Thank you. Would you describe the design and capabilities of the bullets which killed Mr. Carson?"

Charlie continued, holding the bullet in the palm of his hand as he explained. "It is a .30-caliber, 150-grain bullet with an expanding silver tip designed to deliver maximum shocking power and destruction on any solid object it strikes. By design, the bullet is intended for use on large game, to match the capabilities of the rifle."

Dupree now paused for the first time, scanning his notes to be certain he had covered everything with his witness. Satisfied, he raised his head and said, "That's all, Chief Fawcett. Thank you. Defense may cross-examine."

Both judge Boyd and Dupree were mildly surprised when Ben broke his pattern and rose and walked to the lectern. He laid his file down and looked directly at Charlie with an amiable expression, then at the bailiff.

"Mr. Bailiff, would you please deliver defense exhibit 1 to the witness?" He waited while Roy Durfee got it and handed it to Charlie. "Thank you. Chief Fawcett, would you please take that exhibit and state's exhibits T and U to the corkboard and pin them up?"

Charlie finished and Ben continued. "Thank you. Chief Fawcett, with state exhibits T and U on the corkboard, please repeat for the jury what these two diagrams represent."

"They are scale drawings, each showing with a heavy red line the trajectory of the two separate shots."

"Correct. Now would you please take a moment to examine defense exhibit 1? When you have, please tell us what you understand it to represent."

Charlie scanned the drawing, then raised his head.

"It appears to be a drawing of the living room in the apartment, giving a horizontal or side view."

"Would you please examine it and verify for yourself that the dimensions are true and accurate? I offer you a scaling ruler for that purpose."

Ben handed the ruler to the bailiff, who delivered it to Charlie. For two or three minutes, Charlie scaled the diagrams against each other, then stepped back and looked at Ben.

"It appears the drawing is to scale and is accurate."

"Now, may I ask you if you know what the two red lines on defense exhibit I represent?"

"Yes. I believe the higher represents the trajectory of the first bullet and the lower one represents the trajectory of the second bullet."

"Do both trajectories have the same point of origin?"

"Yes, they do."

"Would you agree that if the room was in the same condition at the time of the shooting as when you examined it, there was nothing between the person operating the rifle and Mr. Carson?"

"Yes, I would agree."

"In short, this was not an ambush; not a shooting from hiding."

"No, it was not done from hiding."

"The persons involved had equal opportunity to see the other, did they not?"

"Yes, they did."

"Chief Fawcett, do you agree with the *height* of the point of origin of the two shots as shown on defense exhibit 1?"

Charlie examined the diagram and measured with the scaling ruler.

"Yes. Thirty-four inches above floor level is about right."

"I move admission of defense exhibit 1 into evidence, your honor."

"Mr. Dupree?"

"No objection."

"Admitted."

"Chief Fawcett, in your opinion as a highly trained professional in homicide investigations, is it unusual that a shoulder weapon would be fired from a height of thirty-four inches above floor level?"

"Objection as immaterial, irrelevant, speculative, and argumentative, your honor."

"Overruled. The witness will answer."

"Yes, it is."

"Do you agree that from a standing position, the point of origin for the shots would be much higher, and from a prone position, quite a bit lower?"

"Yes."

"Presuming the lights were turned off and the room was in near total darkness, would you agree that the shooting was extremely accurate?"

"Yes, it was."

"Have you reached any conclusions regarding what position a person would have to assume to fire the rifle accurately from thirty-four inches above the floor level, twice—once at an upward angle and once level with the floor?"

"Yes, I have."

"Isn't it true, Chief Fawcett, that a person would almost certainly have to be seated to fire those two shots accurately and work the lever on the rifle between the shots?"

Dupree interrupted. "Same objection, your honor."

"Same ruling. The witness will answer."

"Yes."

Ben shifted his weight slightly and then continued.

"If you agree it was not an ambush, Chief Fawcett, and you also agree that it is extremely unusual for a person to be firing a shoulder weapon from a sitting position, do you have any conclusions as to how the person came to be in the sitting position? Did you conclude it was voluntary? They just thought it would be nice to sit down to do the shooting?"

"Objection. It's a compound question and argumentative."

"Sustained."

"Did you form an opinion as to how the person firing the rifle came to be in a sitting position?"

"I did not. I have no facts on which such a conclusion can be based."

"Chief, could the person have been *knocked* down?"

Dupree interrupted again. "Objection. Speculative and argumentative, and the witness has already made his answer that he has no explanation."

"Sustained."

Dupree knew the question wasn't asked with any hope of getting such a speculative answer. Ben had asked it to introduce the question into the minds of the jury; just how *did* Joan Carson come to be sitting down with her back against a wall, firing a rifle?

Ben closed his file and turned to the judge.

"Your honor, I have no more questions." He turned to Charlie. "Thank you, Chief Fawcett. I presume you will remember to return as a witness for the defense when Mrs. Carson presents her evidence?"

Charlie nodded, acknowledging Ben had demanded he testify as a witness for the defense.

"Any re-direct examination, Mr. Dupree?"

"No, your honor."

"Ladies and gentlemen, it is 5:05. I suggest we recess until 9 o'clock tomorrow morning. Court is in recess."

Dupree elected to walk down the four flights of stairs so he could reflect privately. He had purposely told the jury about the fight between Joan and Les in his opening statement to defuse it as a surprise later; they knew Les had knocked Joan around a bit, so Ben's point of how she came to be sitting down to fire the rifle shouldn't have come as a big surprise. No real damage done.

Ben drove Joan to his office and invited her to return at 8:15 the next morning. Then he pushed himself away from his desk and let his mind run. The case for the prosecution was almost completed. All they lacked was Bowden to give fingerprint evidence tomorrow and the old caretaker to tie Joan to the rifle; then it would be finished. The little shadow of question he had created in the minds of the jury about how Joan came to be sitting down to do the shooting, was really no big deal. The jury probably inferred the answer from information in Dupree's opening statement. Ben felt a rising fear that in his consuming need to defend Joan, he had been too willing to underestimate the power of plain, cold facts.

Wednesday, December 8th

A WET, HEAVY SNOW COVERED Denver in the dark, pre-dawn hours of December 8th. The accumulation turned the streets white, but as the city awoke and began the business of another day, the blanket rapidly turned to brown slush. The marble floors inside the courthouse became wet and slippery from those who walked in from outside.

The last of the jurors took his seat at 9:05 and Judge Boyd asked the clerk to conduct the usual morning roll call. Then he turned to Dupree

"Mr. Dupree, you were going to call your next witness. You may proceed."

"Thank you, your honor. The state calls James Bowden."

Bowden, middle-aged and showing a little paunch and thinning hair, took the stand. He had a file in his hand and looked entirely prepared and professional.

"Mr. Bowden, please state your name and address, and your profession."

"I am James Bowden. I reside at 1337 McKinley Avenue, here in Denver. I am a trained investigator with the Denver Department of Law Enforcement, specializing in fingerprints."

Dupree nodded his head in understanding, turned a page in his open file, and commenced with his prepared questions. Bowden answered each of them with precise, prepared statements.

Bowden's credentials as an expert were beyond question. He had visited the apartment the morning of the shooting in response to a call reporting a homicide; he had gone through the apartment dusting for and taking impressions of all available fingerprints. His search had produced several sets, two of which were fresh and clear. The set discovered on the fore grip and barrel of the rifle proved to be the prints of Mr. Carson, which was verified by taking his prints right there on the spot and comparing them. The other clear set came from the trigger area of the rifle and was female.

"Mr. Bailiff, would you please bring state's exhibits BB and CC to the witness?

"Mr. Bowden, drawing your attention to exhibits BB and CC, can you tell us what they represent?"

"Yes. Exhibit BB is two photographs, side by side for easy comparison. The photo on the left is the fingerprint taken from Mr. Carson's left hand at the apartment. The photo on the right is the male print taken from the rifle. The photos have been greatly enlarged, and I believe it is obvious they are identical.

"Exhibit CC is four photographs. The two on the left are the female prints taken from the rifle on September 18th, at the apartment, and the two on the right are the prints of Joan Carson, the defendant, taken from the police records at the time of her booking, September 20th."

"Mr. Bowden, would you mount those exhibits on the corkboard and quickly indicate to the jury the similarities you have mentioned?"

In short order, Bowden mounted the photographs, and with the rubber-tipped pointer quickly identified their obvious similarities.

"Thank you, Mr. Bowden. Please return to the witness stand and we will continue.

"Were you able to identify the female fingerprints?"

"Yes. As the photographs show, the prints of Joan Carson taken at the time of her booking are identical to those taken from the trigger area of the rifle just after the shooting. The prints on the rifle are those of Joan Carson."

"Move the admission of exhibits BB and CC into evidence, your honor."

"Hearing no objections, they are admitted."

"Thank you, Mr. Bowden. Based on the facts you have indicated thus far, do you have an opinion regarding *when* the prints of Joan Carson were put on the rifle?"

"Within a reasonable time frame, yes."

"On what fact or facts is your opinion based?"

"The natural body oils and moisture that create fingerprints become dry with the passage of time. Her prints on the rifle were very fresh; hardly any of the oils or moisture had begun to dry or evaporate."

"What is your opinion regarding the time frame?"

"The same morning, September 18th, within just a couple of hours of my arrival."

"Do you have an opinion, based upon the facts you have, as to who fired the rifle that morning?"

"Yes."

"What is that opinion?"

"Joan Carson fired it."

"Thank you, Mr. Bowden. Mr. Cooper, you may cross examine."

"I have no questions, your honor."

"Mr. Dupree, you may call your next witness."

"Thank you, your honor. The state calls Judd Finesilver."

An elderly man rose in the spectator section and slowly made his way toward the witness stand, his feet shuffling, his old, pale blue eyes watering slightly.

Dupree walked over to him and gently took him by the arm, assisting him up the step and into the witness chair. Then Dupree returned to the lectern.

"How are you this afternoon?"

The man hesitated, then smiled a little.

"I'm fine, thank you."

"Are you nervous at being here to testify?"

"Well, no, I . . . yes." He smiled through his embarrassment.

"There is no need to be nervous. We need your help. Do you understand why you are here?"

"Yes, I do."

"What is your name, please?"

"Judd Finesilver."

"Where do you live, Mr. Finesilver?"

"Out on Highway 6, across the street from the Tolboy Construction Company."

"Are you employed by the Tolboy Construction Company?"

"Yes, I am. I'm the night caretaker."

Gently, for the first time breaking the relentless cadence of his style of questioning, Dupree patiently led the round-shouldered, quiet old man through the facts he had to offer.

Yes, he had worked there a long time; yes, he remembered when Les started with the company thirteen years ago and became a partner four years later. He remembered when Les and Joan brought some of their things to the apartment, including the old rifle. When he helped them bring their things into the apartment, Joan had told him the rifle was hers and that they brought it because once in a while Les took it with him when he went out on a project in the mountains during deer season. Joan also said that it was good to have something at the office for protection, since it was at the edge of town.

Dupree leaned slightly forward, speaking slowly.

"Thank you, Mr. Finesilver. I have no further questions. Counsel may cross-examine."

Ben stood. "I have no questions, your honor."

"Mr. Dupree, you may call your next witness."

"Your honor, the state has no more witnesses. The state rests its main case."

The judge glanced at the clock and tapped his pencil on the bench as he pondered for just a moment.

"Mr. Cooper, it is just about noon. Do you have any motions?"

"No. The defense has no motions at this time."

"If you wish to begin your case at large now, we will take the noon recess and start about 2:30. I have a sentencing I have to handle at 1:30 and it might take about an hour. It looks to me like you won't get much further than an opening statement and the beginning of examination of your first witness, though, if we start at 2:30 or after. Would you rather wait and begin your case tomorrow morning?"

"That would be preferred, your honor."

"Mr. Dupree, do you have any objections?"

"None, your honor."

"All right. The jury is reminded of the admonition not to discuss this case with anyone until the court instructs you. We will stand in recess until tomorrow morning at 9 o'clock."

Ben picked his way through the slow afternoon traffic, leaning slightly forward over the steering wheel. The slushy, wet streets were becoming treacherous as the late afternoon cold began to settle in. Driving east on Colfax, traffic thinned, and Ben leaned back to relax a little.

"Tomorrow we begin with your case, Joan. I'll make the opening statement and then Dr. Winters is our first witness. He should be there about 9:30. I expect his testimony to take until about 11."

He slowed and turned into his office parking lot.

Once inside, Ben helped Joan with her coat and then removed his own. He gestured for her to be seated, then drew up the other chair and sat facing her on the same side of the desk. He leaned slightly

forward to speak, and from his expression Joan realized he had never
been more intense. She cleared her mind of everything but what he
was saying.

"Tomorrow, just before or just after noon, you will begin your testimony, Joan. I'm going to review once more the few things you must
remember. We've been over it before, but I don't need to tell you that
tomorrow we make it or break it with you on the stand. I don't want
to alarm you, but I can't risk you not understanding where we are.
Get these few things burned into your memory:

"Keep your eyes on me if I'm asking the questions or on Dupree if
he is. Don't look at the jury. Don't let them think you're patronizing
them or soliciting them.

"Under any circumstance, *don't look at me* while Dupree is cross-
examining. If the jury once gets the impression that you are looking
to me for cues or answers, they will never trust you again. Okay?"

Joan nodded her head.

"On cross-examination, Dupree can use leading questions. I've
told you how devastating that can be, but there's no way I can tell
you how it feels on the witness stand. I won't be able to help you very
much. You'll have to be in control. Take your time. Think. If you
don't understand the question, say so. Make him repeat it if it isn't
clear.

"Listen to his questions and then give your own answer. When
you've answered it, stop. Don't volunteer additional information.
Don't ramble. Listen, answer, stop. Listen, answer, stop. Can you
remember that?"

Again Joan nodded, her eyes showing deep concentration.

Ben's voice softened and his speech slowed. "You must remember this. On cross-examination, he's going to force you to say you
intended to kill Les."

He paused as her eyes registered surprise, then fear. Ben had
waited until now to tell her, hoping she could handle this knowledge
spontaneously better than having to dwell on it. He continued.

"You'll know when the time comes. It will come following a
series of questions in which he establishes that you put both bullets
where you intended. He will lead you into admitting you placed the
shots deliberately and then he's going to ask you if you intended
them to be fatal. It will come in some order similar to that. Do you
understand?"

"Ben, how do you know? How do you know he will do that?"

• • • • • • • •

"Because that's how I would do it if it were up to me. Now listen to me. When the time comes—"

Joan cut in, her voice rising.

"Ben, do you—have you convinced yourself I meant to murder Les? If it were up to you, could you prove it?"

"Come on, Joan. I know better. But I can't let you just walk into a grinder like that. He'll do it to you, Joan. He'll do it just like I outlined it. Believe it." His eyes were boring into her.

She sat back, pulling her thoughts into focus.

"Will it sound like I intended to commit a murder? Will I be giving him the last piece he needs to convict me?"

"You'll be giving him what he thinks he needs." Ben paused. "At the same time, you'll be giving me what I think I need." Again he paused, allowing Joan to absorb.

"Joan, no matter what happens, no matter what you think you'll be doing to yourself, or to the case, or to me, you've got to *tell the truth*. That's what I've got to have. I think I can handle just about everything else if you'll give me that to work with. The key to your defense is you, Joan. The jury has to believe you, believe in you. Will you remember?"

Joan had never seen Ben pleading so intensely, nor his eyes so alive with conviction.

"I'll remember."

For just a moment Ben continued fixing his eyes on Joan; then he turned his head and stood. He walked her to the door and out to her car in the parking lot where they exchanged good-byes.

Ben walked back into his office and sat down. Loosening his tie and leaning back, he attempted to objectively analyze the case Dupree had just concluded. Ben knew a prosecutor's case never sounds stronger than the moment he finishes it, before the defense starts chipping away. That's where he was now with Dupree's case. But realizing that, he still had to admit he had never heard a stronger case at this point in any proceedings he could remember. He could find no meaningful weakness. Dupree had started at the beginning, taken every necessary fact and defined it before the jury, and set each in sequence like bricks in cement, until he had built a wall that seemed impregnable. His delivery and handling of the witnesses had been masterful. Ben could see no chink to give him a beginning.

• • •

In his office, Dupree turned off the desk lamp and reached for his coat from the hanger on the back of the door. Turning to put it on, he slowed, his thoughts forming a conclusion on the posture of the Carson case.

Every necessary fact, every exhibit, had gone into evidence more smoothly than he had anticipated. He felt confident by the way the witnesses had responded. He knew the jury was attentive, probably heavily leaning toward conviction. There were no soft spots; every fact was clear, understandable, and presented in the simplest terms.

Granted, he was seeing the case before Ben started banging away at it. Still, he saw nothing that could have been done better or differently. The only nagging shadow in the entire scenario was Ben; not for what he did, but for what he didn't do. He didn't object nor cross-examine. But Dupree knew that whatever Ben had in store could have little to do with the facts. The facts fell one way—against him. Ben had to have something else and that would become evident in the next twenty-four hours. Whatever it was, its chance of outweighing the facts seemed almost impossible.

Dupree started home, smiling slightly at the anticipation of a warm supper with Joyce.

Thursday, December 9th

AT 8:50, THE LAST JURORS WERE making their way up the great, gray stone flight of stairs to the courthouse. Just a few minutes past 9 o'clock, with roll call of the jury concluded, Judge Boyd turned to Ben.

"Counsel, are you prepared with your opening statement?"

"Yes, your honor." Ben rose and walked to the lectern. He laid his file down, opened it to the first page, and raised his eyes to the jury.

"Ladies and gentlemen, I want you to know my expressions of thanks to you are more than just words.

"To prepare you to understand the case for the defense, may I first tell you we will present very little, if any, evidence that contradicts or confuses what has been placed before you by Mr. Dupree. Rather, we intend to supplement it; add to it, if you will.

"Through the testimony of Dr. Leon Winters, as well as through photographs, we intend to reveal to you the brutal beating the defendant received from the deceased the morning of September 18th.

"Through Chief Charles Fawcett, you will hear evidence that the rifle used in the incident was standing just to the side of the archway into the kitchenette in the apartment, placed there by the deceased.

"A psychiatrist and a psychologist will testify regarding the mental state of the defendant at and surrounding the time of the shooting. They will not testify regarding her intent, because by the rules of evidence, they cannot. But they will give you professional insights into what her perceptions were at the time. The evidence will be clear that she did not intend to commit a homicide.

"The defendant will take the witness stand and inform you of the entire incident. Evidence will show that in the four-month period preceding the death of Mr. Carson, he went through a change of personality that was so total in its nature, the defendant—his wife of twenty-seven years who loved him—became terrified of him. He first became argumentative, and then the change evolved into lapses of memory and conversations that he would begin but not be able to finish. Because of business reverses brought on by a heart attack suffered by his partner, and later the death of his partner, those nearest to him thought he was reacting to the pressures created by the failing business.

"Finally, you will be told that for reasons the defendant never knew, he struck out at her and hurt her. The evidence will show he became so unpredictable in his behavior and so violent at times that she was convinced he was possessed—by what, she could never find out. He began staying away from the home for days at a time, without ever accounting to the defendant for his whereabouts or his activities. She tried to discuss it with him but he became physically violent when she did. On the evening before the shooting, he visited her and demanded she come to the construction company apartment at noon the following day to get her things. He wanted to live there, separate and apart from her. The evidence will show that she could not bear the thought of meeting him there alone, so she went out at 5 A.M., hoping to get her things and be gone before he returned from the construction site at noon. She entered the darkened apartment and heard something behind her. She turned, and he was there. He seized her, struck her repeatedly until she was nearly unconscious, then threw her backward, away from him. Her back struck the archway to the kitchenette, and she slid to a sitting position, dazed. The rifle had been placed against the wall just to her right, by Leslie Carson, preparatory to her taking it with the rest of her personal things.

"The jolt of her striking the wall caused it to slide down across her lap. He advanced toward her. She levered the first shot into firing position and pulled the trigger. He went down backward. She worked the action on the rifle and fired a second shot.

"The evidence will show her perceptions were such that under the circumstances, she was incapable of forming the intent required by the law to make her act a homicide. It was not a homicide. It was an act of purest instinct, beyond any conscious thought—certainly beyond the intent required by the law to make her answerable for the commission of a murder.

"May I now ask for your attention as the defendant's case is presented?"

Dupree leaned forward, pulled his yellow notepad toward him, and readied himself to write. The time for wondering and worrying was past.

"You may call your first witness, Mr. Cooper."

"Defense calls Dr. Leon Winters."

Dr. Winters was sworn and took the witness stand.

"Would you please state your name and your profession?"

"I am Dr. Leon Winters. I am a medical doctor, presently practicing emergency room medicine at Denver General Hospital."

"What is your address, Doctor?"

"I reside at 2375 Windsor Drive, in Englewood."

Pacing his questions at a moderate speed and directing his attention only to the doctor, Ben moved him through his qualifications and the preliminaries of how Joan appeared at the emergency room at the hospital. Dr. Winters described the examination he gave Joan and his personal observations of the bruising and swelling that were so apparent on her body.

"Would the bailiff please deliver defense exhibits 2 through 10 to the witness?" Ben turned to Dr. Winters. "Handing you what have been marked defense exhibits 2 through 10, I ask if you can identify them for the jury."

"Yes, I can. They are all photographs of the defendant, except number 10, which is an exact copy of the hospital records of the Joan Carson case."

"Can you describe the circumstances under which the photos were taken?"

"Yes. They are enlargements of photographs taken by your associate, Mr. David Ballantine, on the morning of September 18th, in my presence as I made my examination of the defendant."

"Could you describe them for the jury, please?"

The doctor described them, identifying the specific injured areas on Joan's body.

"Move their admission, your honor."

"Hearing no objection, they are admitted."

"Directing your attention to the photographs, exhibits 2 through 5 and exhibit 9, would you identify the areas on the body of Joan Carson that appear as dark places on the exhibits?"

In clear, precise answers, Dr. Winters went through the photographs one at a time, carefully explaining the area of the body shown, the extent of the bruising, the cracked nasal cartilage, and the split on the inside of her right cheek which had bled profusely down her face and chin and onto her clothing.

. . . .

"In your examination, did you inquire how she obtained these injuries?"

"Yes, I did."

Dr. Winters referred to his notes to be absolutely accurate, and read to the jury Joan's explanation of the sudden, unexplained, brutal beating by Les.

"Do you have an opinion whether the condition of her body as shown in the photographs was consistent with her explanation?"

"Yes, I do."

"What is that opinion?"

"Her factual statements were consistent with what I observed."

"Thank you, Doctor. I have no further questions."

"Mr. Dupree, do you have any cross-examination?"

"Just a few questions. Doctor, did Mrs. Carson explain to you how the altercation with her husband started?"

"Not in detail. It apparently came on suddenly when she turned in the apartment and he just grabbed her."

"The explanation of the bruising and the altercation came solely from Mrs. Carson, is that true?"

"Yes."

"Thank you, Doctor. No further questions."

Ben didn't look at the jury, but he knew Dr. Winters' testimony, coupled with the photographs, had sobered them.

Joan was to be the next witness. Both lawyers knew the pivotal testimony was now beginning. Dupree squared his notepad on the table and reached for his pencil.

"Mr. Cooper, you may call your next witness."

"The defense calls Joan Carson."

An audible murmur from the spectators ran through the courtroom.

Ben sensed now was the time for the photos to be passed to the jury.

"Your honor, while the defendant is being sworn, could defense exhibits 2 through 9 be passed among the jurors? They will assist in the testimony Mrs. Carson is going to give."

The judge looked over his glasses. "Mr. Dupree?"

"No objections, your honor." Dupree didn't want the jury receiving the photographs quite so quickly, but could do nothing about it. He turned his attention to Joan, taking note of her appearance and demeanor as she walked to the witness stand.

Ben began the critical, delicate questioning by which he hoped to have the jury see her as she was, to come to know her and feel comfortable with her. His pacing and manner of questioning were calm and conversational.

"Please state your name and your address."

"I am Joan Carson. I reside at 4441 Hamilton Drive in Denver."

"How long have you lived in Denver?"

"Just over thirteen years."

"Prior to that time, where did you live?"

"In Caldwell, Colorado."

"For how long did you live in Caldwell?"

"All my life, until we moved to Denver."

"You were married to Leslie Carson?"

"Yes."

The questions continued, Ben speaking quietly, letting the spontaneous honesty of Joan's answers capture the jury's attention.

Dupree sat still, waiting to see where Ben was leading. He listened as Joan comfortably described her background. She had known Les all her life, dated him in high school, and married him after her first year of college, his third. They had two children—twins—Chad and Sharlene, who were seated in the courtroom. She had five miscarriages and one stillbirth; they wanted a large family, but nature had denied them. They were in the ranching business, the life they had both known since birth.

They worked together at it; she kept care of the house and the checkbook, he took care of the heavy outside work. She could, and sometimes did, saddle a horse and work the cattle during fall branding season, or drive the truck during haying season. She had used the rifle on the exhibit table since she was twelve; she could shoot it well in all conditions. She brought it to Denver because it never occurred to her to do otherwise. It was just like household furniture to her and Les took it with him sometimes to construction projects in the mountains, so they kept it handy for him at the apartment. They moved to Denver for economic reasons. It became clear small ranches were becoming a thing of the past and they didn't have the money to expand.

Dupree glanced at the jury. They were following Joan's testimony with deep interest. None of it yet amounted to more than domestic background; it was harmless. Dupree still wondered what direction Ben was headed.

Ben paused, looked down at his file and then began on a new line.

"Did your husband have a job when you moved to Denver thirteen years ago?"

"Oh, yes. He had worked the off-season—January and February—for several years for Glenn Tolboy of Tolboy Construction here in Denver, doing maintenance on heavy equipment. Glenn liked him, and when he heard Les might be available he made him an offer to come to work as a maintenance supervisor."

"Would you describe the relationship that developed between your husband and Glenn Tolboy?"

"Glenn was extremely good at doing cost estimates and forming contracts. I mean, he could take an invitation for bid and was a near genius at figuring ways to save money and still do what the invitation called for. But he lacked the gift for handling people. Les had it. Glenn soon discovered it and started training Les to become a foreman and then a supervisor. And then he offered him a full partnership if Les wanted to earn it."

"Going back just a little, what did your husband do when Glenn offered him full-time employment?"

"He came home, told me about it, and we talked it through."

"What did you decide?"

Joan smiled. "It frightened me to death. I had hardly ever been outside of Caldwell and the thought of leaving everything I had known all my life really frightened me. But I knew Les. I knew he had more to give than he would ever be able to if he stayed on the ranch. We decided it would be best for both of us and for the children. We decided to take Glenn up on the offer."

"After moving to Denver, how did the business of the partnership work out?"

"Extremely well. Les became a partner nine years ago, and at that time their gross volume per year was about two million dollars. Last year, their annual volume was just about one hundred million dollars. The successful combination of Glenn in the office and Les out of the office was a very rare blend."

Judge Boyd turned his head to look at the wall clock.

"Counsel, it is 12:05. Would this be a good time to interrupt for the noon recess?"

● ● ●

With the jury back from lunch and the roll call completed, the judge turned to Ben.

"Counsel, you may continue direct examination of the defendant."

"Thank you, your honor. Mrs. Carson, how did Les view his work?"

"At the ranch or at the construction company?"

"Was there a difference?"

"No, not really, I guess. When Les decided to do something, he usually put all his energy and attention into it. When the job was done, he would let up and relax a little. I think he was pretty emotional about his work. It meant a lot to him to do well and to have people tell him so. He worked more for approval than for money, I think. He was a good worker."

"What was his attitude toward the children?"

"He worried all the time that he was spoiling them. He knew—we both knew—what hard work was, in all conditions, and he knew the value of it. He made sure the kids found out and understood what hard work meant. He wanted them to be able to stand on their own feet and take care of themselves. He worked right alongside of them, or I guess it was really the other way around. They worked alongside of him while we were at the ranch. After we came to Denver, he saw to it they had jobs, bank accounts, and learned to handle money. I helped with that."

"Was it all work with the kids?"

"Oh, no. As I said, he worried he would spoil them. He gave them a little money from time to time, for movies and high-school dances, and he let them use the car a lot. When holidays came, he would just close down the ranch operation and we would go with the kids to town and have a time. At Christmas, he always thought he gave them too much."

"How did the children regard their father?"

"They loved him. They idolized him."

"How did you regard him?"

"The same. I loved him, and I . . . loved him." Her eyes dropped for a moment, then returned to Ben's.

Ben paused. The next question was going to trigger the pivotal ruling by Judge Boyd on admission of evidence. If the ruling went against Ben, the damage would be irreparable.

"How would you characterize his attitude toward *you* prior to last spring?"

Dupree was on his feet halfway through the sentence. This was no longer background. Ben's question was entering the realm of the

Wanrow case. Dupree knew the next question was going to be, "And what was his attitude *after* last spring?" followed by "What impact did that have on you the morning of September 18th?" Pandora's box would be opened. Joan would blame Les for her conduct that morning, and a dead man would end up on trial instead of Joan. Dupree made his move.

"Objection, your honor. Some background seems appropriate, but this question is getting into specifics, which do not really deal with the issues of this case. It's *her* conduct that's on trial, not his. We're not here to try Les Carson."

Judge Boyd studied Ben and then Dupree for just a moment. Leaning forward, he spoke.

"Mr. Bailiff, would you escort the jury to the jury room for just a few minutes? Ladies and gentlemen, I expect there will be some statements from the attorneys on this question that might unduly influence you. To give you the best opportunity I can to fairly consider this case, you will be excused for just a short time." The bailiff escorted the jury out of the courtroom.

"Mr. Cooper, what is your purpose in submitting this testimony?"

Ben paused and glanced at Dupree, then back at the judge. He figured with no jury to worry about, he should address the question head-on.

"Bottom line, your honor, the Wanrow case. We intend to show that Les Carson suddenly changed last spring into a man that became progressively more brutal, finally beating the defendant into near unconsciousness the morning of September 18th. If it hadn't been for his violent, unexplained change, the defendant would never have found herself suddenly dependent on her basic instincts for survival that morning and reacted as she did.

"Your honor, this case does not turn on the facts. The facts have been before this court for weeks. We conceded the facts with the filing of the unexcised medical reports. This case turns on the question of the intent of the defendant at the time of the shooting. And we do *not* concede the issue of *intent*. In this case, it is the intent of a *woman*.

"The modern expansion of understanding of the basic human psyche has reached a plateau that will no longer let the law ignore the clear, undeniable fact that in some of its facets, the female psyche is not the same as that of the male. Relating this to the case now on trial, one of those differences emerges when one examines the perceptions of a female regarding deadly force. In our culture, it is a part of the nature of the female to see *deadly* force where a male would not. This case hangs on that difference.

"With this knowledge now accepted by our society, to force this woman to be tried for her life, without affording her the opportunity to set before this court *her* perceptions, *her* instincts, *her* condition of heart and mind at the time of the alleged crime, and to be judged as a female, is to force her to endure a trial contrary to her rights to due process under the fifth and fourteenth amendments of the federal constitution.

"Specifically, the long-standing laws of self defense in this state in a case like this all presume that the attacker and the victim are both men. The language of the jury instructions and the test used to determine justification for a killing in a case like this are cast in the language of 'the reasonable man' and whether or not the victim of the attack had retreated to the wall, and had his back against it, and was justified in killing his attacker because any reasonable man would have done the same thing.

"What about the reasonable woman who is an attack victim? If the male-female differences are such that a woman would by nature react differently than a man in defending her life, then this court cannot deny her the right to explain those differences so she can be judged fairly by her peers. I cite the case of State versus Wanrow in support, 559 Pacific Second, 548, Supreme Court of the State of Washington. I submit this court can do no less than hear before it judges. Thank you."

Ben closed his file and walked to his table.

Dupree didn't hesitate. He walked to the lectern, faced the judge, and waited.

"Mr. Dupree, let's hear your position."

"Your honor, I have struggled with trying to understand how the defense intended using the Wanrow case in any way that would be of help to the Carson case. The Wanrow facts support the decision of the Washington court, but I don't see how they can do a single thing for anyone in *this* case, in *this* court.

"In Wanrow, a woman was so frightened of the reputation of the neighborhood bully that when she turned and he was unexpectedly standing right behind her, she instantly and by reflex pulled the trigger on the pistol she was carrying, specifically to protect herself from him.

"Now, if the defense intends using the ruling in that case as a source of help in this one, the defense is depending on an illusion. They are reading things into Wanrow that just don't exist. In the Carson case there was not just a single shot fired instantly and by reflex. There were *two* shots. The second shot came several seconds after the first one, and there is no way to claim the second shot was by reflex. It was timed, accurate, fatal, and delivered while the deceased was totally and permanently disabled, and known to be such by the defendant.

"The point becomes conclusively clear by asking and answering one question: If Mrs. Wanrow had fired *two* shots, several seconds apart, the second shot coming after the defendant had slumped to the floor totally and fatally disabled, what would the Washington court have done? To think they would have made the ruling we are now discussing is nonsense.

"Properly understood, the Wanrow case cuts *against* the defense, not for it. Need this court be reminded that even after the reversal, and with the benefit of the supreme court ruling to assist the defense, the second trial resulted in a manslaughter conviction of Mrs. Wanrow, as I recall it. May I repeat, on facts immeasurably more favorable than those against Mrs. Carson in this case, Mrs. Wanrow was still convicted of a homicide?

"Until the defendant can show facts comparable to the Wanrow facts, there is no way to use that case to support this one. And even if the defendant here *could* show such facts, she would still face a conviction for manslaughter if the Wanrow case has any meaning.

"Defense counsel strenuously argues that it would be a denial of her right to due process and equal protection under the law if she is not now allowed to go into details extending back over several months, and which will allegedly show that on the morning of the shooting, her female psyche was in such a condition that the killing of Mr. Carson was not a homicide.

"It may have been a denial of due process and equal protection if she hadn't already put medical reports and sworn testimony before this court that convicts her."

Dupree paused while the damning words echoed off the walls in the silent courtroom. Then he continued.

"She had her constitutional rights when she prepared her defense. She filed the documents that now convict her. Under *any* view, background and details will not overcome what she has already put before this court. She shot him down. Ten seconds later, she *murdered* him. All her constitutional rights were protected. She was not *forced* to make those admissions. Having made them, she cannot now complain that she must live with them."

Dupree paused, gauging whether he should say more. "It necessarily follows that the evidence the defense now offers is not relevant nor material. It must be excluded."

Dupree took his seat and turned his face toward the judge.

The courtroom was silent; neither Dupree nor Ben was moving.

Judge Boyd removed his glasses and toyed with them for just a moment.

Caught between the powerful arguments of the lawyers, no one noticed Joan as she sat on the witness stand, listening and waiting. A cold shudder came over her as she tried to bury her unspoken fears. "Don't they understand? I killed Les. My world was destroyed September 18th. Is it possible the law might not let me explain what happened? How can that be?" No one saw her wipe away the single tear that started down her cheek.

Judge Boyd set his glasses down and spoke.

"I agree the facts in this case are distinguishable from Wanrow in a lot of the details—the number of shots, when they were fired, and the fact the deceased was down to stay when the second shot was fired, in this case. Maybe this defendant should have recognized the quality of her acts and not fired that second shot unless she really did intend to commit a homicide. I recognize all that.

"But I am not convinced that is the essence of the Wanrow decision. It seems to me that case was based on the mental perceptions and apprehensions of the defendant, not the number of shots.

"The stakes in this trial are about as high as they can get in the value system of our society. We're dealing with a human being, the constitution, and established law. The law now being challenged and the constitution it is built on were intended to be the safe harbor for human rights, human values. The problem the courts have is recognizing when the new knowledge we generate requires us to change the law. And if the law must be changed, how do we do it and at the same time maintain the principles we all believe in and not do violence to the constitution? I suppose that's why I'm here. I'm the one on the hot seat."

He paused, and his brow wrinkled as he searched for the right words.

"I think the framers of the constitution meant to accommodate change. Times change. Notions of justice change. We have to accept new truth when we find it. The only things they intended would *not* be changed are some fundamental rights, among them being a right to due process and equal protection under the law.

"In this case, I have an uneasy feeling that in view of the current state of knowledge about the female gender, we would be proceeding without due process, and probably without equal protection, if we didn't at least give the defendant a chance to present what she can, be it new knowledge or old. If it's wrong or irrelevant, we can strike it out of the record and ignore it. If it's right, the jury should hear it. I think the mistake would occur if I prevented her from presenting it.

"So I think I have to give her a chance to explain her perceptions and whether or not they justify the shooting, be it one shot or two. I know that if she can't do it, Mr. Dupree is sufficiently skilled to demonstrate it on cross-examination. For these reasons, I must overrule the objection."

Ben leaned his head forward and for a moment closed his eyes and heaved a sigh. Some of the tension drained out of him as he realized that his desperate, unprecedented gamble of filing the unexcised reports hadn't destroyed the defense, and all the testimony regarding Joan's perceptions when she triggered the rifle that morning would be allowed.

Dupree looked down at his file, then back at the judge. Without a change of expression, he picked up his pencil, ready to proceed.

Joan looked at Ben, trying to comprehend the impact of the ruling, but gave up as the judge spoke.

"Mr. Bailiff, would you bring the jury back in?" They filed in and took their seats, looking at the judge and the attorneys, wondering what had happened in their absence. They would never know they had missed one of the most profound oral arguments and decisions these two attorneys and Judge Boyd would handle in their careers.

"Madame Clerk, would you please read the last question just before the jury was excused?"

Marge sorted back through several strips on her tape, and read.

"What was his attitude toward you prior to last spring?"

All eyes were now on Joan.

Ben spoke. "You may answer the question."

"I know . . . he loved me."

Patiently Ben inquired of Les's treatment of her in the little things that are important to a woman. Her answers were spontaneous, convincing. Les remembered anniversaries and birthdays. When he was away for extended periods on projects or other business, he called nearly every day. When he came home, he always brought something for her and each of the children. Once on Valentine's Day, he just took the afternoon off to be at home, and then the family went out to dinner and a movie that evening. He was thoughtful. He was strong-willed and usually had his own ideas about things. If he thought he was right, he'd hang onto opinions, but he'd give ground when he saw he should. Once in a while he'd lose his temper; he'd be a little distant for a while and then come to apologize and talk it over. He never raised his hand in anger to Joan or the children; he had a reputation for being a gentle man among those who knew him best. Physically, he was six feet, two inches, weighed 190 pounds, and was strong and active. In a contest of strength, Joan stood no chance.

"What was the event last May that dramatically changed the course of your lives?"

"Glenn Tolboy, Les'ss partner, suffered a heart attack that disabled him. He died in early September."

"What effect, if any, did this have on Les?"

Joan dropped her eyes, then raised them and told of the tragic decline of the business. Without Glenn's expertise in the highly technical work of doing the cost estimates for the contracts, a logjam began that Les could not control. He tried to hire men for the work but could find no one with the expertise Glenn had. They tried to sell Glenn's half of the business, but with the economic downturn still fresh, no one was yet willing to gamble on buying into Tolboy Construction. Les was trapped, watching their life's work run on a downward slide into oblivion.

"How did this tragic downturn affect your husband?"

"He began to be irritable, and as it got worse, he became argumentative about little things."

"To your knowledge, was this change you are now speaking of the result of the business pressures you have described?"

"I thought so at first. As it got worse, I changed my mind. I don't think so."

"Describe the change as it progressed with Mr. Carson."

Carefully, obviously weighing her words for accuracy, Joan described the increased frequency and force of his argumentativeness. His behavior was at first a concern to her, then became a worry. Then one day he struck her, and she couldn't believe it. Within days he struck her again, and then again, knocking her down and kicking her. She knew by then something was seriously wrong, and on Wednesday, September 15th, she went to her doctor, Dr. Swenson, with her story. He recommended she call his lawyer, a Mr. Tuttle, and arrange for legal action to force Les to be examined. The appointment with the lawyer was for September 22nd.

"Continuing now with the occurrences that preceded the morning of September 18th, what next developed in your relationship with Mr. Carson?"

"He came home the day after Glenn Tolboy died, and he wanted to talk about the business."

"Did he become violent again?"

"No. I left the house within fifteen minutes of when he arrived."

"Why did you leave?"

"It was impossible to know when he was going to lose control of his temper again."

"Whenever he would lose control, what was his appearance?"

"It was like Les was in some other world, fighting against something that only he could see. It seemed like he would lash out at me, or just anything there, trying to fight whatever it was that was happening inside him."

"What impact did this have on your mind, your emotions?"

Joan's speech slowed as she struggled for the right words.

"It was a feeling like . . . like terror. I left because I couldn't face the horrible, strange things he would say and the look in his eyes like he was someone I had never seen before. A total stranger. I don't remember being afraid of the beatings and the pain so much. It was like I was looking at someone possessed, or a maniac. That was what I couldn't stand."

Not visible to the jurors, Joan held a handkerchief in her hands and her fingers slowly smoothed the wrinkles, folding and refolding it.

"What happened next, regarding Les?"

"On Friday, the 17th of September, he came to the house for just a few minutes to tell me he wanted to live separate from me. He had boxed up my things at the apartment and wanted me to come out to pick them up the next day at noon. He was supposed to be at a job site until then. I agreed and left as quickly as I could. Les stayed at the house a little while to pick up several boxes of his things so he could take them to the apartment."

"When did you return to the house and what did you do after your return, the evening of the 17th?"

"I returned long after dark. I estimate about 10 o'clock. He had gone, with his things. I was afraid he might return, so I sat in a rocking chair in the living room all night in the dark, listening."

"Did he return?"

"No, he did not."

Ben cleared his throat and paused before proceeding into the next line of questions.

"Describe your actions immediately after you arose from the chair."

Beginning to show emotion, Joan told of deciding to go early to the apartment to avoid Les, hoping to be finished and gone before he returned from the construction project. Backing the car up to the apartment door, she got out and opened the car trunk, then turned to open the apartment door.

Ben stood motionless and spoke quietly. All eyes were upon Joan.

"After you turned your key in the door lock, describe what you did."

"I stood there in the doorway and let my eyes adjust to the darkness inside. The drapes were closed and the only light was what came in through the open door. I didn't want to turn the lights on in case he might be inside."

"What, if anything, could you see inside?"

"I could see just vague outlines of things. I knew there were piles of things to the right of the kitchenette, and I thought they were boxes. Some other things were stacked and piled on the other side of the archway."

"What did you do next?"

"I waited a few seconds and when I didn't hear anything or see him, I stepped into the room and reached for the light switch."

"Did you turn the lights on?"

"No. I didn't get that far."

Ben paused and leaned forward in the silence.

"Tell us what happened next."

"I heard, or maybe more like felt, something in back of me. I turned to look. It was Les, right there behind me."

The words were echoing slightly off the walls.

"Could you see any detail?"

"Only a little."

"Describe what you could see."

"His hair was uncombed and all . . . awry. His face was away from the door, but I could still see that it looked dark, like he hadn't shaved for a day or two. I could see his forehead was wrinkled, like it was drawn up in surprise, or anger. But the worst was his eyes. Even with his face away from the door, I could see his eyes."

Ben was watching her intently, pacing the questions.

"Describe his eyes. Describe his expression if you can."

"His eyes were opened very wide. I could see his mouth slightly open. He looked like a maniac. I have never seen that expression on another human face."

"How did it affect you?"

"I have never felt a feeling like that in my life. I don't know the words. It was worse than terror. It wasn't Les. He was possessed. I was looking at someone I didn't know. Whoever was inside him, it wasn't

Les." The corners of her mouth started to twitch slightly. She set her jaw to keep control.

"Joan, can you tell us what happened next?"

"He started toward me. He made a sound like a . . . sobbing sound, and his head tilted a little to his right. I saw his hands start to rise and I brought up my arms to cover my face. He grabbed my arm, my right arm, and then he started hitting me with his right hand."

"Describe the force of the blows."

"He hit me hard. The third or fourth time he hit me I didn't feel the pain any more. I felt one hit on my left eye and I thought my eye was put out. My vision was blurred. I remember him hitting my nose and I could feel the blood coming."

"Where did the blows strike your body?"

"All over. All over my head and neck and shoulders."

"Do you know how many times he struck you?"

"No."

"Could you estimate it for us?"

"Maybe twenty. Perhaps more. I know my left ear was ringing from being hit and I remember feeling the inside of my right cheek smashing against my teeth. I tasted the blood. I could feel it running down my chin."

"What did you do to defend yourself?"

"I tried to keep my arms up to protect my face. But there was no way; I couldn't do anything against Les, not with his size and strength. There was nothing I could do to stop him."

"Did you scream at him? Make any sounds?"

"Nothing. After the third or fourth time he hit me, I was . . . it was like I couldn't make my mind focus. I couldn't react or think."

"What caused him to stop beating you?"

"I remember my mind going numb and my legs started to buckle out from under me. It felt like he couldn't hold me up with just one hand, so he grabbed my other arm—my left arm—in his right hand . . . and threw me backward, hard."

"When he threw you backward, what did you do?"

"I remember my legs wouldn't hold me up and my back hit something. I remember sliding down to a sitting position, with my back still against whatever I slammed into, and I remember looking up at him."

"What were the thoughts you had when you looked up and saw him?"

"I can't remember one thought being in my mind. It was numb. I couldn't get control."

"What did you do?"

"I felt something bang off my right shoulder and then slide down my arm and stop in my lap. I glanced down and felt for it. It was my rifle. Les had leaned it against the wall by the archway when he gathered up my things."

"Which side of the archway had you slammed into?"

"The left side, as you face it from the living room."

"Where was Les?"

"He was moving toward me."

Ben paused and leaned slightly forward. His next words were spaced, penetrating.

"At that moment, what were your thoughts and what were your feelings?"

"It was as though my mind wouldn't work. I couldn't force any thoughts or reason. Then a feeling came over me and I just knew what I had to do. It was like something other than my own thoughts had taken over and I just did what I had to do."

"What did you do?"

"I took the rifle in my hands and levered a cartridge into the chamber. I pointed it . . . by feel . . . and pulled the trigger."

"Where did you point it?"

"Just above his belt, in the center of his body."

"As the shot fired, what was he doing?"

"He had started to turn. To his right . . . he was turning."

"From what position were you firing?"

"I was sitting. I couldn't get up."

"Are you capable of firing that rifle that accurately in the dark?

"Yes, I am."

"After the shot struck, what did he do?"

"He fell down backward, very hard."

"Could you still see him?"

"Yes. He was sitting just to the right of being in line with me and the open door. I could see him."

"What was he doing?"

"He was moving a little. I could hear him breathing."

"What did you do next?"

Joan raised her hands to her mouth and for a moment closed her eyes, struggling for control.

"I chambered a fresh cartridge and . . . I shot him. Through the head."

Ben stopped. He was watching her every expression, gauging whether she could go on. He continued.

"What did he do?"

"He fell . . . toppled over onto his right side and quit moving. I didn't hear any more sounds."

"Tell me about the feeling you described just a moment ago. How long did it linger with you?"

"After the second shot, after Les toppled over, the feeling began to leave me. I could feel my own ability to think and reason starting to come back, and I began to realize what had happened."

"What was in your mind?"

"I couldn't believe what I had done. I couldn't make my mind accept it. I thought I was going to lose my sanity for just a minute or two." She paused and looked down.

"Go on, Joan."

"I waited until I could trust my own thoughts and had enough strength to get up. I stepped over his legs, put the rifle on safety, and leaned it against the wall by the door to the outside. I checked the lock, and I walked out and closed the door. I got into my car and drove to your office. I met David Ballantine there and I asked for you. David called you, and you came down, and I told you what had happened."

Then Joan stopped. Her jaw muscles were tightening. She interlaced her fingers and brought her hands up to cover her mouth. She caught her breath with a single sob, but she did not cry.

Ben waited for just a moment.

"Joan, carefully. What were your intentions at the time you fired the two shots?"

Not a sound was heard inside the courtroom. The muffled, faint noise from the corridor went unnoticed. Every eye was on Joan, every ear straining. The media people were motionless, frozen, hanging on the next words.

Joan brought her hands down. Her voice was quiet, firm, and it was obvious she was searching for words that would best tell the truth.

"I had no thought in my mind, and no intent that I can recall. I can't explain the feeling that rose inside of me. I just knew what I had to do. It wasn't Les. I didn't shoot Les. It wasn't Les."

A faint murmur ran through the courtroom for just a moment. Joan reached upward with her handkerchief and wiped away a tear that had started, but her expression didn't change, nor did she make a sound.

Ben looked at her for a second or two, the pain and compassion showing in his eyes.

"I have no further questions. Counsel may cross-examine."

Judge Boyd spoke up.

"Counsel, it is 4:55. Mr. Dupree, would you care to take up cross-examination in the morning or at this time?"

"I believe it would be better in the morning, your honor."

"We stand in recess until 9 o'clock tomorrow morning. The jury is given the usual admonition." The judge banged his gavel and the crowd slowly began to file out.

Returning to their offices, both Ben and Dupree were deep into their own thoughts, calculating the impact of Judge Boyd's ruling on the Wanrow case. For Ben, it was the opening of a door to evidence that he desperately hoped would be enough to rise above the solid, unmoving case Dupree had built. For Dupree, it was a question of whether his case had been damaged or not. He could see no way that the evidence Ben was now being allowed to get into the record was going to really make any significant difference, in view of the fact every element of the state's case was proven by the testimony of the defendant herself.

Joan's testimony? Neither man made any conclusion. Both men knew the most sensational part of it was yet to come. Dupree was going to try to prove the legally required intent to commit a murder when he cross-examined Joan, who to this point had built a powerful image of herself as an understandable, decent wife and mother who had been victimized.

The question was, would the image survive Dupree's blistering cross-examination?

Friday, December 10th

THE TEMPERATURE HAD CONTINUED its drop to ten below zero. The streets and sidewalks were patched with black ice, making walking treacherous. Those entering the courthouse stomped their feet to remove the salty slush mixture tracked in from the stairway.

The courthouse employees were shedding their coats and scarves, and the banter between them carried an air of anticipation. It was Friday. The approaching weekend always made Friday a good day.

On the fourth floor, room 414, the clerk finished roll call of the jury and Judge Boyd looked at Dupree.

"Mr. Dupree, I believe you were about to begin cross-examination of the defendant."

"Yes, your honor. Thank you."

He walked to the lectern and began.

"Mrs. Carson, you understand it is now my duty to cross-examine you?"

"Yes, I understand."

"I must ask you certain questions, to be sure the jury sees all sides of your testimony so they can make a fair judgment. Do you understand that?"

"Yes, I do.

"At times I may be required to ask you rather pointed questions. They are not intended to offend you, but merely to verify that your testimony is complete and understandable. Will you please try to remember that?"

"Yes, I will."

"Mrs. Carson, I would like to know more about the partnership business your husband had with Glenn Tolboy. I understand the business had grown to be rather substantial, coming into the spring months of this year. Is that correct?"

For more than half an hour Dupree continued his general questions, developing a rhythm as he led Joan through familiar, harmless parts of her testimony. Dupree was putting the jury at ease and preparing to move into the critical questions that would result in her confession of the intent to commit a murder.

Joan looked and listened to Dupree, answering his questions directly and simply.

Yes, their business was large and expanding before last spring. She was willing to work and considered herself a responsible person. She did not tend to panic or lose control in sudden emergencies. She knew the rifle and could shoot it accurately by feel. She knew the power of the bullets and had shot enough elk and deer with it to know that a lung shot or a head shot with that rifle would be fatal. Yes, she considered Les and herself to be pretty self-sufficient people; they tried to solve their own problems.

With just a few more preliminary questions, Dupree started into the critical area. Ben knew when it started and leaned slowly forward, waiting to see if Joan would remember to listen, think, answer—and above all, tell the truth.

"Mrs. Carson, do you remember the few seconds surrounding the two shots that were fired?"

"Yes, I do."

May I talk with you about the first shot? Do you think you can talk about it rationally?"

"Yes. What is your question?"

"After the gun bumped off your shoulder and fell across your lap, you felt for it and realized it was your rifle?"

"Yes."

"You worked the rifle and chambered a cartridge?"

"Yes."

"Did you know the rifle was loaded?"

"I knew it was loaded. It always had bullets in the magazine."

"Then you raised the rifle and pointed it at the shape of Les, coming toward you?"

"Yes, I did."

"He was just a silhouette, was he not?"

"Almost totally a silhouette."

"Could you see the rifle? Could you see the sights on the barrel?"

"I could not see the sights. I could hardly see the barrel."

"You had just received a savage beating, and at one point thought your eye—your left eye—was blinded, and you knew your mouth was badly lacerated inside; your left ear was ringing from the blows. Your legs had buckled from under you. Is that true?"

"Yes."

"Now, Mrs. Carson, under those conditions, how were you able to place that first bullet with such precision?"

"I just . . . it just had to be done, and I did it. By feel. When you take hold of the stock by the trigger with your right hand, and the fore grip with your left, you just know where the barrel is pointing. I can't explain it better than that."

"And where did you choose to place that first shot?"

"Through the upper part of his body."

"Through the rib cage, where the vital organs are?"

"Yes."

"Did you know where the bullet struck as soon as you fired the rifle?"

"Yes. I knew."

"You knew you had placed it precisely where you earlier described a bullet should be placed for a fatal shot?"

"Yes, I did."

"With your knowledge of the rifle, did you know you had inflicted a fatal shot on your husband?"

"I knew he was hurt badly. I didn't know if it was fatal."

"When the bullet struck, I understand it knocked him down backward, into a sitting position, is that true?"

"Yes."

"Mrs. Carson, when he went down, you knew he was at least badly injured, didn't you?"

"Yes."

"And you knew he was not going to be able to get up from that shot, didn't you?"

"I knew he was badly hurt. I wasn't thinking about whether he could get up."

"Did you know the bullets were hunting loads, designed to collapse and deliver heavy shocking power?"

"Yes, I was aware of that."

"You had sufficient control of your thoughts to work the action on the rifle, didn't you?"

"I didn't think about working the action. I just did it."

"How long did it take you to work the action, Mrs. Carson?"

"Just a second or two."

"Then you waited?"

"Yes."

"For what, Mrs. Carson?"

"To see if it had stopped him."

"Had it stopped him?"

"No. He was still moving, and he was making sounds and breathing."

"And you waited. You waited for how many seconds?"

"I don't know. I thought six or seven, but it must have been more. Probably about ten seconds. I don't know."

"Did he try to get up?"

"No."

"Did he make any effort to reach you? To harm you?"

"No, he didn't."

"In fact, didn't you have to wait until his head stabilized and became still so you could place the second shot?"

"I heard him breathing and making sounds and still moving. I pointed the rifle and fired the second shot."

"Did you place the second shot where you intended it to strike?"

"Yes, I did."

"You intended it to strike his head, where it actually struck?"

"Yes."

"You knew a shot from a rifle as powerful as this one, passing directly through his head at the place you aimed it, would be fatal, didn't you?"

"I knew it would be fatal."

"And you intended it to be fatal, didn't you?"

Ben slowly straightened, hardly breathing. Now was the time.

"Yes. I intended to stop him."

"Mrs. Carson, you knew at the time the person before you was your husband, didn't you?"

"Yes, I did."

"Was he armed? Did he have a weapon of any kind?"

"No. Not that I knew of. I am sure he didn't have anything in his hands."

Now Dupree's voice dropped from normal conversational intensity to a quieter tone.

"Just a couple more questions, Mrs. Carson. After the second shot, you sat there in the dark for a time, waiting for strength to come back into your legs, if I understood your testimony correctly. Is that true?"

"Yes. I couldn't get up. My legs just weren't working right."

"You rose, stepped over his legs, and leaned the rifle against the wall by the door?"

"Yes."

"Did you have the clarity of thought to put the rifle on safety?"

"Yes, I did. I always do."

"Then you checked the door lock and walked out the door?"

"Yes. I got into my car and drove away."

"You just leaned the rifle against the wall? Why did you do that? Why didn't you just cast it aside in a panic, screaming, and run out of the room as quickly as you could?"

"I wasn't . . . my mind wasn't working very well, but I didn't panic. I think I just did what I always did with the rifle when I finished using it. I put it on safety and stood it against a wall or in a corner."

"Thank you, Mrs. Carson. I have no more questions, your honor."

"Mr. Cooper, any re-direct?"

"Yes, your honor." Ben walked to the lectern.

"Mrs. Carson, you just responded to a question from Mr. Dupree wherein you stated you knew the person standing before you, the one you shot, was your husband. Do you remember the question and your answer?"

"Yes, I do."

"Think carefully, Mrs. Carson. According to your perceptions at that moment, was the person before you Leslie Carson?"

Joan's eyes widened as she realized her mistake.

"No. It was not Les. As God as my witness, there was a monster inside Les. I did not shoot Les. I didn't kill Les."

Her breath caught and she stifled a sob, then settled down.

"I have no more re-direct examination." Ben went to his chair.

"Any re-cross, Mr. Dupree?"

"None, your honor." Dupree already had what he wanted. Joan had intended to kill the person in front of her; her perceptions of who it was would never change the fact it was Leslie Carson.

It was finished. Her testimony was in the record. Neither attorney could gauge its impact, nor was there time to ponder. Judge Boyd paused for a moment, providing a few moments for the attorneys to pull themselves back from the intense concentration that had drained both of them.

"Mr. Cooper, you may call your next witness."

"The defense calls Chief Charles Fawcett."

Charlie came to the witness stand and sat down, prepared.

"Mr. Fawcett, do you recall your previous testimony concerning your investigation at the scene of the shooting?"

"Yes, I do."

"Do you recall that I visited the apartment about mid-morning on the day of the investigation and talked with you about the facts your people had developed?"

"Yes, I recall that."

"That morning, do you recall a brief inspection you and I made of the wall just to the left of the doorway into the kitchenette, at about the forty-two-inch level?"

"Yes, I do."

"Could you describe what you observed?"

"Yes. I noticed a faint irregularity in the wallpaper. It was a very light mark that made a perfect arc, starting at about forty-two inches above floor level and dropping in a perfect arc to the right, toward the doorjamb. It ended at a place where there was a slight bruise in the paint of the doorjamb."

"Would the bailiff please give defense exhibit 11 to the witness?" The exhibit was delivered.

"Chief Fawcett, can you identify this exhibit?"

"This is a photograph taken by Detective Minelli at the time of the investigation. It shows the arc I have described."

"Chief Fawcett, were you here during the testimony of the defendant, when she described how she was thrown backward by her husband against the doorjamb to the kitchenette? The same side of the doorjamb that appears in this photograph?"

"I heard the testimony."

"Do you recall her testimony earlier, of seeing the faint image in the dark room when she opened the door, of something beside the doorjamb that looked like her rifle or a vacuum handle?"

"I recall the testimony."

"Do you also recall her testimony that after she slammed into the doorjamb, something bounced off her right shoulder and fell across her lap? And it turned out to be the rifle now in evidence, state's exhibit V?"

"I am aware of the testimony."

"Chief Fawcett, have you tested the blade of the foresight on that rifle?"

"Yes, I have."

"Is there a relationship between that foresight and the mark on the wall?"

"Yes. The foresight probably made the mark."

"Referring you now to defense exhibit 11, do you have an opinion regarding whether the arc appearing on the wallpaper in the photograph, and the bruised spot on the outside edge of the doorjamb, are consistent with what you would expect to find if the testimony of Mrs. Carson were true regarding how she came to be in possession of the rifle at the time of the shooting?"

"Yes."

"What is that opinion?"

"The presence of the arc on the wallpaper and the dent in the paint on the doorjamb are consistent with the testimony of Mrs. Carson."

"Further, Chief Fawcett, did you hear Mrs. Carson's testimony that she was sitting down when the rifle toppled across her lap?"

"I heard her."

"Did you understand she said she was firing the rifle from a sitting position?"

"I understood that."

"Would her sitting position at the time she fired the shots be consistent with the facts you gave earlier regarding the upward angle of the chest shot and the level trajectory of the head shot?"

"That would be consistent."

"Thank you, Chief Fawcett. I have no more questions at this time."

"Mr. Dupree, do you care to cross-examine?"

"No questions, your honor."

● ● ●

After the jury returned from the noon recess and answered roll call, the judge continued.

"Mr. Cooper, your next witnesses."

The balance of the afternoon was devoted to submitting the testimony of Ann Fenton, Tom Price, Cecil Gilbert, Dr. Swenson, and his attorney, Mr. Tuttle. In each instance, the witness corroborated the statements made by Joan in her testimony. The value of the support was twofold: it gave credibility to Joan and it completed the picture. When Ben finished, there were no holes, no unanswered questions for the jury. It was now becoming undeniably apparent Joan had told the truth about everything that could be objectively proven.

But more significantly, on the single issue of intent that the prosecution could not directly prove except from Joan's testimony, she had looked Dupree straight in the eye and given him the cold truth. Instead of answering vaguely, she openly, coolly, and completely confessed to the necessary intent.

As Ben sat down, Judge Boyd glanced at the large clock.

"Gentlemen, it is almost 5 o'clock. Unless you have reason to the contrary, I will call the weekend recess."

In the fast-settling dusk, Ben turned his car out of the parking lot, glancing momentarily at the back of the courthouse. Beyond the courthouse, the gold dome of the state capitol building glimmered from the last rays of a sun now set.

Pulling his mind from his thoughts, he glanced at Joan.

"I know you've got a lot of questions, Joan. I'm still too close to the case to give you a very good idea of where it now stands. The pivotal point of the case was just finished—your testimony. You couldn't have done better. Take it from one who knows."

He looked at her and realized she needed to know at least a few things.

"I can tell you one thing. You shook Dupree and startled the jury with your answers about intent. Even with the unexcised reports in the file—and he could have used those reports to impeach you later— he wasn't prepared for the head-on way you answered him. It was good."

Joan sat for several seconds, staring through the windshield.

"I thought I told them I intended to kill Les."

"You gave Dupree what he thought he needed, but you also gave me what I've got to have. The jury was moved, Joan. You got to them. They believed you. That's vital to what I have to do when I argue this case to them." He turned his eyes back to the traffic.

"Ben, give it to me straight. How do you think this is going to turn out?" Her need to know and her fear of knowing were both evident in the quaver of her voice.

Bringing the car to a stop at the next intersection, Ben turned to Joan.

"I don't know. It's not over yet. Any guess I make will just be false hopes. As soon as I have an idea, I'll let you know. Can you hang on just a little longer?"

Joan looked at him intently for a moment, then settled back in the seat, accepting his answer.

Sunday, December 12th

"DAD, IT'S WYLIE." LAURA LAID THE receiver down and Ben felt anticipation as he walked over to the phone.

"Wylie! You're home. How are you?"

"Fine. A little light-headed from jet lag, but fine."

"Well, how was it? How was the trip?"

"Just great. Couldn't have been better. Tremendous convention and beautiful weather."

"When do we get you and Mary over here for an evening to share the videos and tell us all about it?"

"As soon as you can give us the time. We've got a lot of footage and I think some of it is going to be pretty good."

"How was your address received? Anyone comment?"

"Quite well, as a matter of fact. It seems the delegation from Russia wanted copies of my research material sent to Moscow."

"Wylie! That's terrific. What did you tell them?"

"Da."

Both men laughed.

"Ben, I thought I'd better ask about the Carson trial. I presume I'll be needed tomorrow morning at the courthouse. How's it coming?"

Ben sobered.

"Wylie, there are some problems. I hate to put this off on you, but if you have a little time later this afternoon or evening, I need to come visit you."

There was a pause.

"Serious? Joan?"

"No. Les. It will take a little time. And I need your advice."

"Certainly. Would this evening at 7 o'clock be all right?"

"Yes. Thank you. I'll be there."

With his briefcase beside him, Ben drove the few miles to Wylie's home. He was greeted by Mary, and within minutes he and Wylie were behind closed doors in the library.

"It sounded urgent, Ben. What's up?"

Ben waited just a moment, then responded.

"Here's the bottom line. I believe Les Carson killed Glenn Tolboy." Ben waited for a reaction.

Wylie looked at him without moving or changing expression.

"That doesn't surprise me. Tell me how you reached that conclusion."

For twenty minutes, Ben repeated the story he had told David about the missing quinidine capsules and all the evidence that pointed to Les's well-hidden plan to substitute powdered sugar for quinidine in Glenn's medication. When he finished, he waited for a reaction.

Wylie broke off his intense concentration and raised his eyebrows.

"This may be the event I've been waiting for. Do you know anything you haven't already told me?"

"No, I think I included it all. I brought a handwritten summary for you, if you want to review it." Ben lifted it from his briefcase and dropped it on the table.

"I will. Can you leave it?"

Ben nodded.

Wylie dropped his head forward in concentration. "I presume you couldn't use this in the trial, at least so far."

"No. There is no way to even consider it. The only value to it is that it might be a clue to what went wrong with Les. But if it is, I can't find it, and nothing *we* received from Bill Heyrend or the coroner's report or our investigation suggested a clue."

"Who have you told?"

"Just David, and now you."

Wylie continued to ponder for a moment.

"Ben, I want to take a little time tonight and put your handwritten report in context with what I have in my file and I'll talk to you about that in the morning."

Ben rose to prepare to leave, but Wylie motioned him to remain for a minute.

"How's the trial coming?" His eyes locked with Ben's momentarily. Ben was reluctant to answer.

"Touch and go. Wylie, I think I underestimated the picture Dupree could paint with the facts. We got our first shot at offsetting it a couple of days ago when Joan testified. She was simply great, but I don't think we got over the mountain. I'm waiting now to see how it looks when we finish with you and Dr. Johnstone. If I can't do something pretty strong, I've got a problem." He pursed his lips and raised his eyebrows to accent his statements.

"If we got lucky and found out what went wrong with Les, would that help?" Wylie waited for a reply, the intensity in his eyes showing.

"It would help, but I don't know how much. I can't see it being too persuasive because proving something went wrong with Les only tends to corroborate Joan's statements that he started mistreating her. I think the jury believes that already. The problem is still the one we started out with—the facts. She waited ten seconds before she fired the shot that killed him."

Wylie nodded his understanding and rose to walk Ben to the door.

"Wylie, we'll need you first thing in the morning. Can you be at my office about 8 o'clock to run through it once with me? You're first on the witness stand."

"I'll be there."

"Are you ready to endure the usual two-hour dismemberment of the art of psychiatry on cross-examination? I know that's what Dupree has in mind. He won't dare challenge you, but he'll do what he can to embarrass psychiatry."

"So what else is new? That I can handle."

"It's good to have you back. I'll see you in the morning."

Ben buttoned his coat and walked out into the frigid darkness.

Monday, December 13th

BEN'S GLOVED FINGERS WORKED slowly and deliberately, selecting the key to the front door of the office building while his breath formed white clouds in the bitter, biting cold. Carefully Ben inserted the key and turned the lock. Entering the building, he turned on the lights and walked up the hallway to his office. He stopped just short of the door to his office, certain he had heard a knock at the front door.

He returned to the foyer, peering at the door. He glanced at the clock on Marie's desk and wondered who would be knocking at 7:20 A.M.

Staring back at Ben through the window, the light full in his face was Wylie. Ben grasped the door handle and threw the door open. Wylie stepped inside and turned as Ben closed the door against the rush of cold air.

"Wylie, this is a bit of a surprise. You're early."

Wylie pulled his overcoat collar down into place and pushed his scarf down below chin level.

"Yes, I have an idea or two we need to discuss. Have a little time?"

"Come on down to my office. Had breakfast?"

"Yes, but a hot drink would be nice."

They both walked to Ben's office, removed their coats, and then walked back toward the kitchen together.

"I expected you about eight. Everything all right?"

"Yes, I think so. I reviewed your memo and my file last night. We need to talk. By the way, am I interrupting something important?"

"No, not at all. I just wanted to go over your testimony for a little while before you arrived. What's on your mind?" Ben started some water boiling and then sat down next to Wylie.

"Let me come directly to the point. I believe the explanation for Les's conduct lies in a mechanical interference or failure in his brain. There's a chance I could yet determine that if I could get a look at it."

He paused to see if Ben anticipated where he was going in the conversation, then continued. "After the autopsy, the brain should have been put into a plastic bag filled with phenol and placed in the chest cavity for the burial. Do you want to think about getting an order to exhume the body and let me take a look?"

Ben looked at Wylie, startled at the suggestion of exhuming Les's body.

"Dig up the body to examine the brain? I can't guess how a jury would take that. Would an examination of the brain now do any good?"

Ben removed the water from the machine and poured cups of hot chocolate for Wylie and himself.

"That's not possible to know without seeing it. Let me explain the importance of this, Ben." Ben caught the seriousness in Wylie's voice.

"The underside of the frontal lobes of the brain is the control center for the personality of the individual. These control centers are quite sensitive. If any unnatural or undue pressure is exerted on them, it tends to create changes in the personality of the individual. The stronger the pressure, the greater the personality change."

Ben slowed the stirring of his drink; when the full implications struck him, he stopped altogether.

"Go on."

"A brain tumor can create that kind of pressure. If a glioblastoma multiforme—a tumor—happened to be located in the right place and had grown to a certain size, it would explain Les."

Wylie could see the sudden intensity in Ben's expression.

"How do you find such a tumor?"

"We use a stain process. Hemotoxylin and eosin—h and e—to stain the cells and the nucleus blue and red, and then you can see the cells clearly under a microscope. Picking out malignant cells is easy once you can see them. It's a simple test, but you have to have the brain tissue to do it. Can we get the tissue?"

Ben dropped his eyes, considering. Judge Boyd had jurisdiction to issue an exhumation order, but he would have to be convinced it would do some good—and most of all, that it would yield evidence that would be helpful to the trial. At this point Ben could guarantee neither.

"Is there some other way to give you what you are looking for?" Ben's voice rose in intensity. "What about some triple enlarged color photos of the bullet wound where you can see into the head cavity? Would that be of any help?"

"Probably not. You really have to look at the tissue under the scope, after the h and e bath, to be sure."

Ben was now beginning to feel a surge of hope and excitement that perhaps they were moving toward the one fact that had remained hidden all this time, leaving so many questions unanswered.

"Then what about that little bag of frozen stuff—the bits and pieces of bone and tissue in the coroner's office? There has to be some of the brain tissue there."

From Wylie's expression, Ben realized he had caught him by total surprise.

"What bag?"

"The little bag that was listed on the coroner's report. It referred to some bits and pieces of tissue that had been randomly sampled and didn't show anything. Dupree suggested they freeze it in case it was needed, and they did, right up front."

Wylie narrowed his eyes as he scanned the coroner's report in his memory. "The coroner mentioned a standard random sampling of bits and pieces of tissue all right, and concluded there was nothing remarkable. That's probably what you're referring to. But they do not say they saved it, frozen in a plastic bag. You're sure, Ben?"

"David was told about it. I presume they still have it."

Wylie paused, his mind working. "Just a minute." He opened his briefcase and drew out the coroner's report, quickly flipping the pages until he found what he was looking for.

"Here's the mention of the tissue you're talking about, and here's the drawing of the brain damage from the bullet. The bullet hit just above ear level, right about where the temporal and sphenoidal bones join. That means it was located about right. Let's see . . . here it is. The pituitary, the optic chiasm were both either unidentifiable or blown clear out of the head. But no mention of a bag." He raised his head, eyes shining in controlled excitement.

"The location is just right. It's worth a try. You bet I want that bag. How long do you think I'll be on the witness stand today?"

"I think until late afternoon—most of the day. Dupree is going to take more than half of it on cross-examination. Wylie, is there really something to this?"

"Who follows me?"

"Carrie Johnstone, tomorrow, probably all day."

"The minute I'm off the stand I'm going down there, Ben. Let's find out if they still have it and if they'll cooperate."

"What about exhuming the body?"

"Second choice. If this fails, we'll give that a try."

Ben leaned forward and spoke slowly. "Wylie, you're serious about this. Do you think there is any real chance of finding tumor tissue in a pound and a half of bone fragments, cartilage, tissue, and who knows what else?"

Wylie spoke thoughtfully. "We won't know until we try. It *ought* to be just a matter of taking the time to test it all. If we can find just part of a glioblastoma connected to the right organ from up behind the nose . . ."

● ● ●

They drove separate cars to the courthouse, arriving a little early. The jury was ushered in; the judge listened to roll call and began.

"Mr. Cooper, you may call your next witness."

"Defense calls Dr. Wylie Benoit."

Wylie was wearing a dark blue suit, white shirt, and a deep burgundy-colored tie. He looked the model of the well-dressed, professional man.

"Please state your name and occupation."

"I am Wylie Benoit. I am a doctor of medicine licensed to practice in the states of Massachusetts and Colorado. I specialize in the field of psychiatry."

With crisp, precise questions, matched by like answers, Ben led Wylie through his overpowering qualifications as an expert in the field of psychiatry. Wylie had completed college, medical school, and his psychiatric training with honors. He'd practiced psychiatry for twenty-two years, authored textbooks, and served as an honorary member of the board of medicine for several universities. Experienced as a forensic psychiatrist, he'd made twenty-seven appearances as an expert witness in criminal trials, and he had recently been appointed to represent the United States at the international convention in Geneva from which he had just returned.

The jury was in awe.

"In your practice, have you had occasion to become acquainted with the defendant, Joan Carson?"

"Yes, I have, through more than eighteen hours of intensive interviews on every element relevant to this case."

For the next forty minutes, Ben carefully laid the foundation for the testimony Wylie would be giving about Joan's condition. He carefully quizzed Wylie about the examinations he had conducted, the tests Joan was given, who administered them, the results, her physical condition, and her mental and emotional condition. Then, with the foundations in place, Ben moved into the essence of Wylie's testimony.

"Limiting your response to the time prior to the spring of this year, do you have an opinion of the perceptions of Joan Carson regarding her husband?"

"Yes, I do."

"Further limiting your answer to the single perception she had regarding his physical conduct toward her, would you state your opinion?"

With simple sentences, Wylie described Joan's perceptions of Les; she saw him as a gentleman and never feared physical abuse.

"Now, Dr. Benoit, beginning last spring, and continuing down to the middle of September, just prior to the 18th, did her perception of her husband continue as you have described it?"

"No, it did not."

"When did the change begin?"

"Not long after his partner, Glenn Tolboy, was disabled from cardiac disease."

"Do you have an opinion regarding whether or not the change in Mr. Carson was related to the disabling of Glenn Tolboy?"

"Yes, I do."

"What is that opinion?"

"Objection. The question is not relevant nor material to this case."

"Sustained."

"What conduct, if any, on the part of Mr. Carson, did Joan advise you of that is indicative of the change in Mr. Carson to which you refer?"

Patiently Wylie recounted the now familiar changes in Les, beginning with his irritability, then his tendency to argue, leading up to the physical abuse.

"Over how long a span of time did this continue?"

"It began in early June and continued until his death on September 18th."

"What, if any, impact did this change in behavior have on the perception of Mrs. Carson, the defendant, in regard to her husband?"

"In her entire life, it had never occurred to her that Mr. Carson would ever be anything other than the man she had loved and respected. To maintain this perception, she was willing to make excuses, both conscious and subconscious, for his conduct. She was able to do this until the last few days of his life, at which time he finally struck her down and kicked her. At that time she concluded he was in need of help. To explain his brutal, totally atypical behavior, she concluded he was beset by something unexplained that was responsible for his actions. Not having sufficient medical knowledge to properly define it, she referred to Mr. Carson as being 'possessed.' She meant he was possessed by something unknown that was causing him to do the brutal things she was experiencing."

"When did this perception of Mr. Carson evolve in Mrs. Carson?"

"It began the first time he struck her and was clearly defined in her mind when she visited her doctor, Dr. Swenson, and called the lawyer, Mr. Tuttle, for help."

"Until last spring, did Mrs. Carson, or did she not, love Mr. Carson?"

"She loved him totally and without reservation."

"At what point in their relationship did this love for him change, or cease, if at all?"

"It never did cease and it never did change. She loved him until his death. She still loves him."

Ben now came straight into the crucial time frame.

"On the morning of September 18th, what were her perceptions of Mr. Carson?"

"At what point, Mr. Cooper?"

"At the point he suddenly appeared behind her and took hold of her arm."

"At that moment, she essentially had no perceptions of Mr. Carson in her consciousness at all. She was functioning on two things: her life's conditioning, and in just seconds, pure female instinct and compulsion."

"Do you understand, Dr. Benoit, that two shots were fired, with a time lag of between seven and ten seconds between them?"

"Yes, I do."

"Was she aware she was firing a second shot, after several seconds had elapsed?"

"Yes, she was."

"At the time she fired the second shot, what were her perceptions of what was happening?"

"She was simply concluding a sequence of acts that were required to stop the physical and mental terror."

"Did she know she was shooting Mr. Carson?"

"She knew she was shooting the person known as Mr. Carson."

"If she still loves him, as you said, how was she able to do that?"

"In her perception, Mr. Carson was already gone." Wylie paused, hoping the jury understood the bedrock significance of that simple sentence; then he continued. "She didn't know what had destroyed him, but in her view, what was facing her in that darkened room was not Mr. Carson."

"For how long did that perception maintain itself in her mind?"

"From just before the time he grabbed her until this date."

"Are you suggesting the defendant is emotionally disturbed at this time?"

"Absolutely not. She's solid."

"Doctor, were the perceptions of the defendant at the time of the shooting in any way related to the fact she is a female?"

"Almost *totally.*"

"Could you explain to the jury, please?"

"Her perceptions of a male are the natural result of two things. First, where and how she was raised; that is, in the western United States where the common perception is that the male is physically superior to the female. And second, the fact she is a female, endowed with the female instinct to survive in the face of a deadly threat from a male. A man in like circumstances would probably not have perceived Mr. Carson as she did that morning. Consequently, her perceptions at the times relevant would have been dominated by the fact she is a female." Wylie waited a few seconds, then firmly added, "I make these statements academically."

Dupree leaned forward, knowing Wylie had set up the next question by his last answer, but unable to see what was coming.

"What do you mean by 'academically', Doctor?"

I mean I can recite these perceptions to you and this jury because I have learned them through twenty-two years of experience. But the fact is, I am a male, and being such I *cannot feel* what Joan Carson felt that morning."

Ben paused. There it was: the male blind spot, laid bare for all to see. He moved on without looking at the jury.

"Have your opinions in this case, and the history and facts on which they are based, been reduced to a printed form, Doctor?"

"Yes, they have."

"Would the bailiff please hand defense exhibit 12 to the witness?" Wylie accepted the heavy exhibit in the large accordion file.

"Can you identify that exhibit, Doctor?"

"Yes. This is an exact copy of my entire file in the Joan Carson case."

"Move the admission into evidence, your honor."

Dupree shifted his hands on the table in front of him, but remained silent.

"Hearing no objection, exhibit 12 is admitted."

I have no further questions at this time, your honor. Counsel may cross-examine."

"Mr. Dupree, it is 11:50. Would this be a good time for the noon recess?"

● ● ●

Following the recess, Dupree began his cross-examination. He stood and selected several books from a stack that was on his table, and walked to the lectern. He knew the impression he wanted to create with the jury, and without being obvious, developed it with deliberate style.

"Dr. Benoit, I understand you have been involved in the general field of psychiatry for more than thirty years now, if one includes your undergraduate and medical school studies in the calculations; is that correct?"

"Yes."

"Without intending to embarrass you, I also understand your career includes some remarkable honors and recognitions. Would that also be true?"

"I have been very fortunate."

"That being true, Doctor, I presume you are competent to address and answer a series of questions concerning some of the more controversial areas of psychiatry, are you not?"

"I believe I have some understanding of the subject, yes."

With his machine-precision style, Dupree ripped into every weakness in the field of psychiatry. In conversational tones that could not be construed by the jury as being offensive, he meticulously referred to marked places in the textbooks, extracting statements from the mavericks of the profession as well as the accepted authorities, all of whom he quoted for the purpose of undermining and discrediting the field of psychiatry.

The lack of accepted definitions by the authorities in the field on such subjects as neurosis, psychosis, psyche, id, ego, mental illness, the mind, and others was paraded before the jury, creating the impression the very foundations of the field were unstable. The open and often radical and shocking accusations and battles between the leading authorities were aired by Dupree as he read quotations from such figures as Halleck, Szasz, Albee, Menninger, Masling, Ziskin, Abramowitz, Wolpe, Cattell, Thorne, and others. The critical weaknesses of psychiatric tests commonly used, as well as the various publications most commonly accepted in the field, were drawn out and dramatized. The shocking, embarrassing results of the Rosenhan study were laid bare before the jury, as were the staggering differences between the two "experts" who examined Sirhan Sirhan following the Robert Kennedy assassination, which resulted in an unexplained gap of forty "reaction points" in their testing, enough to make the difference in calling Sirhan psychotic or normal.

Wylie patiently responded to every question, never losing his composure or control. Ben had the legal right to stop testimony after a while on the basis that the questions were cumulative and pointless, but he refused. He didn't want to risk having the jury think he objected because it was embarrassing his expert. Ben let Dupree continue, knowing that he wasn't going to make a single statement that would challenge Wylie personally, nor his testimony.

At a little before 5 o'clock, Dupree closed his last textbook, then his file.

"I have no further questions, your honor." He left the general field of psychiatry in a state of unrecognizable wreckage, but he hadn't touched Wylie's opinions.

Judge Boyd glanced at the big wall clock.

"Mr. Cooper, any re-direct?"

"No, your honor."

"Are we finished with this witness, Mr. Cooper?"

"Yes, your honor."

"We will take the evening recess. The witness will step down. Mr. Bailiff, escort the jury to the jury room. They are under the usual admonition about not discussing the evidence until such time as it is finally submitted."

While the judge left for his chambers and the jury filed out, Wylie went directly to Ben.

"Ben, will you be home tonight?"

"Yes, after about an hour at the office. Why?"

"I'm going to the coroner's office from here to follow through on our conversation of this morning. I'll call you."

"Want me to come down as soon as I can?"

Wylie thought a moment. "No, I don't think so. Chances are the presence of the defense lawyer would stop things altogether without their lawyers to approve it."

"Yeah, I think you're right. I'll wait at home. Wylie, good luck." Wylie caught the seriousness in Ben's eyes.

Leaving his office later that evening, Ben found himself preoccupied with thoughts of what Wylie had discovered. Twice he reached for the phone to call the coroner's office, then reconsidered. As he sat down to his supper, the phone rang.

"Hello. Ben Cooper speaking."

"Hi, Ben. Wylie."

"Where are you calling from, Wylie?"

"Just left the coroner's office. I'm on a lobby phone at General. We located the plastic bag and they're cooperating. They're thawing it now. They'll start with the h and e stains when Pinnock gets here later tonight. This was his day off."

Wylie paused for a response.

Ben's voice was strained. "What does it look like?"

"When I saw it, it was covered with frost. No way to tell much. I think there is probably about thirty ounces of material in there. We can't do anything until it's thawed."

"Wylie, you're sounding pretty well up for this. Is there any real possibility?"

Wylie read the tension in Ben's voice. "The more I think about it, the more I can't see why not. The problem is going to be identification of the tissue. And we can't even evaluate that problem until we get it out of the bag and spread it out."

"I'll have to notify Dupree about this just as soon as I hang up."

After a pause, Wylie responded. "Why?"

"Even at best, I'm going to have real trouble getting this into evidence. If it looks like I purposely ambushed Dupree, I don't stand a chance. I have to put him on fair notice of this whole procedure as it develops so he can't yell 'foul.' And even then, my chances are pretty slim."

"Why such a problem?"

"I didn't include it in the pretrial conference or the order the judge signed, which locked in all witnesses and all exhibits. I had prior knowledge the bag existed because David was told about it. But neither of us suspected it might become important. Dupree's going to raise hell, I'm sure."

"Ben, I don't think we should mention this to Joan just yet. If nothing comes of it, I think it's better she not even know we had these suspicions. What do you think?"

Ben closed his eyes, thinking.

"I agree. Let's just proceed with the game plan with this little effort off to one side. If it pays off, we'll deal with that when we get there. Okay?"

"Okay. I'll be in touch tomorrow when I have the answer. Talk to you then."

They said their good-byes, and Ben held down the disconnect button while he looked through his handwritten list for the home number of Dupree. He dialed the number and waited for Dupree to answer.

Tuesday, December 14th

"THE DEFENSE CALLS DR. CARRIE Johnstone."

To impress the jury with the critical importance of this witness, Ben turned completely and looked at her as she rose. All eyes followed his.

Dressed in a tasteful light beige suit and wearing almost no makeup, she walked past the counsel tables and approached the clerk to be sworn in. Her appearance was very plain, but there was a frankness and openness about her that shined. She conveyed a sense of calmness and confidence.

Ben waited for her to be seated; then he began.

"Please state your name, address, and occupation."

"I am Carrie Johnstone. I live at 231 Kiowa Avenue, in Englewood, Colorado. I am a doctor of psychology. I practice here in Denver."

Carefully Ben led her through the necessary preliminary matters of her background, establishing her as an expert in the field of psychology. He then began questioning her regarding Joan—how she met her, the interviews and testing she had conducted as she developed the case, and the conclusions she had formed regarding Joan's condition. By 11 o'clock, Dr. Johnstone had thoroughly revealed her understanding of the relationship Joan had with Les from their early childhood to the present time. Then, with the jury prepared, Ben moved into her opinions.

"Have you formed an opinion regarding her perceptions of her husband prior to the spring of this year?"

"Yes, I have."

"What is your opinion regarding how Mrs. Carson perceived his physical treatment of her prior to that time? By that I mean, his tendency to treat her with consideration as opposed to brutality."

"She perceived him as being a husband who physically treated her with respect, tenderness, and consideration. She had never considered the possibility that he might treat her in any other way."

"If you know, on what were her perceptions based, in the time frame preceding May of this year?"

"Her lifelong acquaintance with Mr. Carson since childhood, their courtship, and marriage."

"Based upon your examination of the defendant, did this perception continue after the spring of this year?"

"It did for several weeks, into early June, at which time changes began to appear in his personality."

"What are the changes you're referring to, Doctor?"

Dr. Johnstone quietly and firmly recited the changes that were now familiar to the jury. Ben was preparing her for the final few questions that he so fervently depended on to reach the jury.

After a noon recess, testimony resumed.

"Coming down to the events of September 18th, Doctor, do you have an opinion regarding the perceptions of Joan Carson that morning?"

"I presume you mean surrounding the time of the shooting incident?"

"Yes. At the moment her back struck the doorjamb and she sat down and the rifle fell across her lap, do you have an opinion of what her perceptions were regarding Mr. Carson?"

"Yes, I do."

"What is that opinion, please?"

"She perceived him as being someone other than her husband. She was aware of his identity, but in her view, the person who had abused her was not Mr. Carson."

"At the moment she fired the first shot, do you have an opinion regarding her perceptions?"

"Yes, I do."

"What were they, please?"

"In her perception, she did not shoot Mr. Carson. She shot a personage that represented a deadly, horrifying threat to her life, and which her subconscious knew had to be stopped."

"You are aware of the time interval between the shots?"

"Yes, I am. I understand it was between seven and ten seconds."

"At the time she fired the second shot, do you have an opinion regarding her perception of her husband?"

"Yes, I do."

"What is that opinion?"

"She stopped an unknown person who was killing her. She perceived only one incident in which she fired two shots; she did not perceive it as two incidents, firing two separate shots."

"Do you have an opinion regarding the thought processes of Mrs. Carson at the time of the shooting? That is, did she consciously decide to fire both shots?"

A hush settled over the courtroom.

"Yes, I do."

"What is that opinion, please?"

"No. She did not consciously decide to shoot him."

"Would you explain your answer, please?"

"Within one or two seconds of the time she struck the door-jamb and slumped to the floor, her thinking and reasoning capabilities all but disintegrated. She could simply no longer cope with what was happening. From within her, a compulsion rose that took control of her conduct. The firing of the two shots was a result of the compulsion. She was defending herself against a deadly, terrifying male force, not as a result of her own thinking processes, but guided by an instinct or a compulsion that only a woman can understand."

There it was! Not from the defendant, but from a woman who was also a highly trained expert. The essence of the entire case was finally held up in front of the courtroom for all to see. The impact on the jurors and spectators seemed profound. Seconds ticked by in total silence.

Dupree didn't move, but his instant assessment of what was happening was accurate. He had just heard Ben's last and best shot at destroying the brick wall he had built for the prosecution. Was it enough? Had Ben done it? Dupree didn't think so, but he knew he was going to have to lighten the impact of Dr. Johnstone's testimony.

I have no more questions at this time, your honor."

"Mr. Dupree, cross-examination?"

Dupree looked at the wall clock and walked to the lectern.

"Thank you, judge." He turned to Dr. Johnstone.

For two hours, Dupree cross-examined. He didn't become firm or offensive, fearing that to offend Dr. Johnstone would also offend the jury. He didn't put her through the grinder he had imposed on Wylie; rather he limited his efforts to compromise her to three main areas: illusory correlation, the effect of base rates, and the Barnum effect, as each of them relates to a proper evaluation of a patient. If he could demonstrate the weakness of the standards of psychiatry, he could probably weaken the jury's view of Dr. Johnstone's opinion of Joan and take the edge off the impact of her testimony. Without hesitation she answered each of his questions honestly.

"Doctor, is it fair to conclude, then, that the facts you were able to develop regarding Joan Carson's life, and the facts you were able to develop regarding the society in which she was raised, were necessarily sketchy? And that created a weak base rate that might have caused your conclusions to be somewhat illusory?"

Dupree's technique in attacking her psychological opinions was standard. All psychologists know they seldom have the time and money to develop every fact they would like to have regarding any patient, simply because there is hardly an end to the affairs of life that impact the individual. Psychologists have to develop the most pertinent facts and some of the secondary ones, make their best judgment, and move on.

Without hesitation, Dr. Johnstone responded.

"Under the circumstances, short of interviewing thousands of persons in Jackson County and Denver, which is literally impossible, I believe I have established an acceptable base rate to form my opinion of Mrs. Carson. I readily admit that it would be nice if we who must make these opinions had the time and resources to exhaustively investigate everything; we do not, however, so we reach a certain point where we know we have enough to go on, and we form our conclusions." Then, as if voicing an afterthought, she leaned slightly forward. "But whatever factual background might be lacking is pretty unimportant in view of what I believe to be the one fact that underlies and permeates this entire case. The defendant is a *woman*."

Dr. Johnstone straightened, her expression still one of quiet competence, but her eyes alive with meaning.

Dupree felt the sting. He smiled at Dr. Johnstone and closed his file.

"Thank you, Doctor. No more questions, your honor."

Judge Boyd looked at Ben. "Any re-direct?"

"None, your honor." The last thing he wanted to do was disturb the testimony as it now stood.

Judge Boyd leaned back, moving his arms and shoulders to relieve the stiffness. "It is almost 5 o'clock. Mr. Cooper, do you wish to call another witness today?"

"No, your honor." The timing had worked just right. Ben didn't have another witness, but he had to keep the trial open until he knew what Wylie had found, in case he had to put Wylie back on the stand. Dupree picked up his copy of Ben's witness list, puzzled, knowing Ben had used all the witnesses he had declared. Dupree dropped the list back into his file. He figured he would wait until morning to see what Ben had in mind. Under some conditions, Ben could recall a previous witness, but that would require some special circumstances Dupree couldn't see at the moment. Dupree knew the tumor question was still open, but under any circumstance the most it could amount to, in his mind, would be an explanation of what went wrong with Leslie Carson. And that would be of minor significance, probably irrelevant.

The judge continued. "Is this a good time to declare the evening recess?"

Both counsel nodded and began gathering their papers.

Leaving the courthouse, Dupree was deep in thought. With Ben's case almost completely submitted, now was the time to pause and consider the exact posture of the trial. Walking the few hundred yards from the courthouse to his office across the street, his mind went over the highlights, putting together the bare bones of what Ben had done and trying to understand how he was going to argue the case in summation.

He entered his office, hung up his coat, and sat down in his big chair, momentarily reviewing his phone messages. Then he turned his full attention to finishing his analysis of the Carson case.

Twenty minutes later he suddenly tossed his pencil onto the open Carson file, leaned back in his chair, and started shaking his head, a slow grin spreading across his face.

"Well, I'll be . . ." He spoke quietly to himself, punching each word lightly with a sense of begrudging admiration.

"So *that's* what Ben was doing!"

Filing unexcised reports that laid out every fact necessary for a conviction; making no objections while the prosecution methodically put a flawless case before the jury; telling the jury in his opening statement that he didn't intend to come into conflict with the facts, just add to them; putting Joan on the witness stand and letting her admit intent; having Wylie go just so far and no further in support of Joan; and then, for the finishing touch, putting Dr. Johnstone on the stand. She was the strongest witness Dupree had ever seen in like circumstances. A *woman*. A *woman* psychologist. What a stroke!

Ben didn't intend to *fight* the facts; he intended to *ignore* them. He had taken a gamble that he could swing the jury his way by getting Joan's whole story before the court, and then strongly supporting it with Wylie's and Carrie Johnstone's testimony. Ben hoped to induce the jury to forget the facts, to feel sorry for Joan. He gave the jury a clear option: facts on one hand, feelings on the other. Dupree caught his breath at the thought of how beautifully Ben had executed his plan. He got the judge to change the rules of evidence so the testimony he had could be heard, and he tiptoed through a mine field to get Carrie Johnstone to say it all just right. Heavens, it was good; near genius.

The realization sobered Dupree. He moved on to the key question: Had he succeeded? Dupree gave Ben's case the benefit of every doubt and started weighing his chances. Dupree knew he had presented an absolutely flawless case to the jury, driving every fact home. If he'd been given the assignment of beating his own case, he knew he couldn't do it. The capstone to his case fell into place with Joan's own confession of intent; his case wasn't going to budge nor yield to emotion.

Dupree knew, too, that the sensational, emotional high, which concluded Carrie Johnstone's testimony, would wane with the passing hours. Dupree was confident that by the time Judge Boyd finished instructing the jury that they *must* consider the facts in quiet reflection, not being swayed unduly by emotion, they would have the right perspective on both Joan and Carrie. The testimony Ben would be submitting tomorrow had to be coming from someone who had already testified, and whatever that testimony would be, it probably wasn't going to change much of anything.

So what would the jury do? It was clear they would have to convict Joan of something; they would probably satisfy their emotional need to do something nice for Joan by reducing the conviction from some degree of murder down to manslaughter. But the conviction would be a felony in any event.

Then a thought flickered through Dupree's mind. A hung jury? Could Ben get it that far? Dupree concluded that the possibility was slim, next to none at all. No, the conviction would be some degree of manslaughter. Dupree wondered if he would hear from Ben before the verdict with an offer to stop the proceedings and make a plea bargain. Maybe. He'd be ready.

● ● ●

Several miles east of Dupree's office, Ben laid his briefcase on his desk and slowly shrugged out of his coat, dropping it over a chair. The testimony of Carrie Johnstone had been unexpectedly powerful. Somehow he had gotten everything he planned before the jury—and in better shape than he had hoped.

Giving it his best judgment, he knew both Joan's and Dr. Johnstone's testimonies had powerfully affected the jury, but were they strong enough to carry through to the time of the verdict? The impact would fade with time; the question was, how soon? The standard jury instruction that they must make a cool, rational analysis of the facts, and not be swayed by emotion or personal feelings, was going to hurt. What Ben had to offer tomorrow, if it worked out just as Wylie hoped, wouldn't really add too much to the case. It would not alter the basic facts already before the jury about Les's conduct. Ben's deepest fear was the probability the jury would play their emotional attachment to Joan against the hard facts and compromise—convicting her of manslaughter, not murder. With a growing sense of foreboding, he had the feeling he already knew what was going to happen.

There was but one chance Ben could see. Did he have enough testimony before the jury to get one or two of the women to refuse to convict her? A hung jury? Barely possible. Was he going to finish this case by begging Dupree for a plea bargain—a deal—just before the jury rendered a verdict?

With a stinging sense of failure upon him, Ben leaned forward on his desk and rested his head on his arms. I did it wrong. I was too close. It meant too much to me. I thought I could build a powerful enough image of Joan to sway a jury from the facts and it was basically wrong. I've failed Les and I've gotten Joan convicted. For a long time he didn't move in the silent, empty office.

Eventually he raised his head, hanging onto the single, tenuous thought. Maybe. Maybe. One person could hang the jury and maybe one will.

Ben glanced at the big clock and reached for the phone, slowly touching the number of the county coroner's office. He needed to know what progress Wylie had made.

Neither Ben nor Dupree was aware of the developments that were now just beginning, which would mature in the night to trigger an unbelievable explosion in the courtroom the next morning, shattering the trial and leaving the case in shambles.

Wednesday, December 15th

"MR. COOPER, YOU MAY CALL your next witness."

"The defense calls Dr. Alfred Pinnock."

Dupree pushed his file a few inches away, laid his pencil down and leaned back in his chair, biding his time.

Judge Boyd's eyebrows rose in surprise. He looked at Ben and then at Dupree for some glimmer of explanation, but got none.

"Are you calling Dr. Pinnock as your own witness, or for some sort of continued cross-examination as a state's witness?"

"A defense witness, your honor, regarding some factual evidence just recently discovered by Dr. Pinnock and his researchers. He's not listed as a defense witness because at the time the witness list was made, we didn't know about these developments. If the court will bear with me, I believe it will soon become clear why this testimony is important."

"Okay. Dr. Pinnock will come to the stand." The judge was tentative, clearly suspicious of surprises in a murder trial.

Pinnock walked to the witness stand and sat down. Ben began.

"Doctor, for the record, are you the same Dr. Pinnock who testified earlier in this trial, about nine days ago?"

Dupree pushed his chair back and stood, his motion drawing all eyes to him. He remained standing, silent, serving notice to Ben he was going to earn everything he got. Pinnock answered.

"Yes, I am."

"Doctor, in the past twenty-four hours, have you had occasion to complete an examination of certain portions of tissue gathered from the apartment where Mr. Carson was found the morning of September 18th?"

"Yes, I have."

"Could you explain to the jury where—"

Dupree moved to his right one step, interrupting loudly.

"Objection, your honor. I want to make a continuing objection to this entire line of questioning, on the grounds that—"

The judge interrupted, seeing that a head-to-head argument was forming between the attorneys. He decided to avoid it by coming right to the heart of the issue.

"Excuse me, Mr. Dupree." Judge Boyd turned to the bailiff.

"Mr. Bailiff, would you please escort the jury to their room? Ladies and gentlemen, to rule on a continuing objection will require that I hear some information that might be prejudicial. You will be called back as soon as possible."

When the jury was gone, the judge turned to Ben.

"Mr. Cooper, I would like you to make an offer of proof. What's this all about?"

Ben placed his hand on the lectern and then moved to one side of it. Dupree remained standing.

"Your honor, I propose offering testimony, and possibly some exhibits, through Dr. Pinnock to the effect that within the past twenty-four hours his office has examined some tissue from the scene of the shooting and found tumor cells. The tumor was lodged in the cranium of Mr. Carson, exerting pressure on the underside of the forward brain lobes.

"Dr. Pinnock and Dr. Wylie Benoit will also testify that the size and the location of the tumor were probably the cause of the personality change in Mr. Carson."

Judge Boyd wrinkled his brow in thought, then looked at Dupree.

"Mr. Dupree, your objections?"

Dupree was moving as he spoke, his defiance obvious. He knew of too many cases that had been lost by the last-minute bit of evidence that turned everything upside down. No way was that going to happen to this case. He spoke loudly; no one could miss the cutting edge in his voice.

"Procedurally, your honor, Dr. Pinnock was not declared a defense witness either on their list or in the pre-trial order. The first notice I had of the possibility of this entire line of evidence was two days ago, on Monday night, when Mr. Cooper notified me by telephone of what was going on. And he phoned again last night. Then about midnight I got a call from Dr. Jack Whalen that some cancerous tumor cells had been discovered in the Carson tissue. At just after 8 o'clock this morning, I received my first official report from Dr. Whalen that more than thirty grams of the tumor cells had been discovered, and that it might be possible to relate them to the personality change claimed in Leslie Carson."

Dupree began to pace, his voice rising, his hand gesturing for emphasis.

"Your honor, this is ridiculous. I haven't had an opportunity to examine Dr. Pinnock's findings, nor his testimony. I will be all but flying blind on cross-examination, on highly technical medical evidence. I don't see how the state can be expected to handle it on the notice I've had. With this entire episode outside the pretrial order, I respectfully propose that there is no way this testimony and these exhibits can be admitted."

Dupree turned and walked toward the end of his table, away from the lectern, then abruptly stopped. He now spaced his words for emphasis, his voice rising in pitch.

"Setting aside Mr. Cooper's proposal that we play wild and loose with procedure in this case, I invite the court to take a look at the wreckage this proposal will make of this trial.

"I've known about that bag of tissue since September 18th and the defense has known about it since mid-October. This is a trial for *first-degree murder,* and if they've known since mid-October, common sense *alone* would have said, 'Get it analyzed.' If there was the slightest chance they might need it, the duty was on them to step up and do something about it. They didn't! They just didn't do it! If they are now allowed to use this evidence to support their case, what it will boil down to is rewarding their lack of diligence, totally at the expense of the case for the prosecution. How can the court even *consider* it?

"But even *that* isn't the most compelling argument against it! The strongest argument is the *legal* argument. The offered evidence *just isn't relevant!*"

Dupree paused, his head thrust forward and his hand out-stretched, pointing toward the bench.

"Mrs. Carson has testified repeatedly about the change that came over Mr. Carson. Other witnesses have supported her. The defense built their case on the *change that occurred in Mr. Carson.* It's in the record about as well as it can be done under the circumstances. They have what they wanted. So the question is, what difference does it make as to what caused the change?"

He left his question echoing off the walls. After a long pause, he continued. "The answer is absolutely cast in stone. No difference at all!"

He took a step back toward his chair, then stopped, obviously closing his argument.

"Your honor, there isn't an argument, not one solid, acceptable argument—procedural, equitable, nor legal—that even *begins* to support this proposal. It simply has to fail!" His head jerked forward, punctuating the last word. He closed his file and stood waiting.

Ben's eyes dropped, then raised back to the judge. Dupree's argument was correct all the way; worse, he was pushing his self-restraint and self-discipline near the limit, ready to go full out if this thing went much further.

Ben calmly collected his thoughts. The judge looked at him over his glasses; his brow wrinkled as he spoke and his eyes were alive with intensity.

"Counsel, how long have you known about the material in the bag?"

"In mid-October, during an investigation of the coroner's report, my associate, David Ballantine, became aware of the tissue stored in the freezer at the coroner's office."

Ben paused, waiting.

"Counsel, why the delay in having it tested? Why are we ten, twelve days into the trial before you come forward with it?"

"Your honor, we did everything we knew to find out what went wrong with Mr. Carson. Two medical experts examined every word of the coroner's medical report, looking for chemical imbalance, brain damage, sodium imbalance, tumors—anything— to explain Les Carson, and they came up empty. Apparently the coroner's report listed the random test results on the tissue.

"However, the report did not mention the plastic bag. I presumed the experts would know about the bag from the report, but they didn't.

"Then last Sunday, Dr. Benoit returned from his trip to Geneva and was convinced an examination of the brain would show a tumor putting pressure on the underside of the forward brain lobes. He asked me to get an order to exhume the body so he could look at the brain tissue. I told him about the bag and he suggested that testing it with hemotoxylin and eosin, two stains, might help. That test was completed by the professionals in the coroner's office overnight last night and the first official report was released this morning.

"By using the state's forensic pathologist, Dr. Pinnock, as the expert to put this before the jury, I hoped the court would recognize we are not bringing in a surprise witness to support all this.

"I also want to assure the court that when the evidence is in, it will be obvious there is no disadvantage to the state. The facts are absolutely beyond question. The tumor was there, attached to the optic chiasm, destroying Les Carson one day at a time. A lump of tumor tissue about the size of a walnut is right over there in the brief-case of Dr. Pinnock, and six months of investigation by ten specialists isn't going to change that.

"Mr. Dupree has been made aware of all this right along with me because I've called him and told him. The state sent their doctor, Dr. Jack Whalen, over to check it out, and if it will serve any useful purpose I'll call him, or let Mr. Dupree call him, or let the court call him as its own witness and ask him anything they want, with no objection or interference from me."

Ben paused to let the judge reflect on his offer. He then leaned slightly forward.

"Your honor, the only two people in the world who know what happened that morning are Joan Carson and Leslie Carson, and Les is gone. Joan Carson has told an incredible story about the brutal beatings she took from him the last few days of his life, and right now her statements depend on just one thing: her credibility."

Ben's eyes were alive with intensity.

"Is this court going to rob her of the single independent bit of evidence that the world can offer us to corroborate her story?" He stood motionless for two or three seconds, eyes locked with judge Boyd's. Then he turned and walked to his chair.

Judge Boyd looked at both counsel for a moment, then turned to the clerk.

"Will you hand me state's exhibit M? Thanks." He carefully went through the coroner's report.

"Counsel, if either of you knows, why wasn't that bag listed in the coroner's report?"

Ben looked at Dupree, who refused to acknowledge his silent question. Ben started to respond when Pinnock, still seated on the witness stand, suddenly raised his hand.

"Your honor, perhaps I could help."

"Yes, Dr. Pinnock?"

"A very simple answer. We performed our usual random test of the tissue and nothing turned up. But before we decided what to do with the rest of the tissue, Mr. Dupree came in to examine the body. He requested we save it in case it was needed, so we bagged it right then and froze it, entering it on the records of what was in the freezer.

The coroner's report mentioned the random test, but didn't mention the bag because that is kept on the freezer records—a separate record. We knew where it was, but apparently no one outside our office did."

The judge continued.

"Mr. Pinnock, can you help me with one further question? Have you discovered a tumor that might account for the change in Mr. Carson?"

"Yes, we found a glioblastoma—a tumor—and we know it was in the location to cause a personality change."

"Thank you very much, Dr. Pinnock. Mr. Dupree, did you ever think to give the defense notice of the bag and your request that it be held in case it was needed?"

"For what reason, for crying out loud? I couldn't have cared less what was in that bag and I certainly have no duty to help the defense prepare their case. In any event, they have known about it since mid-October. Lack of notice is a moot question."

"This court will stand in recess for ten minutes. I want to spend some time in my chambers alone."

While the courtroom buzzed, Judge Boyd went into his chambers. After several minutes he emerged, carrying a book in his hands. He sat down in his large chair and brought his eyes to Dupree and Ben.

"Counsel, I think I will have to allow the evidence. I don't think Mr. Dupree necessarily had a duty to tell the defense about the materials, and I don't think the record-keeping at the coroner's office was necessarily defective. I believe the defense probably did exhaust every avenue they could conceive of in pursuing the question of what went wrong with Les Carson. If two expert doctors couldn't find the bag on the report, I think I would be hard put to fault defense counsel for not finding it.

"We're in this for pretty heavy stakes and I feel that if this evidence will corroborate what Mrs. Carson has been telling us, I have to let it in. So far, there's nothing in the record to support her on this issue. I'm aware that if we get surprised later on and need to do it, we can strike it all from the record and continue without it.

"I notice that under our Rule Sixteen, section (e)(2), the court has the power to amend a pretrial order in the interests of justice. I hereby amend it, so far as is necessary to accommodate this offer of evidence.

"But Mr. Cooper, I do want to place some limitations on this. I'm going to hold you to exactly what you have offered and not one inch further. You say you have hard, medical proof of what occurred in the cranium of Mr. Carson. That's fair game. But if you make any adventure into a personality analysis, or a psychological autopsy, or an emotional appeal just for the impact it will carry, I'm going to stop it—with or without objection—and that's the end of it.

"Do you both understand my ruling?"

"Defense understands. Thank you, your honor." Ben moved back behind the lectern.

"The state understands." Dupree threw his pencil onto his open file and clamped his mouth shut. His jaw was set and his eyes were flashing. He knew he was watching the case he'd won erode into something totally uncertain.

"Thank you, counsel. Marge, did you get that acknowledgment in the record, in the event of an appeal?"

"Yes, your honor, I did."

"Anything further, gentlemen?"

"No, your honor."

"Mr. Bailiff, would you recall the jury?"

The jury filed back in, their eyes darted between the judge, Ben, and Dupree, wondering what had happened. Joan was sitting straight up, her mind working to reach past all the legal and medical words and understand what was coming. She knew they had discovered a tumor in Les's brain, and that Ben was trying to get testimony to relate it to the violent change in Les. But she had never dreamed that a simple tumor could turn her husband into a maniac. Tumors killed people; they didn't change them into monsters. She was nearly unable to believe the story that was unfolding before her eyes.

"Mr. Cooper, you may continue."

Ben moved rapidly through the preliminary questions, establishing for the jury's understanding how the tissue came to be in the freezer, the gap in the record-keeping, and the request by Wylie that resulted in the performance of the test. Then Ben slowed, pacing the questions so the jury could not get lost.

"Did you make the tests?"

"Yes, I did."

"Who else was present?"

"Dr. Benoit was there for much of it. Dr. Jack Whalen was there for most of it. Dr. Robert Lowe, of the county coroner's office, was there for all of it. We had Dr. Julie Scott, an expert on malignant cancer cells, advise us and confirm our conclusions."

"Did you stain-test all the tissue?"

"Yes, we did. No, I must correct that. Part of the tissue was bone and cartilage. We did not test that."

Ben then asked the pivotal question. "What were the results of the test?"

Pinnock was nearly impervious to the weight of the moment, absorbed in his usual passion for accuracy. The jury wasn't doubting a word he was saying.

"We discovered about forty-one grams of cancerous tissue. That would be about an ounce and a half. It would make a ball about the size of a walnut."

With deliberation, Ben continued.

"Were you able to determine the location of the cancerous cells?" Again Pinnock referred to his notes and spoke as though he were lecturing at a seminar. The jury was still, all eyes on Pinnock.

"Yes. They had grown to the optic chiasm, which is the point where the two optic nerves from the eyes cross in the cranium. It is located behind the eyes, just at the base of the frontal lobes of the brain."

"What is the medical term used for this particular cancerous growth?"

"It is called a glioblastoma multiforme. A glioblastoma."

"Within a reasonable degree of medical probability, were you able to determine which direction it was growing?"

"Yes. It was growing rapidly forward and upward, toward the underside of the forward lobes of the brain."

"What bodily or mental functions are served by the underside of the forward lobes of the brain?"

"That is the personality and character control center of the human being."

"Do you have an opinion whether or not this glioblastoma was exerting pressure to that area of the brain?"

"Yes, I do."

"What is that opinion?"

"Objection, your honor. It's irrelevant and immaterial. Did the record show my continuing objection to this entire offer of evidence?"

"The record shows it. Your objection is overruled. The witness will answer."

"Yes. In my opinion, it was exerting pressure on the underside of the forward lobes of the brain of Mr. Carson."

"What is the result of unnatural pressure on that area?"

"Almost invariably it results in some sort of a change in the victim."

"If this tumor did involve the optic chiasm, do you have an opinion within a reasonable degree of medical probability what, if any, effect this would have on the vision of Mr. Carson?"

"Yes. From time to time, with increased frequency, he would have experienced difficulty with his vision. He would probably have opened his eyes wide to see people clearly. At times he would have probably looked at people, and they would have been aware of a peculiar, blank look in his eyes, resulting from him trying to focus and recognize them."

The minds of the jurors were working as they recalled Joan's testimony of Les's eyes being "like those of a maniac."

"I have no more questions at this time, your honor."

Ben sat down and Joan placed her hand on his arm, speaking softly, but firmly. Her eyes were wide in amazement.

"Ben, I know they found a tumor, but I always thought a brain tumor caused death. Can it really *change* a person? Did it change Les? Wasn't Les in control of his own mind when he—" Ben quietly cut her off.

"Joan, we didn't have an official report on it until Pinnock walked in this morning just before court time. Yes, I think we found out what went wrong with Les." The judge cut off any further conversation.

"Mr. Dupree, you may cross-examine."

Ben lowered his voice. "Listen to Wylie when he testifies. He'll explain it. I've got to watch this."

Joan turned her face toward the witness stand, her eyes narrowed in puzzlement.

Dupree looked at the judge.

"Your honor, the state requests permission to reserve cross-examination until a later time."

"Under the circumstances, you may reserve. Mr. Cooper, call your next witness." Ben hadn't anticipated calling Wylie to the stand so soon, but he hid any appearance of surprise.

"Defense calls Dr. Wylie Benoit." As Wylie walked to the stand, Dupree rose and stood silently, now trying to dominate the courtroom. The tension was building.

"For the record, are you the same Dr. Wylie Benoit who testified earlier this week in this trial?"

"Yes, I am."

"In the past forty-eight hours, have you had occasion to visit the coroner's office regarding the examination of some tissue related to this case?"

"Yes, I have."

"What did the examination reveal?"

"There was a malignant tumor, a glioblastoma, growing in the forepart of Mr. Carson's cranium, just ahead of the optic chiasm."

"Were you able to judge the size of the tumor?"

"No, we were not. We recovered enough of it to know it was at least about the size of a walnut. How much bigger the whole tumor was we don't know."

"Do you have an opinion, based on a reasonable degree of medical certainty, as to whether this glioblastorna affected Leslie Carson?"

"Yes, I do."

"What is that opinion?"

Dupree moved so suddenly his foot caught his chair, skidding it backward several inches.

"Objection! This is calling for a conclusion based on medical evidence that is so slight, so shaky, as to be totally worthless. Perhaps worse than useless. Mr. Carson is dead. We're playing a guessing game through doctors as to how this tumor might have affected him. It's ridiculous!"

The judge turned to Ben.

"Mr. Cooper?"

"Two medical doctors have expressed some conclusions based on evidence they have seen. The question is, is there *enough* evidence to support their conclusions? These doctors believe there is."

Ben stopped and waited. Dupree threw his pencil back onto his open file and waited, his eyes almost challenging the judge.

"Objection overruled. It is admissible and the jury will have to decide its significance. You'll have your chance on cross-examination, Mr. Dupree. The witness may answer."

"Yes. In my opinion, the tumor *did* affect Leslie Carson."

Ben moved straight to the point, using common language instead of legal jargon.

"How?"

Dupree interrupted again, his hands raised as though to stop the trial.

"*OBJECTION.* I want to ask some questions in aid of my objection, your honor."

The judge leaned forward. "Ask your questions."

Dupree didn't take the time to walk to the lectern. He leaned against his table and began.

"It is an absolute impossibility for you to know how that tumor affected Leslie Carson, isn't it, Doctor?"

"To know?"

"Yes, to know. To form a competent medical opinion."

"It is not impossible for me to form a competent medical opinion. I've already done that." Wylie remained calm.

"At least, Doctor, you are in agreement that *no one,* not yourself, not Dr. Pinnock, not Dr. Whalen, not anyone, can competently state *how* such a tumor will affect the individual or *the extent* to which it will affect the individual. Correct?"

"In the abstract, I agree with that. But regarding Leslie Carson, I have a firm opinion."

Dupree, trying to stay composed, turned to the judge. "I renew my objection."

"Overruled. The witness may answer."

"It is my opinion that the pressure exerted by the glioblastorna on the underside of the frontal brain lobes caused a personality and character change in Mr. Carson that accounts for the radical change in his behavior."

"Specifically, Doctor, what change?"

Every eye in the courtroom was now centered on Wylie. No one was watching Joan as she sat alone at the defense table, leaning forward, stunned and shocked. She could hardly believe the possibility that a simple tumor could change Les into a monster. Could this be the answer behind all her questions? The color left her face and her eyes were open wide, staring.

"The changes began with a tendency to become argumentative, critical. Those around Mr. Carson thought his behavior was the result of the staggering business load that fell on his shoulders when Glenn Tolboy became incapacitated. The tumor progressed and he began having some head pains. Then the tumor began to choke off the optic chiasm, causing him to squint and then open his eyes very wide from time to time. Those closest to Mr. Carson thought he didn't recognize them at times. He began having memory lapses, slurred speech, and then an inability to make a coherent sentence. His anger was so out of control that his arguments became violent. His violence was first displayed toward those nearest him, his wife and his partner. Then, just several days before his death, he became totally irresponsible for his actions. His increasingly brutal treatment of his wife, including the horrible beating he gave her the morning of the shooting on September 18th, was totally outside his control. Essentially, the person in the room with Joan Carson that morning was not Leslie Carson. The body was, but the person inside was not. Had he lived, he would have finally lapsed into a coma and I believe died from—"

That was as far as Wylie got before Joan blew the trial wide open. Suddenly she stood, speaking as she rose, leaning forward on her extended arms, palms flat on the table. She was conscious only of Wylie. Her voice was pitched extremely high, nearly cracking under the strain. Her sudden outburst stunned everyone into total silence.

"Wylie, are you telling me Les couldn't help it? He didn't know? It wasn't really Les?"

Wylie's impulsive answer came immediately. "Yes, Joan, that's what—"

Judge Boyd's gavel came down with a crash that shattered Wylie's answer. He interrupted with almost a shout.

"*Doctor, that's enough.* Mrs. Carson, you're out of order, Sit down and don't say another word. This courtroom will come to order, *right now.*"

Joan slumped to her chair, and her loud, racking sobs filled the courtroom. She folded her arms on the table in front of her and leaned forward, burying her face in her arms. Her shoulders shook and she was beyond making any attempt to control or hide the flood of tears. The weeks and months of unbearable pain and guilt poured out.

Suddenly, as though by some silent signal, understanding broke clear in the minds of the judge and jury what they were witnessing.

Since that tragic morning of the shooting, Joan had thought the fault for Les'ss behavior rested with her; somehow she had failed Les. And then she shot him. She had loved him with all her heart and only at this moment did she finally understand that the brutal actions against her weren't really *Les'ss* actions. Les was *gone* before the morning of September 18th.

Dupree was livid. He had been standing a step back from his table when Joan shattered the trial, and now he lunged forward as though catapulted, his face red and his voice rising to a shout.

"*I MOVE FOR A MISTRIAL.* There is no way in the world that I'm going to stand still for this—-production. This is *EXACTLY* what the court instructed both counsel and this witness to AVOID, and—"

Ben had started over to Joan when she stood, and was nearly to her when Dupree made his outburst. Suddenly Ben turned and pointed at Dupree, cutting off his words by shouting, *"DON'T MAKE ANOTHER ACCUSATION UNTIL YOU—"*

The gavel hit the block again and Judge Boyd came to his feet, his voice rising above Ben's.

"Counsel, take your seat, and hold your peace. Bailiff, please escort the jury to the jury room. Right now. Ladies and gentlemen, please disregard the disruption of the last few minutes. I will instruct you more completely when you return to the courtroom. In the meantime, counsel, I want you both in my chambers. Move. *Move."*

After Dupree and Ben had entered, the judge slammed the heavy door to his chambers, the sound echoing. He didn't wait for either man to be seated; he swung around to Ben, head thrust forward, eyes flashing.

"Did you know that was coming? Did you know Joan Carson was going to do that?"

Ben spoke with animation. "As God as my witness, I'm as stunned as you are, Judge. No. I didn't know."

"Why hadn't you explained to her about the effects of that tumor *before* Wylie got on the witness stand? What kind of *idiot* procedure was *that?"*

Ben's eyes narrowed, and his voice raised.

"Stop right there. I got to this courthouse about two minutes before we began this morning and hadn't had a single second to worry about what Joan knew or didn't know before I got here. We were up half the night last night sorting through the bloody pulp that was all we had left of Les Carson, and we finished preparing Pinnock and Wylie to testify just in time to drive like crazy to be here by 9 o'clock. Before then, I had told Joan exactly what I honestly could tell her, and that was that we *might* have something, which would help us understand Les. If it was all wrong, then it was all wrong, and I'm sorry. But I'm *not* going to back away from it, and if you strike it from the record it will be just after the biggest courtroom brawl you ever saw."

Dupree had been facing the judge to see how he was reacting, and now jerked his head toward Ben, his face red and his anger causing him to speak in quick, loud bursts.

"Stay in the record? You're right it's going to stay in the record! I won't let it out. It's the most blatant grounds for a mistrial I've ever seen." Dupree gestured wildly. "It couldn't have been staged better by a

producer and director out of Hollywood. With the proper promotion, that could be the best production of the year! And the leading lady? She ought to be given an Oscar! How many dress rehearsals did it take? How long did you work on it? How is she paying your fee, Cooper?"

Seven or eight feet separated the two men, with Judge Boyd standing to one side of the line between them, his leg touching the large table in the center of his chambers. As the last sentence fell from Dupree's mouth, something snapped inside Ben. He clenched his right fist and started for him.

Judge Boyd momentarily froze at Dupree's statement, then his face blanched in shock at Ben's reaction. He stepped between the men just as Ben was closing with Dupree, and jammed the flat of his right hand against Ben's chest, pushing with all his weight. He slowed, then finally stopped Ben. His voice boomed.

"You take one more step toward Dupree and it will cost you five thousand dollars for contempt of this court and twenty-four hours in the slammer across the street. Do you understand that? Make your choice right now." The judge's nose was less than six inches from Ben's face. Not the slightest hint of reservation or fear showed in the judge's expression.

The judge waited, his hand maintaining pressure on Ben's chest as Ben battled the rage inside. Slowly, tenuously, he regained control and relaxed his fist and took a step backward.

Judge Boyd turned and faced Dupree, who lowered his hands from the defensive position he had assumed when Ben made his lunge.

"*You idiot.* After making a statement like that to him about Joan Carson, you're lucky to still be on your feet. I wouldn't fault him for one second if he'd knocked your fool head off. If you got any more dirty remarks to drop somewhere, you go to the john and flush them down the toilet where they belong. One more crack like that in this proceeding and I issue a restraining order against you personally, barring you from making any further appearances in my court for 180 days. Do you understand that?"

Judge Boyd stood firm, his eyes boring into each of them for several seconds.

"You two are seasoned officers of this court. You're going to conduct yourselves accordingly or you're going to pay the price. Ben, you got any quarrel with that? Dupree?"

He continued to stare at each one of them until he saw the fire and anger in them begin to burn off and come under control. Then he walked over and rolled a secretarial chair to the end of the big conference table.

"Now sit down. Both of you. Let's get this behind us. Get your heads back into the business of this trial."

Slowly they both drew chairs out from the big conference table and sat down opposite each other. The judge sat at the end of the table, between them.

"All right. Dupree, you have a motion for mistrial in the record out there. You going to pursue it?"

"You better believe it."

"I won't rule on it until we get out there and you put it in the record, but if you want to discuss it, what specific grounds are you looking at?"

Dupree looked incredulous.

"*What grounds?* There isn't a chance, not a glimmer of a chance, that jury can make a rational decision after what just happened out there. Come on. Get real! Cooper and the defendant just blew this trial out of the water."

"Okay. I understand. Now I want to spend a few minutes to think through this—mess—and figure out where this thing is and whether or not we can resurrect some semblance of hope for a competent trial." The judge jerked his head forward in emphasis. "The *defendant* takes over cross-examination, right while her own attorney is conducting direct. Where in the annals of recorded trials do you find a precedent for *that* one?"

Judge Boyd stood, shaking his head, racking his brain as he searched for some acceptable way to take hold of the wreckage.

"Counsel, would you both give me about ten minutes to let this thing settle in my mind? Are you both okay now?" His eyebrows raised as he looked at both of them, judging whether he could trust them yet or not. "I won't have a repeat of this nonsense!" He looked at Ben.

Dupree nodded, and Ben walked out of the chambers back into the courtroom to find Joan. The twins were beside her, Chad with his arm around her shoulders and Sharlene quietly talking with her. They both straightened when they saw Ben, and Chad got up from Ben's chair. Ben nodded his thanks and sat down beside Joan.

She didn't speak at first, not knowing what to say. Finally she said, "I'm sorry, Ben. I don't know what happened, what came over me. Am I in trouble with the judge?"

"No, you're not in trouble. I think the judge understands. But Dupree is going to make a motion for a new trial. I don't know how the judge will rule on it. Could fall either way. Are you all right?"

"Yes, I'm okay. Ben, did I understand Wylie right? Les was gone the morning of the 18th? It wasn't really Les?"

"Les was gone quite a while before that, Joan. It wasn't him that hit you and kicked you. It was a total stranger that died the morning of September 18th."

For several seconds Joan buried her face in her handkerchief and her shoulders shook as she silently sobbed. When she calmed down, she raised her eyes once more to Ben.

"Would it have killed him?"

"Wylie says it was inoperable. He would have been dead within six months."

Her jaw was working and she swallowed hard. While she stared down at her hands folding and smoothing the damp handkerchief, she whispered to herself, "He didn't have a chance. He didn't have a chance."

Ben glanced up at Sharlene as she began to quietly cry, and then at Chad, wiping his eyes with the back of his hand. Ben felt helpless, not knowing what else to do or what to say, hating the hurt he saw in these people, hating the fact that Les was dead, hating what the system was doing to Joan and her twins.

Everyone's thoughts were interrupted by the sound of Judge Boyd coming back into the courtroom.

"Mr. Bailiff, inform the jury we will be a few more minutes. Mr. Dupree wants to finish his motion for a mistrial. I want to hear this out of the presence of the jury."

Ben collected his fragmented thoughts and turned his full attention to the proceedings. He was only vaguely aware of the crowd of spectators that had now gathered. Every seat in the courtroom was taken, every available place a person could stand was occupied, the doors were being held open out into the main corridor, and people were standing outside hoping to catch a glimpse or hear a word of what was going on.

"Mr. Dupree, I'm ready to hear your motion and your argument."

Dupree walked to the lectern.

"Your honor, I now restate my motion for an order of this court declaring these proceedings to be a mistrial at this point, and granting the state a new trial. The new trial is requested pursuant to Rule

Thirty-three, and I shall submit it in writing as required within the fifteen-day limitation. The mistrial is requested an the grounds that the unprecedented procedure that developed just before the recess has removed any possibility the jury can reach a rational, reasoned, unemotional decision in this case."

When Dupree finished detailing his argument, Judge Boyd looked at Ben,

"Mr. Cooper?"

Ben responded by making it crystal clear the incident was purely spontaneous and unexpected. His counterargument was simple. A new trial would gain nothing; the second jury would be required to hear the transcript of the incident and their judgment would be one step removed from what this jury already knew firsthand.

Judge Boyd leaned forward and removed his glasses, fingering them while he spoke.

"I understand the basis for the motion and I agree with Mr. Dupree that there is some merit to it. I've had to push aside all the emotion and outbursts and get to the bottom of this issue.

"If we did have a new trial, the new jury would hear the transcript of this incident before they could make their judgment of the case, so I don't see much gain. If there are grounds for a mistrial, we'll see them clearer when we finish than we do now, and Rule Thirty-three gives us latitude to correct it then.

"So, bottom line, I think I have to deny the motion for a declared mistrial at this time. This doesn't prevent the same motion from being made at a later time by either attorney. Mr. Bailiff, would you recall the jury?"

An audible wave of comment swept over the courtroom as the bailiff brought the jury back to their seats.

"Ladies and gentlemen of the jury, I have ruled on the motion made by counsel just prior to you being sent to the jury room. I want to admonish and instruct you now on what happened. Through impulse, the defendant interrupted direct examination of a witness and asked a question that was improper and totally outside lawful procedure. The question was answered. I do not want to repeat either the question or the answer, but rather I want you to blank them both out of your mind. Disregard the interruption. If it had an emotional impact on you, think it through carefully and disregard the emotion of the moment. Keep your mind in a state of cool reflection, so far as possible. I trust you can do that."

He studied the jury for a moment, then continued.

"Mr. Cooper, you may continue your examination of the witness. I trust the defendant will allow you to complete it uninterrupted."

Joan looked at the judge and nodded, her embarrassment obvious.

"Dr. Benoit, do you recall if you had finished your answer before the interruption?"

"Just one or two more things. In my opinion the tumor was inoperable. I believe Mr. Carson's abnormal behavior would have increased until he lapsed into a coma, and he would have died within six months."

"I have no more questions."

After a noon recess, the judge turned to Dupree.

"Mr. Dupree, you may cross-examine."

"Your honor, I request permission to reserve my cross-examination until a later time."

"Granted. Mr. Cooper, your next witnesses."

"Your honor, the defense has no more witnesses. The defense rests its main case."

"Mr. Dupree, what's your pleasure?"

"I request the court to grant a half-hour recess. I need to confer with my rebuttal witnesses before continuing."

In the conference room, Dupree spoke first to Adamson and Two Boys.

"Thanks for all you've done, but it looks like we won't need you on rebuttal. Joan Carson gave us the right time interval during her testimony, and we won't need to impeach her. You did good work. Thanks again."

They both nodded and rose to leave. Dupree turned to the other men and continued.

"Dr. Whalen, was there anything said by Benoit or Pinnock concerning the presence of the tumor that you disagree with?"

"No, I don't think so. We were all right there, working on it together. I think we all see it exactly the same. Wylie laid it out pretty well."

He looked at Pinnock, who bobbed his head, nodding agreement.

"Okay. Then let's talk about the effect it had on Carson. Dr. Ratachek, as a psychiatrist, what exception do you take to the testimony of Dr. Benoit on that question?"

"Not much. He was a lot more firm than I'm prepared to get, but that's because he knows a lot more about Les Carson than I do. I agree with his statements that the tumor *could* have caused the changes; I can't contradict his opinion the tumor *actually did* cause the changes in Carson that are in the record."

Dupree closed his eyes and lowered his chin.

"Is there any sense in cross-examining you, Dr. Pinnock? This is pretty weird, asking you that, but under the circumstances I have to. Is there any weakness in what Cooper asked you that would make any difference?"

Pinnock pondered a moment. "Not that I know of. I know the tumor was there. I also know it would have caused some kind of a change, although I don't know *what* kind of a change. But if Mr. Carson went through the change that everyone is talking about, that must have been it. I think I said all that and I can't think of a way to say it differently."

"How about Dr. Benoit? I'm reluctant to cross-examine him because he'll burn me if he can. Unless I have something that will really reach him, I don't want to lay myself open. Anybody want to help me on that?"

The four men looked at each other and none spoke.

"That's what I thought. Dr. Meadows, are you still prepared to talk about the testimony of Dr. Johnstone?"

"Yes. I think I can help with that, just the way we discussed it."

"Okay. We'll use Dr. Meadows and the rest of you are excused. Thank you. I'd like to use all of you, but if I did we stand a chance of getting hurt more than helped, and the gamble isn't worth it. Let's go back and get started."

Dupree walked back into the courtroom and took his place at the prosecutor's table. Everyone waited for just a moment while the judge came back in and the jury returned.

"Mr. Dupree, how do you want to proceed?"

"I waive cross-examination of Dr. Benoit and Dr. Pinnock, and I call Dr. Chris Meadows as the only rebuttal witness."

Dr. Meadows was sworn in and took the stand.

After developing Dr. Meadows' qualifications as a psychologist, Dupree laid the foundations for his opinions by establishing his examination of Joan and his close scrutiny of the reports of Dr. Johnstone. Then he proceeded into the opinion that would contradict Dr. Johnstone.

"What were Joan Carson's perceptions of her husband in the several seconds surrounding the shooting incident, specifically the second shot?"

"The first shot was fired in fear and terror, which probably robbed Mrs. Carson of a conscious decision to shoot him. She knew the shot was disabling, however, and her mind was clear enough to wait, then work the action on the rifle, and continue waiting until the head of Mr. Carson stabilized. The interval was about ten seconds, during which time she brought herself under control, then fired the second shot. That shot was not the result of fear and terror; it was a conscious, considered act."

"Thank you, Doctor. No more questions."

"Mr. Cooper, cross-examination?"

"I have no questions, your honor." Both Ben and Dupree knew it was useless; an hour of cross-examination would result only in further erosion of the field of psychology and not one single word of the opinion of Dr. Meadows would be changed.

Judge Boyd looked at the big clock and pondered a moment.

"Do you both rest your case?"

"Yes, your honor."

"Ladies and gentlemen, it is now past 4 o'clock. Considering the events of the day and the things counsel and I must accomplish before giving the case to you, I am going to declare the evening recess. Counsel and I will go into my chambers and work out the jury instructions. I will deliver the instructions to you in the morning, and counsel can argue the case. Counsel, any objections?"

"None, your honor."

"Court stands in recess until 9 o'clock tomorrow morning. Counsel, may I see you in my chambers?"

With the two attorneys seated at the old conference table in his chambers, the judge hung up his robe and loosened his tie.

He opened his files and selected a large sheaf of papers.

"Marge, you ready?"

"You bet."

"All right. For the record, Counsel and the court are met in chambers for the purpose of selecting jury instructions. The court has received and reviewed the proposed instructions from both parties, and has read their briefs in support of their various proposals. The court will rule on the controversial ones right up front, so we don't have to go back and redo some of the others later. We'll start with number seventeen.

"Okay, here we are. Number seventeen. Self-defense. I'm going to change the standard one slightly, by putting in some things requested by the defense. I'm going to put in the words 'according to her perceptions at the time of the occurrence' after the words 'deadly force,' so it reads she can use deadly force against deadly force according to her perceptions at the time of the occurrence. Any objections?"

Dupree spoke. "Yes. I object. The standard instruction is correct, without the proposed modifications. Objection is for the record."

"Noted. Marge, did you get it?"

Yes, sir."

"Number twenty-three. I'm not going to put in the things requested by the defense. I'm going with the standard instruction. But I am going to let you include the perceptions of the female gender at large, and of Joan Carson in particular, in your closing arguments. That way, you get your chance to cover the evidence of the doctors. Any objections? Ben?"

"How wide a latitude do we get in closing argument?"

"Whatever the record will support."

"No objections."

"Al?"

"I don't object to the standard jury instruction. I do violently object to throwing this thing open to heaven only knows what in the summations."

"Noted."

It was done. In the heat of the crucible of conflict, law that had controlled the state for almost 150 years had been added to and expanded, just a little. Just enough to embrace the female gender.

Thursday, December 16th

AT THE FRONT OF THE COURT-house, Joan glanced at the dull, purple-gray heavens as she and Ben made their way up the stone steps. The familiar hush had settled over the city. The air stood dead under the heavy clouds, as though nature was holding its breath, waiting, expecting. By habit, Ben unconsciously made his estimate as to when the snow would start and how long it would hold. The air was crisp, but the deep, biting cold had lifted when the storm moved in, as it always did before a major snow.

Leaving the elevator in the main corridor of the fourth floor, Ben and Joan slowed their pace as they approached clusters of people gathered near the entrance of the courtroom. Amid the buzz of talking, they began working their way through the crowd.

Inside the courtroom, every seat was already filled. Extra folding chairs had been placed at every point allowed by the fire code, and in those places where seating did not occupy floor space, people were standing. The doors were open, and the entry was filled with people, the crowd spilling into the hall.

The media filled the first two rows of benches on both sides of the aisle. Prepared with their pads and pencils and battery-powered recorders attached to directional microphones in their laps, they passed the time with quiet, idle talk, waiting for the judge to enter.

In the early hours before dawn, Ben and Dupree had each independently reviewed the trial, preparing themselves for the summation now before them. Each had concluded that the emotional, wrenching experience of yesterday had impacted the trial enough that no one knew where it now stood. Both had looked past the impact, however, far enough to see that once it was analyzed coolly, the evidence given of the tumor that had destroyed Les shouldn't really change the general structure of what had occurred to that point. Dupree's case should have survived it nearly intact; Ben's case was bolstered a little because of the corroboration and support it gave to Joan's statements about Les. But basically, the case was one of hard fact being confronted by some sort of inner human prompting that Joan should be given some consideration because of her female reactions at the time of the shooting. And last, both lawyers knew that no matter what reasoning or conclusions they tried to force on the shape of the trial at this time, the verdict was ultimately up for grabs.

At 9 o'clock the chamber doors opened and Judge Boyd took his chair while the jury filed in and took their seats.

"Ladies and gentlemen of the jury, it is now my duty to instruct you in the rules of law that you must use in making your decision. Following these instructions, counsel for each party will be given time to present their arguments on the evidence. Each party will be given one hour. The state will be allowed to divide the hour, giving opening and closing argument in this case, in any manner it chooses. The defense will make its entire argument at one time. Do not take notes on these instructions, as I will deliver them to you in written form for your deliberations. I now invite you to give me your utmost attention while they are read."

For just over an hour, the judge plowed through the instructions. Fifteen minutes after he started, no one in the room even pretended to be able to absorb everything while he droned through it. After he finished, the judge turned to the jury. "Thank you for your attention, ladies and gentlemen." He then closed his file and raised his face toward Dupree.

"Mr. Dupree, it is ten minutes past ten. You may open your argument. Do you wish to be notified when you have used a certain amount of your time?"

"No, your honor, thank you."

Dupree rose. In his mind, he reviewed his notes from his conclusions and preparation, reminding himself to stay with the facts. In the long pull, facts win.

"Mr. Bailiff, would you please bring the state's exhibits to this table? Thank you."

Dupree moved to his place behind the lectern and turned it until he was facing directly toward the center of the jury. He watched while the bailiff laid out the exhibits on his table, next to him.

"Ladies and gentlemen, may I first thank you for the keen attention you have demonstrated thus far in the case. I am aware of the burden this case is to you. I shall do what I can to aid you in making a correct decision. It will of course be yours; Mr. Cooper and I can only assist you in reaching it.

"You will recall in my opening statement I made a commitment to you. I committed the state to put proof before you that the defendant, Joan Carson, with deliberation and intent to cause the death of her husband, did in fact cause the death of her husband, Leslie Carson. Proof of those rather simple propositions constitutes proof of murder, as the judge has just now instructed you, and *proof* depends on *facts."*

Dupree paused for emphasis.

"In this case, then, the state must present *facts,* sufficient in their number and clarity to convince you beyond a reasonable doubt that Joan Carson both intended to kill her husband, and with deliberation did so.

"Before reviewing this evidence with you, there are two other propositions that I want to present for your consideration.

"First, as judge Boyd has already instructed you, your decision should be the result of reason. Not emotion, nor sentiment, nor pity, nor empathy. Just cool, considered reason, based on the hard evidence now before you.

"The second proposition I think you should reflect on, is the quality of the act we are considering. It is the act of murder. In the recorded history of civilized nations, the act of murder is one of the few that stands universally condemned. You must remember we are not talking about theft, fraud, robbery, or any of a number of other crimes. We are considering the ultimate violent act one human being can inflict upon the person of another."

Dupree paused, then turned toward the exhibits arranged on his table. "May I now summarize the evidence, the hard facts, which are before you?"

For half an hour, with methodical precision and in conversational tones, Dupree reached back into the minds of the jurors and blew away the smoke and the clutter that had crept into the trial. One by one, he brought each of the hard facts back before them, holding them up once more, laying each in order, rebuilding the brick wall that had somewhat crumbled during the defense testimony. All the facts were there: Joan's pre-dawn arrival, Les appearing behind her, the beating, the rifle tumbling across her lap, the working of the rifle to fire the first shot, the ten-second pause while she worked the action again and waited, the shooting of Les a second time, and the expertise which enabled her to place the second bullet accurately. Dupree paraded the sickening photographs one at a time, forcing the jury to again deal with the grisly destruction Joan's act had inflicted on Les.

Then he paused, moving toward his final remarks before turning the lectern over to Ben for his argument.

"You now know it was the second shot that killed Mr. Carson. It is *that* shot which must be measured by the law. If it was fired with intent and deliberation, then it was a murder."

He paused again and stepped back from the lectern for a moment, then moved forward.

"Was the shot fired with deliberation and intent to kill? I asked her if she knew the power of the rifle, and she said yes. I asked her if she placed the second shot where she intended, and she said yes. I then asked her if she knew when she fired it that it would be fatal, and she said yes. When I asked if she intended it to fatal, she replied that she did."

The argument was firm, sealed by the testimony of Joan herself on the single issue that might have remained in doubt: her intent.

He turned and looked at the clock in back of him, gauging his time.

"Ladies and gentlemen, before yielding the lectern to Mr. Cooper for his summation, there are one or two more propositions that I want set before you.

"After all the evidence is considered, at the bottom of it all is one irrefutable fact. It was Joan Carson that had the rifle that morning, not Mr. Carson. The capability of inflicting instant death was in *her* hands, not his. Complete command of the situation was *hers,* not his. She used that capability to kill him, at a time when she *knew* he was totally incapable of rising from the floor, or presenting further harm to her person.

"This proceeding doesn't revolve around what the prosecution came here to prove. We have proven a murder. We have proven it by the words of the defendant herself.

"No, this case revolves around what the *defense* has come here to tell you. So far as I understand it, they have agreed that Joan Carson indeed *did* murder her husband, but, under the circumstances, she ought to be excused. After all, she's a *woman.* She needs to be understood and forgiven, and not held accountable.

"It is impossible for me to think that the facts are less compelling simply because the defendant is a *woman. I* can't begin to calculate the revolution that will take place in our society if it is suddenly enough to say, yes, this person blew the life out of her husband by putting one bullet through his chest, and then ten seconds later, with him down, helpless, dying, she put a second one through his head. Just to be sure. Just for reasons known only to her. Just because she is a woman. And that's a complete defense, so we won't bring her to accountability for it."

He paused, then changed course slightly.

"I won't have you believe I am trying to put down women as a gender. Exactly the opposite. I am trying to say that they *are* competent, intelligent human beings as a gender, and it is precisely for that reason they must stand accountable in a court of law. To require less of them would be an open accusation that they are less than what they are. To give them license simply because of their gender is to acknowledge an incompetency in them that is simply not there. They *are* competent and responsible, as a gender.

"While Mr. Cooper is presenting the defense, would you please try to remember that?" He closed his file and looked at Ben.

Judge Boyd leaned forward.

"Mr. Cooper, your summation and argument. You will get the usual warning at fifty-five minutes."

Dupree picked up his file and took a few moments to reorganize all the exhibits on his tabletop. Ben glanced at the clerk's exhibit table, where all the defense exhibits yet remained, while Dupree picked up his file and sat down.

A quiet murmur passed through the jammed courtroom as the people prepared their minds to hear Ben's closing argument.

Ben had his head tipped forward, his eyes staring at the top of the defense table. Dupree's argument presented an impregnable, closed circle, as he knew it would. Ben's mind was swamped with fleeting commands to himself. Stick with the game plan—avoid the facts—don't even try to fight them—Joan and Wylie and Dr. Johnstone have given you your best chance—the dramatics yesterday helped—you can't get an acquittal, but there's a chance for a hung jury—get one or two of the women jurors to feel something for Joan—remember the lesson learned from the little old lady in the second row of the jury box who didn't know the why of her decision, she just *felt* that way—go for it, clear your head and act like you know what you're doing—go for it!

Ben slowly closed his file and pushed it away from him. He looked over at the clerk and shook his head in the negative. Startled, the clerk silently asked with his eyes if Ben wanted his defense exhibits. Again, Ben shook his head. The clerk raised his eyebrows in surprise and settled back into his chair.

Ben stood and walked to the lectern empty-handed.

Judge Boyd suddenly leaned forward and dropped his chin, eyes peering out over his glasses. He was puzzled as to how Ben would present a summation without the exhibits and a file.

Dupree appeared unimpressed.

Ben began quietly. "Ladies and gentlemen, I won't presume to lecture you, nor do I intend taking an undue amount of your time. I see nothing to be gained by repeating to you what Mr. Dupree has so accurately presented in his closing argument. The exhibits, the photographs, the rifle, the bullets, the diagrams—I doubt anything I can say will add to your knowledge concerning them and what they mean in this case. It will startle you, or at least *should* startle you, to know that I agree with what Mr. Dupree has said about them. It will probably confuse you when I tell you that I am in full agreement with what he has presented to you in the trial and argued to you in his very able summation.

"I don't think I can do much to add to, or detract from, the facts, the exhibits, the diagrams, and the rules he has called out to you.

"There is but one dimension I feel I can add to this case as it now stands that might be helpful to you as you now consider your verdict. Perhaps that single dimension is best defined by contrasting it with what you now have before you.

"You see, as of this minute, Mr. Dupree has done a master's work in presenting you with all the objective facts he needs to legally prove a murder."

Ben paused, waiting for the low buzz of whispers to stop. Those in the room who had law and courtroom experience leaned forward, astounded, wondering if they had just heard Ben admit a murder.

"If you will take the time to write down a checklist of all the necessary elements to sustain a conviction in this case, you will find all of them satisfied by the evidence. In fact, most of them are provided for you by the words of the defendant, Joan Carson.

"If that is all you require for a conviction, then your duties from this point on are simple. You need do nothing more than make out the checklist, put the check marks in the appropriate places, total them up, and convict her. That you can do in half an hour, with the jury instructions, the exhibits, and the testimony of Joan Carson. You need not consider anything more than that.

"But respectfully, I must suggest that there is something inside of each of you that rebels at the thought of dealing with a human life in a checklist fashion. There is something in each of us that says there has to be more. We aren't machines. We aren't cattle. The sum total of the check marks, be they good or bad, is not the sum total of our lives. We are more than that. Surely we are more than that.

"That is the one dimension I feel I can address and assist you in understanding."

Ben shifted his feet, and his eyes dropped to the heavy lectern, his hand rubbing the surface. He looked back at the jury and continued.

"We *are* more than a checklist. We *are* more than the exhibits and the diagrams and the photographs and the testimony. That is what the doctors, Benoit and Johnstone and Ratachek, have told you these past few days. Each of them correctly pointed out to you that the professions of psychology and psychiatry, dealing with the essence of the human being, must necessarily include some vagueness, a sense of being indefinite. Have you pondered why? It is because human beings are infinitely *more* than any science, any other thing on the earth. *None* of the three doctors I have just named can define the mind or the essence of the human being because no one has ever reached the limitless dimensions and capabilities of the human being to give them a view sufficient to define what is there! In the context of this case, Joan Carson is infinitely more than any, or all, of the checklists or the exhibits or the testimony."

He paused to allow the jury to reflect on his statements.

"Please, may I review the elements of this case that extend beyond the checklist? Beyond all you see spread on these tables before you? Will you listen as I try?

"You know Joan and Les were raised in Caldwell, in the high mountain ranch country, north of us. You know about their early lives, their schooling years, their later courtship and marriage. You know about their children.

"They decided to leave their beginnings and moved from Caldwell to Denver to try to improve their position and fortunes. Les found his place in life to be the construction business. He blossomed. His natural talents were given full opportunity for growth and expression. He worked hard. The business grew until he earned a full partnership.

"Through it all, you know Joan was there beside him. You heard what she and Les had. They shared it all, the good with the bad, the wins and the losses. They had trust and faith and confidence. Did you see the little expressions on her face as she described their relationship and life together? Can you doubt what Les meant to her and she to him? Is there any question they loved each other more than anything else in the world?

"Then Les's partner, Glenn Tolboy, suffered his first heart attack. From that moment on, the construction company was all but doomed.

"Because he was the man he was, Les refused to buckle. He worked to salvage the business until he was drained in body and soul. It was only because he loved Joan and Glenn that he finally agreed to sell, in a last-ditch effort to save something from their life's work.

"Then, small, seemingly insignificant happenings began to appear. Les began showing unexpected signs of irritability. He began arguing occasionally with people he worked with. They were surprised, but explained it away by saying, 'Glenn is incapacitated. Les is carrying the whole load. Give him some allowances.'

"It became worse. He began forgetting things. His arguments became temper outbursts. His closest friends at the company began noticing he had been drinking. Occasionally he couldn't remember what he had done five minutes ago. Those who had worked with him for thirteen years were shocked by his inability to recognize them. Ann Fenton couldn't believe it when Les instigated a shouting argument with Glenn over money.

"None of those incidents compared with what was happening between Les and Joan.

"He began arguing with her. Then suddenly one day, he struck her. Within days he had struck her twice more, the last time knocking her down. When she tried to rise, he kicked her, cutting her above one eye with the toe of his shoe. She began leaving when she knew he would be home because it was impossible to predict what might trigger him and what he would do. The expressions that came over his face when the explosions occurred were terrifying to her. She had never dreamed Les could be capable of such conduct.

"It never entered Joan's mind to do anything but try to help him. When she knew he was in trouble, she went to her doctor, and from there called a lawyer, Mr. Tuttle, to *force* Les to get the help she knew he so desperately needed. The appointment with the lawyer was scheduled for Wednesday, September 22nd.

"But on the evening of September 17th, events were set in motion that resulted in the heartbreaking incident that brings us here today.

Les came home and told Joan he wanted to live separate from her. She was to come to the apartment at the construction offices the following day at noon to get her things. To avoid the possibility of saying anything to him that would result in another beating, Joan agreed and quickly left the house, returning late that evening. She then spent the night in the dark, sitting in a rocking chair, terrified that he might return."

Ben paused and looked directly at the jury in silence for just a moment. His jaw muscles were working, his voice taking on a slightly husky tone as he struggled.

"He didn't return that night. The following morning, about 5 o'clock, Joan decided to get to the apartment and remove her things before he returned from a job site, afraid of what he might do if she met him.

"She drove directly there and opened the door with her key. She paused to listen, to be certain he was not there, and then she stepped into the dark room. When she reached for the light switch, she heard the footfall behind her.

"She turned, and even in the near total darkness, she could see his face, his eyes. She knew he was possessed by something. It was not Les. She was looking at a horrifying, mindless brute.

"She raised her hands instinctively to protect her face. He seized her arm, and with his free hand, he struck her in the face and head and neck, repeatedly. Her mind went numb and she couldn't focus or think. Les was a powerful man, hardened from a lifetime of rough work; she didn't have a prayer of a chance in a combat with him. He struck her until she was semi-conscious and her legs buckled out from under her. Then he threw her backward."

Ben paused, searching for words to convey the emotion.

"Her back slammed into the doorjamb to the kitchenette, and as she slid to a sitting position, her old rifle—hers since earliest childhood—slipped down the wall where Les had put it, bumped into her shoulder, and stopped on her legs. Les made some grotesque, hideous sounds, and advanced toward her.

"At that point, Joan Carson had no conscious intent of doing anything because she had no conscious thoughts. She had been beaten nearly senseless and her mind was numb. Her nose was bleeding, with some of the blood running down the back of her throat. Her mouth was bleeding, the blood running down her chin, onto her sweater. Her left eye was blurred and she thought it was blinded. She couldn't run from him; she couldn't even stand.

"It was the body of Les advancing toward her, but she knew whatever was inside was not Les. Her single clear impression was that this brute was advancing to beat her again. She knew he could kill her with his hands and she knew he probably would."

Ben paused and again brought his eyes to bear directly on the jury.

"Understanding what happened in the next few seconds is the key to understanding why we are here today." Ben spoke with intensity.

"The unbelievable change in her husband from the man she had known to this raging brute, followed by a night of terror, sitting in the darkness, and culminating in a merciless, horrible beating, all but destroyed her mind. Joan did everything she could to tell you that she knew her thinking and reasoning power ceased to function. A feeling. A compulsion. An instinct native to a woman. Something inside her, from a well deeper than anything she had ever known, rose to defend her. She was not in control. She simply did what her natural instincts required of her. She faced and destroyed the deadly force that to her perceptions would kill her in the next few seconds. Native instinct she neither understood nor challenged destroyed the maniac before her.

"Then, with the crisis past, the compulsion retreated back to its source and allowed her conscious thoughts and reason to resume control. Slowly she realized what she had done. In her own words, for several minutes she thought the realization was going to cost her her sanity.

"Dr. Carrie Johnstone, with a woman's natural instincts and an uncommon expertise that allows her to understand them, explained to you that what Joan struggled so hard to say was all true. Joan was powerless to do other than what she did."

Ben stopped for several seconds, deciding not to reiterate what he had just said.

"After struggling for several minutes to hold her sanity, and after the strength returned to her so she could, she stumbled across his body, leaned the rifle against the wall by the door, set the automatic lock, closed the door behind her, and drove her car to my office."

Ben cleared his throat, attempting to control his emotions.

"I—each of you saw the price Joan paid on the witness stand while she told you all of this. Then yesterday, when you learned the truth about Les from Dr. Benoit, could you doubt the truth of what she had tried so desperately to tell us?

"Do you recall her actions when it finally burst into her mind for the first time what had gone wrong? Why Les had become a thing of terror for her? How does one describe the heartbreak she felt when she realized that Les was not to blame; the flood of tears she could finally shed, knowing he had loved her until he was no longer Les? I don't know the words. I can only trust that you know them.

"Now may I suggest what I believe each of you is beginning to see? Allow me to articulate and summarize it.

"A good, strong, decent man had risen to the heights of his profession. He had most of the best things life can offer. A good woman, two fine children, and a future that looked solid because it was built on a past filled with hard, dedicated work.

"A malignancy began its work in his brain. And with its growth came the beginnings of his destruction. In a rather short period, it was robbing him of his mind, his memory, his personality, his character. This man rapidly became a thing of brutality and terror to the one person he loved the most, and who loved him above all. By intuition—call it what you will—Joan sensed the person facing her that morning in the apartment was not Les. She did not know why, but she knew that person was capable of destroying her.

"From that day on, she has lived with torment in her heart as to whether she was right or wrong, until yesterday. The truth came out in the testimony of Dr. Benoit. Joan had been right. It was not Les that she had faced that morning. It was a stranger.

"Now, ladies and gentlemen, with that much committed to words, can you agree with me regarding what we have described?

"You and I and this court have been witness to a pure, simple *tragedy*. *You* know now that Les was not responsible for what he became. Les was the victim of an insidious, destructive cancer. If that is true, was Joan any less the victim of the same cancer? Which of the two, Les or Joan, has suffered and will continue to suffer the most from it? Have you pondered what the tumor in the brain of her husband has cost her? Taken from her?

"The prosecution has suggested Joan is asking that she be given license; that she be excused, forgiven, not held accountable.

"She asks none of these. To the contrary, weeks ago Joan voluntarily submitted herself to examination by the state's psychiatrist and psychologist. She told them every detail in the entire incident, holding back nothing. Then, with my concurrence, she permitted the entire record to be submitted to both the prosecutor and this court, and you have it in the exhibits. To this moment, she has not changed a word of it, nor has she made excuse. Avoid accountability? She *begged* for it."

Ben allowed a second to pass before he drew the jury's attention for the last time.

"Ladies and gentlemen, I have tried to present the truth to you as simply and as cleanly as my understanding and my limited capabilities will allow. I recognize I have used less than half of the time allotted me, but in this case, unnecessary words somehow seem to be a disservice to you. I have but one final proposition to put to you and then I am finished.

"Down inside each of you is a private, quiet place where you ponder and decide the deep things in your life. It is away from the clutter and the pressures of living. In this case, it is away from the interference of the exhibits, the diagrams, this courtroom, and the conflict the law has forced upon you. In that private, quiet place, you face only you. You are totally alone, accountable only to yourself. It is there your life is justified—or damned."

Ben paused, hoping desperately in his heart some of them knew what he was talking about. Then he continued.

"I can only pray to God that each of you is familiar with your own place of judgment."

He clenched his hand and brought it up in front of his chest, leaning forward, his face drawn with intensity.

"If you do understand, and if you can find your way into your own soul, then it is there you must face yourself and ask the single question on which the judgment of Joan Carson must stand or fall.

"You must ask yourself, 'Knowing what I now know about Joan Carson, knowing she is a woman with a woman's instincts, and knowing her part in the tragedy of the morning of September 18th, can I convict her of murder?'"

Ben dropped his hand and paused for a moment, then lowered his voice slightly.

"If you can answer the question 'yes,' then you must convict her."

He paused, knowing the shock of his suggestion would cause the jury to recoil a little before they would refocus and wait for his conclusion. He didn't move until he knew they were totally prepared for what he hoped would be the single proposition that would bring them face-to-face with their moment of truth.

"But if you cannot answer 'yes,' then for *your* sake you must set her free. You *must* set her free."

In his face, his eyes were thoughts and feelings he could not speak—a pleading that could not be put into words.

A silence held for three or four seconds while he searched the eyes of each jury member.

Then he turned, walked to his chair, and was seated.

The silence continued, unnoticed by Ben while he stared at his tabletop, trying to believe he had somehow met and turned the crushing weight of the facts for one or two jurors, at least enough to make them refuse to bend; to hang the jury.

Around him the silence still held. The jury hadn't moved since he finished. In the spectator section, it was as though no one dared break the spell. Richard Frazier, seated by David, sat leaning forward while he stared and silently whispered to himself, "My goodness." Chad and Sharlene sat motionless, eyes wide and staring.

Ben raised his head and looked at the judge.

"Mr. Dupree, you have about twenty minutes to close."

Dupree stood and slowly assumed his position at the lectern. Ben's summation was just about what he expected it to be. He knew he had to gently bring the jury back to the real world, and yet not offend. Just show them the brick wall one more time.

"Ladies and gentlemen, after hearing the very powerful remarks of Mr. Cooper, I trust you will have some sense of understanding and compassion when I tell you that I do not face these matters with feeling of anticipation and comfort. There are times when it is not easy to remember the rules society must impose on me, and in this case on you, to protect itself, and keep its affairs in order. At times it requires a price, and the price can be hard to pay. Sometimes it can be heartbreaking. But ladies and gentlemen, wisdom born of experience dictates that finally, the rules must prevail and you and I must abide by them.

"I am compelled to now remind you that when you were examined as to your fitness to sit on this jury, one of the questions you were asked, at least twice, was whether you would be willing to listen to the instructions of the judge and make your decision accordingly, regardless of personal feelings or emotional reactions. I must admonish you to remember your commitment to read the instructions given you by Judge Boyd, and consider the evidence before you, and then make your decision in a calm, reflective, cool state of mind as you were directed. The single question you are committed to answer is, has the state presented sufficient evidence to persuade you beyond a reasonable doubt that Joan Carson, with deliberation and intent to do it, in fact did commit an act that took the life of Leslie Carson?

"Counsel for the defense has just confirmed that she did. I don't recall the last time such a concession was made in a trial of this nature, but if you will recall, you did hear it.

"Ladies and gentlemen, as I suggested before Mr. Cooper addressed you, the thrust of his summation finally boils down to one proposition: Mrs. Carson committed a murder, but under the circumstances, she should not be held accountable.

"You cannot let that argument succeed.

"Consider for the last time the facts before you."

Quickly, in summary form, Dupree presented each salient fact in its proper order, creating the brick wall for them for the last time—the image they would carry with them into the jury room to make their judgment.

Then he paused, allowing time for the minds of the jury to catch up with him.

"I have puzzled over what tactic the defense would use to avoid accountability for the murder. Now we know. A 'compulsion.'

"May I give you the bottom line of that argument? When compulsions become excuses, murder will become king. Think about it. The entire argument of the defense is put to rest in that single thought.

"One more thing. I am sure you are perceptive enough, wise enough, to try *Joan* Carson and not *Leslie* Carson. All the evidence of what went wrong with Les is interesting, but not at issue here. The sole question is, did Joan murder him? Try Joan Carson in this case; if necessary, we'll try Les later on.

"Last, I want to mention just a word about the testimony from the psychologists and psychiatrists. I doubt any two of you will agree on what they said, so I doubt it will be a threat to the right result in this case. Use your good sense. Don't be drawn off your own views by those who have admitted theirs are no better, and often worse.

"The time allotted for summation is almost ended, I must conclude. I am confident you can, and will, meet the duty you have to carefully, objectively, weigh all the evidence and facts. Then make your verdict. It must be guilty. Give Judge Boyd what he must have to render a just, fair, factual sentence. Thank you."

He closed his file and walked to his seat.

The hush of the courtroom was broken by movement among the spectators, then the jury.

Judge Boyd dropped his pencil onto his yellow pad and rocked forward in the huge chair. He looked at the jury.

"Ladies and gentlemen, the time has arrived for you to go to the jury room and make your verdict."

The judge gave the bailiff the usual directions, banged his gavel, and the jury filed out. People began standing, stretching against muscles that had become taut during closing arguments. The buzz of conversation began as Dupree and Ben gathered their papers and put their files in their briefcases. Ben nodded to those who came to offer their remarks, while he waited for the twins to come to be with Joan.

When they approached, he spoke to them quietly. "Could you come over to my office for just a few minutes before you go home?"

Back at his office, he helped Joan with her coat and was just removing his own when the rap came at the door and the twins walked in.

"Thanks for coming. There are some pretty important things we need to talk about and time is short. Before we do, would you care to give me your impressions of closing argument?

Chad looked at Sharlene and then turned back to Ben.

"They were good. For both sides. If you want to know how we felt about yours, I don't know how it could have been better."

Sharlene nodded, as did Joan.

"Thanks. The one up there taking the shots never knows how the battle looks to the observer. But I didn't ask you here to talk about that, much as I'd like to."

He turned to Joan.

"I have to tell you all that we're at a point of no return. I can still go to Dupree and probably cut some kind of a deal. The good part is, you will have some input as to what the deal is and it will stop the whole thing right now. The bad part is, any deal will have to include a felony plea. If we decide to do it, I have to do it right now. Today.

"I wouldn't tell you this if I didn't feel that as of this minute, you stand a strong chance of a felony conviction anyway."

He waited for their response. After a pause, Joan spoke.

"Do you think they'll convict me?"

"The hard facts are all one way, Joan. We knew that going in. I think we made a monumental assault on them, but I doubt we got clear past them. The trial took a bizarre twist yesterday when you stood up, and none of us can even guess where it left us after it all settled down. Don't misunderstand me. What you did, and the impact it had, could only help you, but even with that, I have to tell you my strongest hope is just to get a hung jury."

He waited, but no one spoke, so he continued.

"You'll have to tell me now of your choice about a plea bargain. What do you think?"

Joan held back for a moment, then asked, "What's your advice, Ben?"

"I can't give you my thoughts. I must have yours."

Joan slowly nodded understanding and walked over to the windows, watching the first flakes of snow drift lazily downward. The twins watched her for a moment, then stood waiting.

She finally turned.

"I have to know, Ben. I can't make a deal."

Ben looked into her eyes long and hard, and then nodded.

"Okay." He began to move, his thoughts leaving the weight of the decision Joan had just made.

"It's what—1:30? I don't think we'll get a verdict today. I recommend the three of you go home and wait there. Don't leave the phone. When they call me I'll call you and meet you at the courthouse. The earliest should be tomorrow some time. If it goes past that, it's anybody's guess."

The Verdict

DUPREE GLANCED AT HIS WATCH as he turned the last corner in the broad marble-floored corridor, and patiently pushed his way through the crowd into the courtroom. The time was 3:40 P.M. The jury had taken almost twenty-seven hours.

Inside, the courtroom was jammed to the walls with a sea of faces. Ben was already seated at counsel table with Joan, waiting.

Dupree walked to his chair and sat down. Bruce went back toward the banister and stood.

To both Ben and Dupree, nothing seemed real. The noise of remarks being made by those nearby all seemed distorted, out of place, not relevant, too loud. The thoughts going through their minds seemed odd, as though they didn't relate to anything going on. Both men accepted the familiar lost feeling as part of the strange phenomenon that occurs while attorneys wait for a murder verdict.

The door to Judge Boyd's chambers swung open, and he walked to his bench and sat down.

"Be seated, please. Mr. Clerk, are all the parties present in the courtroom?

"They are, your honor,"

"Thank you. Mr. Bailiff, has the jury reached a verdict?"

"They have, your honor,"

Ben audibly sucked in his breath. A verdict! A verdict meant there was no hung jury. He'd failed! Ben's heart sank with the knowledge Joan had been convicted. Of what? How serious? Murder? He tipped his head forward and closed his eyes, trying to keep his composure.

"Would you bring the jury in, please?"

The bailiff rose and walked down the aisle in front of the large windows, toward the door marked for the jury.

Joan was sitting wide-eyed, counting his steps, wondering why he was moving so slowly, when in fact he was walking at normal speed.

The bailiff disappeared and in a moment he emerged with the jury following behind him in single file. The judge rose, and all in the courtroom rose to their feet, waiting for the jury to be seated.

Every eye that could see was studying the faces of the individual jurors as they walked the distance to the jury box and took their seats. When the jurors were seated, the judge sat down, as well as all the spectators who could.

"Would the foreman please rise?"

A man on the second row stood with a piece of paper in his hand.

"Mr. Foreman, has the jury reached a verdict?"

"We have, your honor."

"Would you please hand it to the bailiff?"

The bailiff walked over, accepted it folded, and handed it to the judge. He opened it, examined it to see that it was properly entered, then folded it again. The judge handed it to the bailiff, who took it to the clerk.

"Mr. Clerk, would you please read the verdict?"

The clerk opened the folded paper.

"In the District Court for the Second Judicial District of the State of Colorado, in and for the County of Denver. The case of the State of Colorado versus Joan Carson. Criminal Number 2127. We, the jury find the defendant, Joan Carson, not guilty."

Joan jerked from the shock. She was totally stunned.

Ben gasped and felt himself sag against the table. He caught himself and instantly turned toward Joan. She also turned and closed with him, locking both her arms around him with all her strength, her cheek against his chest, saying nothing at first. Then she began quietly repeating over and over, "Thank you. Thank you. Thank you." But it was lost in the commotion and heard by no one. Ben wrapped both his arms around her and held her tightly, dropping his cheek to her hair. They stood there, locked together, oblivious to the unbelievable din that had spontaneously exploded when the verdict was announced.

Reporters instantly jammed through the doors in an avalanche, fighting to get to the elevators and the telephones so they could return to their offices in time for the evening editions and newscasts.

Dupree had recoiled in disbelief at the reading of the verdict; then a look of wonder and puzzlement crossed his face. He slowly shook his head.

The judge sat in his chair, momentarily stunned by the verdict; then a smile flickered across his face and was gone. From the bench, the judge saw there was no chance the jury could hear him. He rose and caught the attention of the jury, giving a hand signal to remain seated. He didn't try to gavel the court to order. He just sat back in his chair, waiting for the flurry of activity to subside.

Without regard for the restriction against it, spectators flooded past the banister into the area reserved for members of the bar, and crowded around Ben and Joan.

Wylie made his way to the corner of the jury box and simply waited, savoring every moment of the drama. The twins were laughing through their tears, working their way to Joan and Ben.

Finally approaching them, Chad grabbed Ben and threw both arms around him. Sharlene embraced Joan, and as they stood there together, Joan began to weep. David walked up and Ben didn't hesitate. He freed an arm from Chad and grabbed David, pulling him into the circle.

Minutes passed and the courtroom would not clear. The judge became concerned, and finally he stood and walked down to the jury box. He thanked them, commended them, and told them they were officially discharged from further duties in this case and could leave when they were ready. Then he returned to his chair, gathered his file, and walked through the door into his chambers, pausing only to take one last look at a scene he had never before witnessed.

Dupree waited for an opportunity to shake Ben's hand and congratulate him, but it soon became obvious that the chance would be a long time in coming. So he finally quietly made his way out, intending to call Ben first thing in the morning.

When he could, Wylie worked his way to Ben and was quickly brought into the circle, Joan stepping over to embrace him, Sharlene right behind her.

Fifteen minutes passed before the crowd began to settle down and thin out. Ben was interrupted a dozen times to shake hands and hear praise from well-wishers, receiving their compliments by deferring all credit to Wylie, Joan, and David. As things began to return to some semblance of normalcy, Ben took stock and turned to look for Dupree. He realized he had gone, and made a mental note to call him in the morning. Ben finally shook his head and spoke to Joan and the twins, David and Wylie.

"I know I'm not able to put this all together and say it right, not now anyway. Would you all come to the office tomorrow morning, say, 10 o'clock, for just a few minutes? It won't take long."

BEN PULLED THE DOOR OPEN, smiling while Wylie stamped the snow off his shoes and walked into the foyer.

"Good morning, Ben. Has the world settled down for you yet?

"Let me help you with your coat, Wylie. Yes, I think I'm about back with the real world. How are the roads? Getting plugged up?"

Ben had been there for over an hour, shoveling the sidewalks clear of the sixteen inches of snow, which had been falling steadily since just after noon the previous day. David had arrived to help, and the sidewalks, with shoveled snow banks nearly three feet high on both sides, were already starting to disappear again under the soft, large flakes.

Ben hung Wylie's overcoat on the foyer rack, then walked with him back toward his office where a tray with a pot of steaming cocoa was waiting. Ben paused and called, "David, got a minute in my office?"

As the three sat down, Ben glanced at the clock and his expression sobered.

"We've got just a minute or two before Joan arrives. There's one thing I think I would like to put to rest. Only the three of us know about my conclusion that Les killed Glenn Tolboy. Under the circumstances, I don't think Les was responsible. I think he was gone by then. Unless either of you see it differently, can we agree to just let it end right here?"

David nodded, and Wylie spoke.

"Forgotten. Good idea." Then Wylie continued while he filled a cup with cocoa. "See the newspapers this morning?"

"Yes, Laura brought them in and read them all to me before 8 o'clock."

"That verdict is being hailed as a state landmark in the advancement of the status of women in court proceedings. Now what do you think of that, my barrister friend?"

Ben looked at Wylie, a smile tugging at the corners of his mouth. "Did any of those guys mention how close that came to being a prize-winning fiasco?"

"Well, no, but I think I can talk with a couple of them, and with a little luck I can get them straightened out on that point and—"

Ben's laughter cut him off and Wylie grinned his ingratiating grin. David smiled, reaching for the cocoa.

"Wylie, did you read the article—about half a page—where the state bar had its resident forensic psychologist explain in detail the mental processes the jury went through to get the verdict?" Ben was smiling in anticipation.

"I read it. He's a nice guy who has been cloistered in his ivory tower too long. His explanation was so neat and tidy it was a thing of beauty. The problem is, it had little to do with what really happened in that jury room. He never did consult with the true authorities on the verdict—the people who made it. He should have listened to the little old lady in the middle of the back row—you know, the one who didn't know why she voted for acquittal, she just *felt* that way. That's the answer. The ultimate answer."

Ben looked at Wylie and their eyes locked for just a moment as they reflected on the profound depth of that simple statement. Then Ben smiled and nodded his agreement, reaching for his mug. He slowed his hand as he paused to listen.

"I think they're here." He rose and walked out his office door, followed by David. Wylie waited.

In the foyer, Chad was helping Joan with her coat and Sharlene was still tapping the last of the snow from her shoes. Their faces were a cheery pink from the cold and their eyes sparkled. Ben stepped toward them, speaking.

"You made it. I was a little worried about the streets with this snow. Let me help you."

Within minutes they were in Ben's office, helping themselves to the cocoa and making small talk. After a while, Ben spoke, knowing they were waiting expectantly to hear the purpose of the visit.

"I just wanted a minute with you all because I think there are some things that need to be heard.

"Joan, I was the one that stood at the counsel table and did the talking and had the high profile in this case. The papers have my name in them this morning, along with yours. I just want to be sure each of you understands that it isn't my name that should head the list. It should be you people here. Wylie, Carrie Johnstone, David, and Joan. Mostly Wylie. That's the closest I can come to letting you know how I feel about who was responsible for what happened. I've called Carrie and told her this, earlier this morning. To say thanks is almost an insult. I can only hope you all understand how much that trial meant to me and what I feel for each of you for what you did. I can't say more than that."

No one felt uncomfortable with his frank, honest statement. And no one responded, not wanting to detract from the sweetness of the moment. Ben continued.

"I want you all to know, too, that Al Dupree called me at home late last night and congratulated us all on what happened. He will not appeal the case to the Supreme Court. Joan, he made me promise I would tell you that he has reconciled himself to the verdict and extends his sincere wishes for your future happiness. He meant it, Joan. If you see him again, walk up to him and shake his hand and tell him how you're doing. He'll be glad to know. Chad and Sharlene, you too, Okay?"

"There's one more thing. I've been swamped by reporters since last night. Joan, how about you?"

"We finally took the phone off the hook."

"Do you want to give any of them an interview?"

"No, I don't, Ben. At least not right now. I'm leaving tomorrow with the twins to go up home and visit Dad. I've got to tell Jesse what happened. Will you be coming up for some of the Christmas vacation?"

"Yes, I think so. Laura wants to go up."

"Would you come see us and tell Jesse all the details that I'll forget? He'll want to know. Will you come?"

"Sure I will. I'd love to."

Wylie put his cup down and interrupted,

"I believe there is one thing either of you can do that will be of great professional interest to me. I believe it would be very enlightening to visit Caldwell for a day or two and make a personal appraisal of what it is up there that causes you guys to be . . . how does that go, Ben? Tough as saddle leather and—"

Ben and Joan both started to laugh, cutting him off. He grinned.

"I'll be going up just after Christmas Day, Wylie. Ride up with Laura and me. We've got a guest room that will be fine for you and Mary, and I can't think of anything I'd enjoy more than showing you what God's country really looks like in deep winter snow."

"Done. Let me know the details when we get closer to Christmas, Ben."

Ben looked at David.

"David, what are you doing between Christmas and New Year's? Want to ride up there, too? Laura and I would love to have you along."

"I hadn't thought about that at all, Ben. I've got family back in Pennsylvania and I'd planned to be home."

"I understand. If your plans loosen up, will you let us know and come?"

"If it works out, I'd love it." The thought of Laura flashed through his mind.

"Well, I think I've covered my agenda. I'll be happy to spend the rest of the day here if any of you have items you want to cover."

The small talk resumed again while they finished their cocoa. After a while, they all started toward the foyer and Ben held the front door open while they said their good-byes.

Ben and David stood in the snow outside the entryway, watching as Wylie's car backed out and crawled to the street, followed by Joan's car, with Chad driving. As the Buick stopped at the street, waiting for the traffic to open, Joan and the twins turned their heads and waved to Ben and David.

Ben was standing with his shoulders hunched against the chill of the air, eyes squinting slightly, and he raised his hand and waved back.

After they drove away, Ben stood for a moment without moving. "I couldn't bring it all back, Les. But I did what I could. I did what I could. I think she'll be all right now." Ben didn't realize his softly whispered words could be heard by David.

"Did you say something, Ben?"

Ben looked at him and smiled. "No, it was just . . . no, nothing, not really. Hey, did you ever see this old town more beautiful than when she's wearing a clean white dress?"

Ben turned his head, his eyes sweeping the neighborhood, as he paused to ponder the beauty of falling snow. The trees were laden, their limbs thick and white and still. The shrubs lining the parking lot were now a hedge of white velvet. The nearby buildings and homes seemed to blend together into one continuous line of pristine white mounds.

Ben turned and smiled at David, then started back into the office with David falling in beside him.